Terrence Hill

# THE HEART
# OF A POET

Leonardo da Vinci was a restless genius,
an intellectual and artistic giant

The main intrigue of the novel is the sanity or lack of sanity of the main character. What should grip the reader is the incredible story and the unknown fate of this man

Title | The heart of a Poet
Author | Terrence Hill
Cover image | © faradia - Fotolia.com
ISBN | 978-88-91142-01-6

Youcanprint Self-Publishing
Via Roma, 73-73039 Tricase (LE) - Italy
www.youcanprint.it
info@youcanprint.it
Facebook: face book.com / youcanprint.it
Twitter: twitter.com / youcanprintit

2014

Rf TERRENCE F HILL

E:MAIL  HILLTERRENCEF@gMAIL.COM
LIVES NOW IN ROME, ITALIN

This is an earnest request from the Creative Community of Palm Springs to have you consider the works of Humanitarian, Playwright, Poet and Novelist, Terrance Hill.

Having read his works over the years I have witnessed his dedication and growth. As a creative individual, his work has been an inspiration. His Humanitarian point of view has continued to inform his Works.

As a retired Navy Veteran of the Iconic Vietnam War, his quest has been, to contribute to the literary conversation.

His published work "War and after" is provocative in it exploration of Contemporary problems initiated by that conflict. He draws from his own experiences, such as his struggles with PTSD and adjustment to civilian Life. His close connection and interview of his creative contemporaries, has enabled him to confront large questions, as "can Civilization survive its own Technology" and "the conscience of man as the Reality of War"

These new works are in touch with the unconventional struggles to explore the contradictions of conscience. For your consideration

BERNARD HOYES
ANTHONY SILVA
PLEASE
Google

3

*THIS IS THE CITY IN WESTERN CANADA, THAT I GREW UP IN*

# REGINA

A poem by T.F. Hill

The wheat fields are our walls,
The broad blue sky our horizon,
Glass towers glisten in the sunlight,
People strut to work and go home,
What can you really say about this place,
Other than that.

But there are dreams here, big dreams,
As if the sky and fields thought,
The wind blows for hundreds of miles,
The snow comes,
And people love each other in that cold,
Even at dawn, the red horizon breathes life.

And in the spring,
The muddy streets splash all over,
The many car washes are busy,
As people struggle for the dry green grass,
And in other places, seeds are planted,
Hope is high on the prairies,
Merchants pray and the clouds in the sky,
Hold the truth.

The pools open, the buses run,
Children leave school,
And it's all for the weekend at the lake,
The roar of planes landing, people travel,
And it's not all business,
The churches are busy,
And there's no nude dancing,
This is Regina,
New faces - new families,
Young and old.

Industry, tall buildings,
Trust and maybe even a free cup of coffee,
Not in Toronto but in Regina, Yes,
The Y.M.C.A. where young men go and old,
Somewhere in between things,
A big park - many,
And no heroin addicts here,
Just maybe some puffers,
And no skid row here,
People bottom out in the detox.

There's a life here in Regina for all,
As the ducks fly over in the fall,
It's real, it's nearly undiscovered.

### CANADA

Poem by Terry Hill

THIS LOVELY LAND, CANADA
CRIES OUT TO ME
SING MY SONG
NOBODY HAS HEARD IT YET
LIKE A BASKETBALL IN THE NET
WE PRAY FOR YOU, O CANADA
TO BE THE LAND OF LA, LA, LA
HOME TO MANY LOST DREAMS
WE ARE ALONE, SO IT SEEMS
DEAR CANADA
ANSWER ME BACK, FROM
YOUR GREAT PROSPERITY
TO US WITHOUT A FEE
O CANADA, WE LOVE YOU
SING YOUR SONG, FOR US TO
LIVE YOUR LIFE
BY YOURSELF
LIKE A WINDOW ABOVE A SHELF
YOU LONG TO BE
SO WE CAN BE FREE
HERE, NOW, WE ARE
A PART OF YOUR GRAND DESTINY
LONGING TO BE
THIS SONG, THIS DREAM
LIKE A LIGHT BEAM
TO THE STARS
WE SEE WHAT IS OURS
THIS COLD GREAT LAND
WE WILL BE IT'S DESTINY
LIKE RAIN AND FIRE
WE BREATHE OUT HOPE
SO YOU CAN FIND US
WORTHY OF YOUR GRAND DESIGN
OH NOW WE TALK OF THIS
AND MORE BECAUSE
WE KNOW THAT HERE, THERE IS NO WAR.

## POEM STORY

Anthony Quinn stood before a pace theater and said "When I won the Oscar, there was a ten year old boy standing next to me who asked 'Is this what it is all about, the limozenes and the awards?' I said, no, I suppose it isn't and the ten year old boy looked up at me and said 'you promised me you wold change the world'".

One begins, because of a natural discontent, to reach for the crack cocaine or whisky of life, which leeds to enlightenment by death or a living nirvana. One will either find God in death or in the joy that passed and understanding that the world cannot give or understand.

The Russian winter took the armies of Napoleon.

In America, the Road took all the great ones (Buddy Holly, Whitney Houston, Elvis...).

A priest in San Felipé Mexico ministering to the married celibacy state of Mexican families explains his own priestly celibacy as 'what it is that he has found that the world cannot understand'.

"I come as your friend" – Alexander Solzenicyn said to America.

Jerry Baren said "Terry, looked into the eyes of the marine captain when I said "Terry came down from Canada to help America".

## Poem

We will remember those who suffered.

We will remember those who stopped for a coffee, for a cola, for a dream to go whit life.

We will remember those as young as the sun on the clouds of the late evening. That seems early, earlier than the morning.

We will remember the women we kissed, so softly and politely to hit the high note on the trumpet.

One has to think high.

## Poem

We don't want to enjoy life

We want to touch the sandels and dirt under the beggars feet we want to live forever.

We want to continue to listen to God.

We want to always feel the voice of the angels.

We want to live in the beauty of what touched the heart of God.

We want to go toward

A goal that will leave us penniless on this earth but able to hear a song sung by the angels.

# THE ARAB

*a novel by T. F. Hill*

But I guess you could live in a rooming house in Toronto and not be involved with the materialistic struggle - oddly enough at the kindness of capitalism. One would want to go to Paris, just to walk on the streets but is it realistic. Could I really survive there. One has to be rational and after all, I have called it quits. The struggle of my life is over. Whatever I've managed now is what I have - and, all I'll have. My rent of 451 dollars a month, along with my telephone bill , is paid from my father's account at his office. I receive 100 dollars a week spending money - wired into my bank account. I have a VISA credit card with a 300 dollar a month limit. I also receive 263 dollars U.S. as a military pension for emotional damage from the Vietnam war. So I do indeed live, but I am poor and hardly an eligible bachelor. At the present time, I'm working in an art gallery - Alphonso's,in the afternoons - just for commission. I sold a painting and earned 49 dollars last week. My bank account reads 1,321 dollars and some cents.

Really, I imagine myself to be one of those writers who is unknown in his own time - quietly making my way for coffee in the morning or sometimes in the early afternoon. I pray that God might save me, but it does seem to be my life, and although I'm unhappy, it is the life I chose for myself.

The only thing I didn't choose was Toronto. I would have preferred Madrid or Paris, however, I do love my own culture and people and I suppose I am happier here.

Part of my life seems to have been an endless insanity - of going from one place to another, often in a complete paranoid state and half crazy with alcohol. I do now live on an anti-psychotic drug, a low dosage and of which seven doctors disagree about. All but one think I'm well. However, I believe the one that doesn't because I know the way I feel, and that is not well. I look well and that's the disillusion.

Inside, I'm either a beautiful,

sensitive man or a sad tragic person.

At least two members of my family believe the latter. Some people think I should be a janitor - others a postal clerk. I wish to be an artist, a writer, and it is my undoing. The time I have on my hands is endless and it seems to lead to mental depression and imaginary insecurities.

I detest my friends, but I must have friends - someone to know, to see who is interested in me.

When I gained 50 pounds, I virtually eliminated the opposite sex from my life, although some people still tell me that I am a good looking fellow.

I've been invited to my parent's place in Palm Springs for Christmas, but don't feel well enough to make the trip. A short train ride is about the extent of what I can travel. Airplanes send me into a state of panic and terror.

I don't feel there will be any resolution of anything. Quite likely, I will make an attempt to lose some weight and I may move somewhere. Perhaps Toronto is too big a place for me, with too many people.

I know that I should quit drinking, but with all the time I have on my hands, it turns out to be one of my main activities.

One of my major problems is that I don't trust my father. This may be the source of my psychiatric difficulties. I feel that at any second he may drop a brick on my head, similar to the oil barrel that hit me on hill 1105 in Vietnam. I suppose I want this to be a story of some kind, a novel. The novel is really about a man who wanted to be a writer - who wrote plays and novels that didn't seem to amount to much. Oh yes, one of my novels is listed in the library, but it wasn't ever reviewed.

# CHAPTER I

Alphonso, at the art gallery, has a nephew in Damascus, Syria, who apparently has large financial interests at bay to invest in Canada. He says we can become rich by being the Canadian representatives. Alphonso, however, doesn't even know how to write a letter. He wants me to write it - and if he doesn't sell some paintings, he'll be out of business within a month.

I asked my so-called partner, Andrew, a young social dilettante, to write the letter and said he could be a partner. However, Andrew is nearly as incompetent and I doubt that the letter will make much sense. Of course, I could write the letter myself, once having worked at a senior level of business, but I really don't want to - don't want to be rich and really don't want to hustle for a business dollar. Simple things make me happy.

Of course there's the other story, when I called my father from Mazatlan, Mexico.

"Hello dad", I said. "I'm in Mazatlan, Mexico". There was a long pause on the phone. Finally he said, "you are not well, Paul and you shouldn't be in Mazatlan".

"But look", I said, "I want to be a writer and that's all". Somehow, I couldn't go back. I had to find something felt like, in North America, one is essentially competing with a hamburger stand. One night I had gone insane and thought that I was on the Nixon clean up list. I had written a dissident Vietnam war novel (the one I'm tested for)

I flew to Paris to seek political asylum, but I was in such an emotional state, I could hardly function. I lived with a French artist's daughter for a time and then ended up in jail for not being able to pay for lunch. This went on for a time, enjoying my freedom on the streets of Paris until the Canadian Consul contacted by father - a well-to-do businessman from Regina. He brought me back to Toronto and forced me into psychiatric care. I lived a lonely life after that, writing in a small room on St. George Street. But that is that story.

Now I'm well and trying to write a good novel.

There certainly seems to be lots of time - time to go back to Paris and live on the streets - time to go to Montreal - time to do anything. And what really will happen - probably nothing at all as long as I have enough money for coffee. There certainly seems to be time to be a writer and do something other than compete with a hamburger stand.

My experiences often weren't stories. They were merely things that happened. For example, when I was living at the Y Chalet in Banff, trying to write a novel, one day I walked about a mile out of town, thinking about mountain climbing. I looked in the direction of the wind, above the evergreens to the middle section of a mountain. I was sitting on the grass, which was the filthy dusty grass after a snow thaw. To the left I could see the top of a mountain that stood to one side of the view. It was the highest point – snow covered, virgin, alone. On top of this, something was moving - a climber. He moved for awhile, then began to fall. I saw it, because at that second, I happened to be loocking. It wasn't really a story, it was a tragedy. I do wonder if he found that which he sought.

# CHAPTER II

I'm going to go out this evening, to Benny's Delicatessen in the hopes of meeting a Pakistani, who lives on the streets. I would like to buy him dinner and listen to him talk about Islam.

I arrived at Benny's and sat at the small bar by the window. I looked for the Pakistani, Armin, but he hadn't arrived yet so I ordered a draft. Two drunks were on either side of me, but they quickly left. I sipped my beer and asked about one of the owners, John, who often handled the bar. He still worked they said, but not until Thursday evenings. It was a damp Tuesday evening.

Seven o'clock passed and no Armin. I ordered another draft and thought about Armin. He was a true existentialist character. He owned nothing. He had nothing. He lived by totally his own choice. He wanted nothing and was, in a sense, a free man.

After my third beer, I realized that Armin was not going to show up. This , even more so, enhanced my respect for him because I knew that he probably hadn't eaten all day but had still chosen to do something else.

My fascination with Armin was so great, that I wanted to be like Armin - but not in Toronto - rather on the streets of Paris. A free man in Paris. I wondered whether I possessed the mental toughness of Armin. Armin didn't have a woman because one loses them to the culture.

This, however, was still better than a man who had everything, but didn't have a woman. Armin was at least free.

This would be the great irony of Hell - that, what you lusted after would mean nothing to you by the time you got there. A women's bum wouldn't even be something you would be interested in looking at,

One thing I was sure of and knew for certain was that there is no meaning in life what-so-ever - meaning only exists in God.

# CHAPTER III

I managed to light a small fire in my apartment - oh - it was in the fireplace.
The wood didn't bum well and I thought that, were there a real fire,
the wood of the house would undoubtedly burn very well. Perhaps this wasn't
a good piece of wood - it can happen.
Just a good piece of dry wood - wood that wouldn't burn. But the best
telephone number I have is a blank piece of white paper. In other words, who
will I call - it's all there on that paper - I have to be, first of all alone with
myself.
The following evening, Andrew invited me to his apartment for dinner. He
cooked and we washed the dishes after. I had checked into the Y.M.C.A. to do
a Postinia - a spiritual retreat, to get away from the schedules and pressures of
my association with middle class life.
I hoped of course, to dry out from the beer and rum I had been drinking - to
not get lost in endless days of drinking. I was reminded of the leopard tracks
in the mountains that shouldn't have been there. My life seemed like that - that
only who was very innocent could possibly be tempted by
sin. To the rest, they are without hope and live in it - that is, sin.
It took an American to say it about the poverty and deprivation of the world.
Larry said one night at the Pioneer Inn, Maui, "I'm not him, how do I kn0w if
he'll find a job or what will happen to him".
This vas shortly after he had described the dead of a fellow diver.
" He dove down and never came up- that's what happened- he didn't want to
come back up".

# CHAPTER IV

One thing I've learned is that you have to work - the alternatives are grim. I washed out because of alcohol and I should have found a way to stay in Spain. The total terror of flying - going to Madrid - the economic insecurities of running out of money there. The terror - but I would do nearly anything to correct my spirit - to regain my integrity - to take away that sick feeling from my stomach. Maybe I'm a social drinker but I have been an alcoholic - and even social drinking leaves me in remorse and depression -soI can't drink at all.

At least I know that if I slip, it won't be into total consumption of alcohol.

I'm writing because I have no one to talk to at this hour of the evening. I sometimes feel as if I've cheated my father. I don't work and he pays my bills. Am I worthless?

Lou said something interesting - that they work and I live of their sweat and then feel resentfull of their success. He called me a slob, indirectly. I began to read Mexican history - it disgusted me. I then realized that one of the European countries was my only hope for living in a romantic world - which i wanted to live in. I didn't like the reality around me in Canada and America - and most of all, that you had to work for a living, I mean really work - like work, work. Doing things that were hard. I couldn't take it. The incentive and motivation, really wasn't there for me.

For me, at least, I didn't believe in working. I knew that you had to in one sense, to get anywhere but I wasn't sure where that was. I think I would be happy if I had someone to talk to.

I was still romantic about prison and being rehabilitated, although I had been called incorrigible , I still rehearse my academy award acceptance speech. Tonight it was:

"I'm glad I've finally made a contribution, hopefully to God and to humanity. Thank you".

Maybe I can write my way to Madrid. I think my spirit might right itself there and I might lose weight and not look like such a slob.

"Dreams Were Your Ticket Out". I want this to be a novel that I write in 3 weeks - like some of the last I've written. I don't know what the story is yet although I know that this is a story.

I've been told that I'm not crazy but if I was, I would truly go insane - like the man of La Mancha - only it would be that insane feeling inside my head that I lost human worth and had to be locked up out of control of myself.

I suppose my father has seen me at my worst - but I've certainly seen him that way as well. He had Christ - I hope I have God.

I'm so arrogant. I should hang a sign up - don't bother people unless they've told me I could bother them. I now know what it's like to be insane. I've written myself into insanity instead of out of it. I'm teetering on the brink - I fear I will go insane and my father will be past caring. My God - what a fate. I would pile bricks just to be sane again - although I'm too lazy.

Thank God, for God - He is my last hope - will he save me - no - but I'm not yet insane. I would need to do something that would make me insane.

This is now 4 years later - I got out after I went insane. I lived like a monkey behind bars - my food was nearly thrown to me - they can't explain it.

I need some medication - but I'm out of it. You can probably guess - I'm still here. Will I phone someone? - I think not. This would be a suicide note. The last thing I write but for the ridiculous hope that it somehow is a novel.

I'm a despicable person - but like the elephant man. "I am a human being". It's a cruel world but people are very kind to me.

I think sometimes that my insanity is genius but it hasn't been recognized as such. I've passed it off as a play for the stage or a novel but really it's just me - insane.

Nothing is going to happen to me, I know this - unless I provoke it myself. I'm in control - I'm not on acid.

Maybe I'm a potential murderer - but I doubt it. I can't escape into alcohol anymore, it depresses me. Maybe I would try other drugs - but I doubt it. I have one - a shot from a nurse - the anti-psychotic they give prisoners. I'm not on it now. Should I take it again or is Norman Mailer right - it interferes with the soul. I could be a genius rather than a psychotic. My fears might be the way the world really is - the C.I.A., the F.B.I. and so on.

So and so might be an inhuman monkey- there might be monkey revolutions - maybe I'll be taken in the night by two big black men out of money - gunmen, mutilated , for nothing. Is Capitalism that cruel? To some, obviously yes. It is cruel to make a man work like a slave.

Maybe I should try to build an office building or a shopping centre. Maybe I could do it.

I wouldn't want to be the one to say that I had nothing and did it - saying "I'm the President of this little enterprise, simply because I am the President". This brings up a thought - the guy on the lower scale should be paid more - what is this, slavery? The minimum wage should be tripled - including teenagers.

Maybe I should be in Politics. "I built a shopping center down in Phoenix and now I Kant to be Prime Minister" - but I can't fly, I'm too paranoid to get on an airplane.

I read back over this - it was lousy. Nothing anyone would read. But near the end there was hope.

I'm not a writer that people would read. Maybe somewhere I have an audi ence. I hope.

This is like my previous writings. Is there any hope for me?

This is styled after Herzog by Saul Bellow. But I hear a publisher now saying, "this sure as hell isn't Herzog".

Well, Henry Miller wrote like this too - what's the difference – that this isn't Paris.

Am I insane? I must be. Everything is too hard. I can't make it.

What have I published - a novel myself - it was terrible.

Nobody will ever read what I write.

But I get some satisfactions from writing.

A. A. holds out a promise. This is the real thing that's going on.

I'm probably exactly what I most fancied being.

I was really happy a week or so ago - thinking of myself as a writer - enough money in my pocket etc. I was happy. But when I came back from Indian Wells I was bummed out.

# CHAPTER V

But this is the real thing- real life- the beautiful –the terror- the serenity – the bliss – the unforgettable.

I remember what the guy who lived on the boat in Maui said " All I worry about is which way the wind is going to be blowing in the morning"

I've failed, lost the battle of life. I'm on a street corner watching the world go by me. The dreams and hopes are gone. All illusion has faded.

I'm not rich and never will be. Most of life has become meaningless to me.

It began when, "to be somebody", I decided I would become a writer. I went to Spain, where Hemingway had gone. Unfortunately my first novel was not "The Sun Also Rises" - as if it could be.....

But I had raged a great battle - an imaginary foray in my mind - a battle with the bottle. It went on for years. My writings were, of course, nearly insane. At the very least, I was insane when I wrote them. Of course, no one was interested. I seemed to continually destroy myself, reduce myself to the streets and jail in Paris, Frankfurt etc. It's a miracle I lived at all.

Once, I sought Political Asylum in France. I was later returned to an asylum in Toronto. Everybody else's life seemed to be real. Mine seemed fragmented, surreal.

When I sobered up, the only job I could find was as an usher in a movie theatre - and I had often said I was a film producer.

Still, I am only 34 and would think that life still had something in store for me. Perhaps it does.

I stopped at the library to read Walt Whitman on Rejection - a soul lost and Nabokov was worse - a poor widow in Italy. There was a man who slept in the seat next to me. His trousers appeared to be made of burlap. However, the heals hadn't wore off his shoes, so I thought he still had some standing in society.

I sometimes wished that I'd had money before they gave me shock treatments. I would have liked to drink, write and be my crazy self - until I died. Because what did they save me for - an existence without hope or meaning - and perhaps they've changed me so that I can no longer be myself.

Now that I think back, I've been an alcoholic since I was ten years old. It's amazing that I got as far in school as I did. Today I'm sober, but it was just yesterday that I had my last drink. I hope tomorrow that it won't be the same.

17

I wanted to go to San Francisco. I thought that the answers might lie there. After all, I had been released from the Marine Corps there - from a psychiatric hospital. Perhaps I could find my way from there. I didn't know 1 had about 2500.00 dollars in the bank. Perhaps that's what I should do. But I seem to lack the courage to go.

This evening, I have a date with a Vietnamese girl from Saigon. She doesn't think our effort in the war was right. I don't feel like doing much.

I don't know what I am going to say to her.

I found the Cafe Eden on Davenport not too far from where I lived - in an old mansion. I think the part I lived in must have been the garage.

From at least 15 years old, I lived in an alcoholic illusion - of seriousness, of confusion, of distorted and unrealistic thinking. Essentially,

I had attempted to escape normal consciousness through the use of alcohol and schizophrenic withdrawal. My inability to face the reality around me was either due to that reality – (a combination of school and parents) or due to a mild case of schizophrenia. Only time will tell. As I don't drink and that original reality is different. I may not be schizophrenic at all (bio-chemically). My illness may have been environmentally caused. Therefore if those social causes are removed - the school situation and the alcoholic parents - after an extended period of adjustment, I could be well.

I decided to leave Phoenix after arriving there from Toronto. It is

just to take a 6 week trip to Spain to hopefully finish a screenplay idea.

Undoubtedly I'll run into my old friend Tom Entwistle, probably in the alemenia off the Plaza de Santana .

It has always been my objective, to get back to Madrid and write. Now I'm going to it for 6 weeks.

I saw Armin in Toronto. He was homesick for Pakistan - still living on the streets and I lent him 5 dollars. He won't work - but he's free. The spring has come and he'll see summer

I have a couple of rooms in Toronto and an apartment and car in Phoenix.

I doubt that I'll lose it all just by making a trip to Madrid. But my father could cut my allowance off and I might have to go to work, when I get back.

A week has passed. I decided I would not go to Madrid. Maybe I'll go back to Toronto where Armin, the Arab is. Maybe it's the best thing. Perhaps

this is all God's will. But it's a shame I'm not successful - but perhaps, in that, I am. Arizona, the heat, the hot summer days. It is spring and 96 degrees in the shade. I suppose I should stay here and work the A.A. program- stay sober and find a job.

I thought about going to Paris - probably the freedom I would feel there - French women and the beauty of the city. I can imagine myself sitting across from Notre Dame Cathedral, having coffee in the morning.

I thought of writing a novel or a play titled "The Love Between a Father and A Son". I had in mind the great love my father had shown for me and of course the love I had for him.

How could I be 34 years old and have no track record of employment - no career, very little money, nearly nothing - not even a girlfriend. But it could be worse off and I'm conscious of that. Sometimes it seems as if there's very little hope for improvement. I seemed to have failed, for good, and others seemed to have succeeded - for good as well.

Last night I thought of going to San Francisco. Each night it is something different , a trip - a novel - a new start in a new environment. As if that is going to add something to my life or make it happy. It is an illness, even to a man in a prison cell.

I think one has to change from the inside and see what is around you, differently, rather than what is around you being différent. The new hope rests primarily for me, in my soul.

To hear the birds on the trees in the morning - to see the sunset. It is after all, here, rather than there. There is merely another "Here", when you get there.

I would enjoy the sound of the ocean crashing against the shore in the late hours of the night.

I have this imaginary thing however of hitting skid row in Vancouver, Canada- It's sort of a romantic idea - being a writer etc. - the complete existential man - answering to no one - Free. But I wonder if I would suffer, Would the beauty of the mountains be enough and the occasional view of the Bay.

I say my psychiatrist today. He re-assured me that nothing drastic would happen to me.

My heart obviously beats to a different drum than others - to write - to live in a room in Paris or elsewhere -- to let the world go by me thinking that in the mad rush they have all accomplished nearly nothing. Of course, I would keep my visa card to eat on, and have my allowance.

# CHAPTER VI

At least on Maui, one could hear the pounding of the surf, the ocean slapping the rocks at night. I can think of little else that has meaning in life.

Then I read an article in Time Magazine, titled "The dollar talks in Europe", about how inexpensive Paris is. I thought, it would be perfect if I could go to Paris and write.

Then I thought, half the world must be paranoid schizophrenics man of them with good reason.

The existential man, the Arab seemed to me. I was not bound by materialism - I owned nothing but my clothes and papers. The question I was asking myself was - could I go on living this way and be happy. But I

definitely am a borderline schizophrenic, with a slightly paranoid view of things

This is the flaw that holds me back.

Well, it's another night and I'm up all night. I'm thinking of going to Las Vegas to work in a casino and become a successful writer

# CHAPTER VII

I never liked decorating the Christmas tree. I didn't mind buying it or picking it out, but I didn't like decorating it. This was when I was an adult. I also seemed to be pre-occupied with women. I found beer and scotch a healthy form of escape. I loved to dream - to live in fantasies.

I suppose the first real insight into what made me tick was when I decided to be an enlisted man rather than an officer in the United States Marine Corps.

I wanted to share the common realities of life, not live above them. I suppose, in essence, this made me either a Communist or Christian. I still don't know which I am. I felt much later, that it was my destiny to live slightly above skid row, or actually on skid row. Most worldly ambition seemed immoral. I also had dreams about success - a quiet academic life - a land developer or perhaps a very moral writer.

I suppose it was moral to raise a family in affluence, but even of this,

I was uncertain. The real purpose of life besides a moral survival seemed to be love. I had seen so much worldly success and very little love. In fact, what I mostly saw around the wealthy in Palm Desert was depression.

My parents let me live there during the winter. I suppose they didn't know what to do with me. I had been emotionally damaged by the war in Vietnam and seemed incapable of doing anything. I would constantly sober up for a few days hoping my father would see something in me and suggest a course of action such as opening a small business. But this never occurred.

He was a tough man, sure to win a fight. One sensed this about him and was very sensitive to what one said or how one behaved in his company. He really reminded me, perhaps in 'a priori* sense of a great man. There seemed little in life that he dealt with improperly - even when he drank a bottle of scotch a day. Being a paranoid schizophrenic, I could never be like him. I looked a little like him and some people thought that I would probably achieve things as he did. This was very unlikely.

At times he had wanted me to face the nitty gritty of earning a living.

This seemed a horrifying notion to me - to be plummed into the working world with no way out but malnutrition.

I did receive a small pension from the Marine Corps, and might with luck be able to obtain a room and buy cigarettes. My drinking would be a problem and in these- circumstances, I might well hit skid row again. I say again, because

I've been there before - in New York, where it so scared me, that I bounced a check for 200 dollars rather than accept the frightening hospitality of the city. In the state of mind I was in, I had to drink. I imagined Frank Sinatra was going to back me to fight a revolution in Canada.

I was also introducing myself around as a playwright and was sure I would be a great success. The women I had loved I imaged I had shown the ultimate act of love by sending her home to return to University. I thought my fate awaited me alone in the stars.

I used to sit in a pub on the lower east side imagining I was a General in psychic battle with the other people at the bar - and the bartender, through psychic thoughts, announcing my greatness - librettist, General in the war etc. Some years later, I thought I might even be God. When I was in Paris I thought that the French accepted me as the Leader of the Revolution in the lies tern World - perhaps even someone similar to Napoleon Bonaparte. I was living with a French artist's daughter near the Odeon Theatre. She supported me, but I did absolutely nothing but drink Polish vodka - the damage I must have done to my brain and body. One day, 1 left to go for a holiday outside of Paris. She gave me 3000 francs.

When I returned she was gone and I was lovesick, broke and very ill. Thence ensued a charade of restaurant and hotel capers that repeatedly lauded me into the French Prison System.

There's something very beautiful about a recovered drunk living just above skid row. It is as if all the rest of society was nearly bullshit. He has seen the essence. After all, the Egyptians lived better 5000 years ago than they do today. I suppose these thoughts were also a part of my makeup and my ambition to" Hit skid row. Everyone else wanted to go up, I wanted to go down. I recovered from the Bohemian life, now totally disinterested in it. Many end their own life before coming out of it. It was a certain persistence that saw me through.

I am way ahead of the story. More jails and skid row's awaited me in my relentless enthusiasm for being on the bottom.

I sometimes think of one or other of my brothers enjoying financial success. They don't sit on an island in the summer interested in philosophy or history - painting and writing or tending to horses. What moment will they ever have outside of business - is there even such a thing, as a moment outside of business.

I fail to see that you have to be a business executive in order to be happy. After all, not everybody's talents are suited to such a thing. Physical poverty isn't as bad as mental and spiritual poverty. I do feel sorry for the guy who wants to go to Honolulu and can't afford it. However, it's not as bad as starving to death and outside of Africa one is unlikely to do that unless your a member of the I.R.A.

I met the head of the I.R.A. and he gave me his private address in Dublin.

I wanted to write a novel there. But it wasn't meant to be. I discovered

That I loved other people more than I loved myself. That's why I was always on the bottom. My soul and my heart were not at the bottom.

# CHAPTER VIII

It was at about this time that I started to believe that the large cultural group against me were preceeding to moves I made and substituting their people - with whom I didn't click. I left San Francisco for Monterrey to apply for a job with the newspaper. There of course, I thought the staff had been changed with the people against me and naturally I was turned down. I thought my room was again on a closed circuit monitor, probably publically broadcast.

As I left Monterey, I thought the Mafia put a contract on me because they thought I knew about the monitor. Thence began a game where I had to appear as if I thought everything was normal.

I then flew to Vancouver. On the flight, somebody offered me a cigarette and I thought there might be a drug in it. In Vancouver, I managed to borrow 1000 dollars. By this time, I was convinced I needed political asylum in Paris, France.

I should add that there was some degree of mental torture and anguish involved with this. As well, I had become totally addicted to alcohol - mostly scotch and beer.

Well, I've already told you what happened when I got to Paris. So I'll leave this story alone.

I'm now in Regina and thinking that my cup is overflowing. I'm having a scotch and I don't really care about what might happen to me. I've faced the worse. I've been there. I've been around the world. I'm home and I'm probably going to stay.

I'm the guy on the street corner, waiting to either be run over or escorted to Paradise.

I thought the whole thing was to be free - along with being a writer. I found out that most people don't even respect writers and that as far as being free is concerned most people call that being a bum.

is concerned, most people call that being a bum.

This has gone on for 12 years, ever since I returned from Vietnam. I live in a dream world. I always have. I don't feel I have to do what other people do. I don't feel I have to live as other people do. It doesn't appear as if anything terrible will happen to me. I'm on the lookout for some kind of destiny, hoping I won't meet fate.

Probably, I would be much happier working as a clerk in an insurance office. But then, I would never know what was waiting for me out in the world.

Christ was a wanderer.

I know there are people who would like to crucify me

When I lived on the streets of Paris, I was free and I was happy. I suffered from severe delusions. I'm not so sure that curing me was the wisest thing. I had to have my beer, but that has now all left me due to shock treatments.

Now that I live in reality, I find it is awfully discouraging. What can I now do, having only prepared myself to be free. Perhaps I could go back to delivering newspapers.

When I was crazy, I slept well at night and every day was exciting and the reason I didn't succeed was because of conspiracies. It was all so simple and all I wanted was to live in simple rooms and have my beer. Now I seem to need a certain degree of affluence which I am unable to achieve for myself. My father pays my bills.

"Can't you go to sleep at night and get up in the morning*', I said to Bill one day, not too long ago.

"Well, I'm for whatever helps me make it through the night", he said.

"So you don't think giving up drugs and alcohol will help", I said.

"No", he replied.

"I see", I said. I thought I had seen the light in sobriety. But waking up to where I was at having done with my life as I had, wasn't easy - and the nights were tough on me. I was a nobody who had written 3 unpublished novel, 4 plays for the stage (unproduced) and two screenplays (unseen)

In six months, you'll be begging to shine my shoes", I said.

That ended the conversation. I had seen a lot of people go down the hill quickly on the bottle to incomprehensible states of mind and being.

# CHAPTER IX

A week later in Regina, at the Plains pub, he was trying to bum a ten.

A day after that, I left for California for the winter. My own drinking had tapered off considerably and I was managing to stay sober for 4 or 5 days at a time. People used to comment on how well I looked. But I still thought the middle class dreamed and worked their way into obscurity and oblivion - simply another passive face at a 75 dollar dinner.

I secretly believed what Sartre had said - materialism is death to the soul, or something like that. I very much admired him. The party was over when I discovered that to be true. There was nothing left to celebrate. It was a greater delusion than the mentally ill suffer.

The party had definitively ended for me. I was now seeking contact with God and a destiny for myself. Maybe one day, I'll have to struggle to survive.

But I would probably give up very easily seeing, even to that, very little purpose. If I had a family to support, I would probably make them all work as the solution - otherwise, I might put a gun to my head because I couldn't keep up with my neighbors.

It is doubtful that I'll ever take on that responsibility.

I feel I live by the grace of God myself, so what would I do if there were others. Besides, focus on Ray attitude - which has been my attitude since I was 17 - is that I resent having to do anything. After I fought the Vietnam war, I resented any expectation that said I had to do this or that. Was somebody going to execute me - hardly, therefore, I just stayed free. There were of course, millions of veterans who were similar to me. At times, the system seemed inhuman, fartougher than the war.

The war was in essence, still a great adventure of life and death - somewhat similar to mountain climbing. However, it didn't leave you feeling that way after it was over. It left all in varying degrees of of emotional illness.

Still, one never knows what will happen. If something can happen it might.

This certainly isn't the bunker on a Vietnam perimeter. How exciting to be sitting there with a machine gun, looking out on a field at night. Now, I am in San Diego - a nice apartment, a health club, aerobic dance classes, a pool, palm trees, women, the works. Yet, I wish in the deepest part of my sub-conscious that we were in a war zone.

There, I knew the rules and my role was easy. Here, it is not.
so easy. What is the point to all this. I am reminded of the 50,000 suicides of Nam veterans. What exactly is the point to all this. We are all more or less action junkies, seeking that escape from ourself that only war can satisfy. The pursuit of sex is one way to go, the pursuit of God, another. First I went one way then to the other. My libido is succumbing with age and my thirst for meaning in life is growing.

I went to the A.A. club regularly for meetings even though many times I would drink after the meetings. Something in me wanted to hit skid row again. I was talking to Charlie the other night. He told me he had been an engineer but had given up after about a 10 year career. He said, "I've been on skids ever since, staying sober for 6 months at a time, from time to time. I went down to Costa Rica after I quit working but I was lost. I ended up back in the U.S. and have ridden the rails over 70,000 miles."

"But where do you sleep?", I asked. "In a sleeping bag by the school", he said. "And how do you eat?", "Well, I don't think about it", he said. "Could you use some money?", I asked. "Sure", Charlie said. So I slipped him a twenty dollar bill.
There was something very moral about Charlie's life since it still is a starving world.
What impressed me about Charlie, was his peace of mind. Something like the humility of Peter, the dishwasher and- immensely content man whom I know in Toronto.
A fellow in A.A. in Regina always haunted me. I couldn't help but think some of this was genetic. By his features, he looked like a skid row bum. Are we what we look like?.
My rent and expenses are paid by my father. I don't really know the reason why, although I asked him once and he said; "Because you are my son".
I also receive a small pension from the United States Marine Corps, for apparently chronic emotional problems stemming from my experience in the Vietnam war, I don't seem able to compete or manage my own life very well. I've certainly been very sick and on skid row - really suffering. But I know, I'm also a chronic alcoholic. The only way to arrest it is to stop drinking.
I would like to go to Paris and just be a writer but there are a number of

problems associated with this. One is that it seems to be taboo with my family. Another is that I would probably fall into a drinking pattern and become very sick. Another is that even if I didn't drink, I would probably become very lonely and forlorn and perhaps unable to write. It would be like I was doing something bad. But one of the things that motivates me, is that I can't help but think that after all most people are doing, is surviving, particularly, the A.A.'s.

I always wanted life to be about so much more than survival.

When I drink, the next day I'm not even well enough to go to a movie. It was my great escape all my life - to drink and dream.- to lose myself in the wanderings of the mind caused by alcohol. I become very sick now - unsocial, intollerant, incapable of functioning or thinking clearly. It has truly run it's full course with me. It took about 19 years, from 17 to 36. The rest seems to be insanity and death. It's time to put the bottle away. Last night, I poured the two remaining beers in my fridge, down the drain. When I woke up late this afternoon, I read from the big book of Alcoholics Anonymous. I'm just now getting on my knees to ask God's help.

I didn't see my doctor today and I missed getting my shot of modicate.

I know it deters the imagination and my ability to write. I hope I don't become schizophrenic again. I have to chance it.

I put on another pot of coffee, remembering when I tried to seek political asylum in France, suffering from schizophrenia. I ended up in prison outside of Paris from not being able to pay restaurant and hotel bills. My father rescued me and took me back to a psychiatric hospital in Toronto. I thought my problems were merely financial. I was out of it and drinking heavily.

I was just thinking, maybe our minds are interfered with by radio and T.V. waves. I once thought that I could pick up psychic thoughts from radio and tv vision - what a delusion.

I walked in the cold winter night. I slid on the snow. It was home - Regina. I remembered the many rum and cokes - the numerous women and the warmth of my family home.

It was hard to believe what had happened to me. I felt the same as I once was, but 13 years had gone by like the wind. I had been another person - insanely trying to be a creative writer.

I learned that you've got to have hope and dreams to live life.

I now think that I should be in business for myself. My sleeping disorder prevents me from working for anybody else. I also now value work and starting within the system. I can see that it produces happiness. But I gave my life to God the other night. I was at our beach cottage at Lake Katepwa. I feel better I now have a bible to read and recently I have known peace of mind.

I was coming out of my father's office building this morning and someone representing an investment company from the east offered to loan me 10 million dollars. But it required a letter of credit from the bank. I've flirted with starting a business career.

We had coffee in the plaza and a near bum from A.A. came up inquiring how I was. That was all I needed. He was unshaven and looked like he was from the Salvation Army.

I was just thinking that perhaps a person hasn't lived a full life until they've been insane and perhaps in prison. I've been there. - It hasn't exactly been a cozy middle class life. But I didn't want that. I wanted excitement and reality. I found both - the real issues - hunger and cold - freezing on a Paris street. I've been there. That's probably the reason I can appreciate a quiet simple life now. The terror and suffering I've known have been unreal. I know something that other people can't quite be certain of. That's basically what I am - a man who knows something that other don't.

I went down to the Georgia Hotel for a couple of beer. It's sort of a Bohemian place for dopers and down and outers. I met some people there. They seemed to like me and respected the fact that I was a published writer.

I slept then, I woke up and had coffee - real early - like 3:30 in the morning. The movie Jesus came on. I watched part of it and felt called to go to Madrid. I then went for coffee at the Bus Depot. A local artist joined me and we were talking about blackouts. I told him of the blackout I went into in Los Angeles. A couple of days later, I had hotel receipts from Cuatamala in my pocket. Apparently, I had been staying in two hotels at the same time. This was shortly before my parents cut me off and I was on the streets in Regina. They had the police arrest me and take me to a psychiatric ward. I was there, except for one escape, for 30 days in which I had shock treatment. This was the same time that they finally cured me of the schizophrenic delusions. It is with a drug called modicate - a shot in the ass every two weeks.

# CHAPTER X

I have fought hard for my right to be a writer in a free society - whether I'm published, successfull or whatever, even never read. I chink the fact that one writes makes one a writer, and I think many people are jealous of that or simply refuse in their own minds to give you credit for that. They ask you if your making a living at it and so on - what ignorance.

Writers are special people who articulate the ideas of their times, even if they're unread. It's a special existence to live with the pen.

The bottom line world has missed something, - like a nice pot of tea on top of a mountain.

I can remember telling my psychaistrist all this when I was under court ordered care and probation in Toronto. I convinced him and my probation officer that it was just fine for me to write, and that's all - my right in a free society. Now I have some income laid on me, a nice apartment and plenty of paper. So I can be a writer today, but very few people respect me for it.

I was just thinking, that I should be happy here in my apartment because of those filthy missions I used to sleep in and the Y.M.C.A.'s across Canada, and begging for food. It was atrocious.

So, this is me again, up all night, waiting for the bus depot to open for coffee. I hope to see Emile and Nfurray there. They both take modicate for schizophrenia, Emile has been threatened by social services that he'll lose his $524. a month if he doesn't take his shot.

He told me that he hears voices from God the father, Jesus, Mary and in male and female voices, the devil. Emile is a writer.

But it makes me feel good to see and talk to these people that I have something in common with, - even though I don't consider myself as disabled as they are. However, the inability to work seems to be common place amongst my fellow schizophrenics. Maybe we should all be thrown to the wolves, then Canada might have a national schizophrenic dishwasher association. Imagine every dish in Canada being washed by a schizophrenic.

But I think most of the laziness is a side effect of the medication. I think it is every man's decision whether or not he will take this drug. has to weigh it and ponder it.

Lake Katepwa is a good escape for me. My parents let me use their cabin whenever I want. So my main activity seems to be driving back and forth between Regina and the Lake, 60 miles away. Mow would I explain this to a girlfriend. The days seem to be over when older women would take me on as their younger lover - but never over 40. I've had a lot of sex in my life but since coming back to church, I've tried to remain celibate. It's not easy and I think of women constantly having been used to such a normal sex life.

But being overweight now, and 37, I don't seem to have the same opportunities. It's not so important to me because I realize that it's just something that lives in my mind apart from reality.

It's all so hard. What is the point of any of this - get a bottle of Haig and get high - dam tomorrow.

So I did. I only drank 9 or 10 ounces and then went to bed. I slept until 4:45 this morning and got up and made coffee. 1 then went to the Bus Depot for more coffee.

I met Jimmy, who lives at the Salvation Army. He's on the same medication I am, as well as an Anti-depressant. 1 bought him a package of cigarettes and lent him a dollar He seemed pleased. I gave out over 200 dollars in hand-outs last week. I don't know if it's right or not.

It's hot today. I've gone all day without a drink. I'll try to go till this evening

Maybe I would be happier in Paris. I certainly would like to have a companion. Someone

to talk to - who believes in my dreams - shared my reality

Well, I've succumbed to a few scotches - dreaming about Paris. But the ordeal of the

flight over might well be too much for me. The other thing I thought about was buying a gasoline station.

I was also thinking the trouble with the Conservative is that they are so hung up on honor and principal that nothing gets done because of the principal of the thing.

Whereas, the Liberals are free flowing and seem to facilitate getting a problem solved.

July 4, 1984. I woke up this morning, or rather at 1 P.M. this afternoon, thinking that the right thing to do would be to jump out of a window. It just seemed correct. Later, I met Shorty for coffee at the Bus Depot. He's been committed 6 times at the

General Hospital, but he's happy. He thinks that St. Teresa appeared to him and called him, "His Majesty". He thinks he should be King of Canada. I was once like it, shortly, before shock treatment and modicate.

What bothers me is that I should have achieved more before I became ill.. Then I would be able to plug back into that level of society. But in trying to be a writer, I pretty well left myself at the bottom - big dreams and a hard fall to the pavement.

I have my second play being read by various people at the moment. Maybe something will come of it.

Perhaps it's time to say what I formerly was. I was formerly the Executive Assistant to the President of Jackson-Smith, a big developer. I was formerly, the Assistant Manager of the Gateway Corporation, a house builder. I was formerly an outstanding non-commissioned officer in the United States Marine Corps. - a real marines' marine.

I was the best field radio operator in Vietnam. I was a former all-marine football player. I was a former Varsity football player. I was a former prisoner in Paris -

a former prisoner in Toronto and a former psychiatric patient in Regina, San Francisco and Toronto. I'm a published author and a published free lance journalist. I'm a former great lover of women - many women - a father and a former husband.

I'm a former resident of Madrid, Paris Toledo, Spain, San Francisco, Los Angeles,

San Diego, Phoenix, Palm Springs, New York, Montreal, Winnipeg, Vancouver» London, England and Halifax, N'ova Scotia. In a few of these places I was actually happy, but what I was searching for, I don't know,

I actually worked for the Wall Street Journal for one day.

I'm writing this, sitting in the Lebret pub, listening to the juke box and looking out across the lake to the green slopes of the valley. My mother found a copy of my second play for the stage and I sent it all over. Maybe I'll be produced finally and achieve some acclaim.

Scary- a drunk can really scare the hell out of you - and when you look at them, you know they are slowly going insane.

There's something he can't face - the drunk on the street. For the most part it is that he is responsible for himself. Never the less, some people have it worse than others.

But a bum walking down a street in New York is of more value than most people think. It is Annin, the Arab. He has no hope and no future yet he is not a terrorist - is not a criminal - he values his life and most of all, his freedom. He won't compromise this freedom. He chooses to be where he is.

The Preacher said something one morning that caused me some thought . He said, "we are living in darkness". This caused me to think that possibly everything we believe in, our total system could be wrong - that we are living some kind of Mamon life, not knowing' the difference. "For what does it profit a man to win the whole world and lose his soul".

How this ties in with what I have previously written is that the Arab and the bums on the streets might be saints, in this light.

Get it for me - I don't care what you have to do to get it, or what you have to pay for it - just get it..

# CHAPTER XI

Nestled in a comer of the room amongst posters of PRINCE and MADONNA was a picture of Jesus, holding a lamb, standing amongst sheep. This was the music room of a self-help club in REGINA - mostly for psychiatric patients. It was there that I first saw Elaine - a beautiful native girl of 18.

George was talking to me as I watched her at the sink.

"You Know Harry, we should just go off into the night and never come back - what do people do these things for? - there's a better life somewhere, maybe in Bermuda or Jamaica !

It was months later when I had Elaine over at my apartment. I thought of what Shorty had said about her.

I was sitting beside her and I asked her if she was married. She said "no, but she wasn't living with her parents either". So, a deal was struck up between us. I had tobacco, a bottle of wine and a place to stay. She needed a place to stay and something to do. Apparently she had watched her boyfriend hang himself. Elaine liked to watch rock videos, so I put the T.V. on Much Music. I was amazed,as she could sit there for hours watching this - without saying much of anything. She liked Chinese food so I ordered some.

She would call me in the afternoon after she had moved back to her parents place. Apparently she wasn't supposed to drink.

She would always ask me to get her some smokes. So I would. She insisted that she could handle this and wouldn't drink. She was the type of person I couldn't say no to and she apparently had the same effect on others.

I'm always thinking this is it, or that is it - that this must be it - or that I'm going to find something that will be the meaning of life, bat I never do, and it depresses me. I can't seem to find it. The closest I've come is the feeling of a fresh hundred dollar bill..

Once I thought I had found it, but the others in my life couldn't see it and I couldn't see what they found - meaningful work, discipline, early evenings, rationality and, I think, a form of peace . What I had found, bordered on the irrational - the logic of a dreamer, a playwright, late evenings, beer and whiskey, Spain, the bullfights, an international comerade- none of which I or anybody else could afford. But I wanted

it anyway. It turned me into a beggar - the boulevard of broken dreams.

The wind howling outside my window reminds me of a premonition - that I would lose everything, even my sanity and would be walking down a street, maybe in Paris, and it would be cold and windy, and I would be forever alone - too old to fit in - and scarred mentally so that it would indeed be too late for me - wretched, alone, never able to return home, lost in a hell and destined for a hell beyond; a bad deal with the devil instead of God. Somehow apart, having missed it - that grip on something in life; having thrown it all away just to be a writer (which wasn't it).

The prairie wind howling, reminding me to stay at home * leaving the world to those it had not beaten. It was the schizophrenia that finished me, not by ideals and now I'm afraid to try again. I value little things now - having coffee with a friend in the early afternoon; a piece of pie in the evening; a walk in the park at dusk.

I guess I'm rather like an old man, grateful that it wasn't worse than it was, because it could have been.

I remember checking into the military hotel, while waiting for a free lift to Europe - the tormentor would always check in with me and I would pick these thoughts up - tormenting me until I would say a simple prayer asking God to let me out of this life for a simple existence somewhere in the world. But I kept on panhandling for

beer in Frankfurt, begging for food on the streets. There seemed no end and then suddenly a drug called modicate and it sent the tormentor away. Suddenly I was well, but the street had done its damage. Writing wasn't worth it anymore. I saw those happy faces going off to work in the morning and knew that the point of all my plays and novels was erroneous. North American life was good, healthy and prosperous. To think I had thrown all that away for the ambiance of a French cafe. But I wasn't alone. There had been many.

However it still comes back to the schizophrenia. But for that I may have earned the equity to live on international life and most certainly would have made it as a writer. What did God have in store for me now - a warning to other lost youth, and what a precious treasure they are - the young people, eyes glistening, smiling, full of faith in the system and their chance to have a happy prosperous life - and it's true, .it's there for the taking. Yet I somehow feel that their faith is not well placed - those innocent smiles - life is not that easy - they may be cheated - things weren't totally fair. We've let them down, its a tragedy. We didn't change enough, soon enough. These generations will hate us, eventually. If there was only a writer to fill them in - to let them know, then it would be all right.

I was just thinking, I nearly lent that Arab 1200 dollars to go home to Pakistan. He had become hardened with the cruelty of Torontonians - work or starve, and he having a Masters Degree in Philosophy on top of it all. Yes, the dollar rules.

Fine

## TOUGH DREAMS

*A NOVEL BY DAN AND TERRENCE HILL*
*I THOUGTH I'LL GIVE THIS NOVEL TO GOD– THEN I THOUGHT*
*ABOUT IT, AND IN fACT GOD HAS GIVEN THIS NOVEL TO ME.*

He woke up at 3:00 a.m. Jim Harris was in the midst of what the famous Harvard professor Erik Erickson called an identity crisis - and like Erickson himself, found wonder lust to be the solution - to wonder through the great cities of the world until he found himself. Jim wanted to be a writer.

His brother, Mike, joined him for coffee around 7:00 a.m. in their family home. Their father was an American journalist posted in London, England. They had grown up there and both had recently graduated from high school. At the insistence of their father, they had both read *"The History of Western Philosophy."* Neither wanted to continue school.

So Jim said to Mike, "I'm leaving and may be gone for many years. I have 1,000 quid saved and that will get me started."

Mike said, "Why don't you try to get a job in business like myself. We could do really well."

Jim said, "It would be very selfish of me to do that - please tell Mom and Dad after I've left of my plans. I want to be a great writer."

Jim was 18 and Mike was 19.

Jim took the morning train to Paris. He arrived around 3:00 p.m. and took a taxi to Notre Dame Cathedral. He prayed there and then set out to find a hotel room in the poor area near the Gare de Lyon. The first he entered had a staircase and halfway up was a beautiful woman. He said in French that he was looking for a room. She said to him "No, you want some love."

He said, "Combien." (How much)

She said, "30 francs."

He could not control himself and obliged her. He tried to kiss her but she said no, implying he might pick up an infection. It was 1993 and AIDS was rampant.

He then found the Hotel Julius Caesar - a cheap place near the Gare de Lyon. Paul's Restaurant nearby became his hang out. He started to write a novel. It was a take-off on the loss of the early writings of Ernest Hemingway. Hemingway's early writings had been stolen or disappeared and the person who possessed these manuscripts would have no idea of their value.

Jim did a lot of drinking and after a few months he was broke. The hotel said he could have credit there and he was hoping the same from Paul. But after eating a meal and telling Paul he needed credit, Paul said "No" and called the police.

He said to Paul as the police took him out, "Paul, we were friends." Paul just shook his head.

Jim was thrown into jail at the Bastille. It was a cell with six men in it and a hole in the middle of the cell. Soup and bread were passed to them through a slot in the door. After 10 hours, they were led out and gave their belts to a guard. Jim did not want to do this and the guard pulled back his fist to hit him in the mouth. Then Jim gave him his belt. After this, they were told to take off all of their clothing and bend over so they could see up their bums for drugs. He was stunned and did not believe what was happening.

Later in court, he said to the judge, "Was it a crime in France to be hungry?" The judge said this was not a serious matter and sentenced him to 8 days in prison.

He was sent to a modern prison outside of Paris. He had his own cell with music and tobacco. They were let to see a movie and twice a day they were let out in the exercise yard.

# CHAPTER XII

Mike's story is a bit different and his view of the world was a bit different than his brother Jim.

Mike had met a priest philosopher who was his mentor and ignited in Mike's heart a longing for spiritual truths, which Jim had also but in a different way. Although Mike was a good athlete at school and generally a leader among his peer group he had an ache in his heart that was longing to be healed and he did not know where this ache came from. Perhaps it was involved in the family and his ancestry. Their grandfather was a stone cutter and a builder in London and had made a lot of money doing this and somehow had very strong connections with the establishment but when Mike asked his father about that background for some reason he was shut off from learning about it. Mike's feeling was that clearly were secrets that he was not to know about but at the same time these secrets were holding both Mike and Jim in some sense in bondage and Mike felt that until these things were dealt with there would be no true spiritual liberty which in Mike's view was J always more important than material liberty. But for that matter looking around at his friends Mike's family was not particularly more dysfunctional and in more pain than similar families in Chelsea at the time. His schoolmates and families had their complicated stories. Fathers with mistresses, illegitimate children who were rejected, mothers who were alcoholics and kept hidden, emotions of both anger and despair having not been dealt with; these were the things that affected Jim and Mike as they set off in their respective careers which only later would be revealed and discovered. Mike's first job came about as a result of an introduction by his mentor of a very

successful man of the City. And because Mike felt uncomfortable in his home he was very excited to get on his own and give his hand at achieving financial independence which could only be a Band Aid for the spiritual freedom he really longed for. This business opportunity to allow Mike to become a partner in real estate ventures in rural counties where the population was growing. Mike always believed that one day he would meet that special lady who God had planned for him to spend his life with. He'd had girlfriends over the years but they were never the right one and finally one night almost by accident in a pub he met that great lady that he believed he was destined to meet. She felt the same way. They began to date and within a year were married. Her name was Sara and she was from a large family. They had many things in common, commitment to family, dedication to hard work and a deep spiritual foundation that was only in the early stages of development.

It wasn't long after he got started that it was clear that Mike had very good instincts for the real estate market. He could see things and make deals that were very attractive and within thirty months he became a millionaire. His peers were astounded and even Mike felt a bit overwhelmed by the speed of his success and because his deepest yearnings were spiritual he was never attached to the money or the success but he did feel a certain confusion from this world where all things are measured by money. Yet in his heart he knew that was false. He knew there was something more and he knew that Jim was right and was searching for that deeper spiritual truth and liberation that could not be found in the material world. So Mike had a certain envy for Jim's courage and freedom.

Both Mike and Jim had the same dream of harmony, joy and peace but this was a tough dream because the world they saw and experienced was one of dislocation, anger and turmoil. If only that their tough dreams would come true one day.

# FRUTTIVENDOLO

Quando quattro anni fa mi trasferii a Vancouver, una famiglia coreana possedeva e gestiva un piccola frutteria sulla West Broadway. Notai che la scelta delle merci era limitala, che la frutta era stantia, e non c'era nessuna insegna o altro per pubblicizzare i prodotti. In realtà, pensai che l'unica cosa che il fruttivendolo sembrasse voler vendere fosse la figlia diciottenne, seduta seminuda dietro la cassa. Col passare del tempo, cercò di compensare la mancanza di entrate aumentando i prezzi. Il negozio si svuotò di clienti. Un giorno gli parlai e mi disse che gli affari non andavano bene e che si sarebbe trasferito in Cina.

Il negozio fu presto rilevato da un'altra famiglia asiatica, ma non cambiò nulla. Non si erano dedicati abbastanza a imparare la lingua

Di lì a poco, il negozio cambio ancora proprietà. Fu un'altra famiglia a rilevarlo. Le arance e gli altri frutti furono subito freschi e i prezzi diminuirono. Gli scaffali erano pieni di merce. Comprarono un terminale per la lotteria, l'accesso a internet e una fotocopiatrice. C'erano insegne ail'estemo con le offerte speciali e tutti i servizi offerti Gli affari cominciarono a esplodere.

Ho riflettuto per più di quattro anni sugli eventi di quel negozio Le prime due famiglie pensavano che l'economia canadese andasse male. Ma il negozio si trovava in una posizione eccellente e al quartiere un negozio di alimentari serviva. Intorno c'erano sopratutto appartamenti con bassi costi d'affitto.

Tutto questo mi fece pensare all'influenza asiatica di Vancouver di cui il governo ci aveva tanto parlato. Era ovvio che, in quel negozio, furono l'impresa individuale e l'ingegno a fare la differenza. 1 sogni di due famiglie si erano infranti, quello di un'altra si era avverato.

Ovviamente, il successo non dipende soltanto dallo stato dell'economia - c'è chi ha successo e chi no - Chissà perché?!

# LAZARUS

*A Novel by T.F. Hill*

He couldn't get Lazarus off his mind. Lazarus seemed to be everywhere - the panhandler and plain beggars. He felt compelled to help these people, partly because of the biblical story where Lazarus was carried up to heaven by the angels and the rich man died and went to hell for not sharing his bounty with the poor.

He was plagued by a memory from Paris - a well-healed middle-aged Parisian woman waking by a suffering soul and uttering "C'est justice "

He was in Vancouver having recently arrived from Regina. He moved from city to city, always spurned on by the delusion that someone was going to murder him.

He wanted to take on the responsibility of feeding the world. He wanted to do - research to come up with an economic plan, it was a terrible thing that two billion people went hungry each day. While most were taking up golf in the developed world, many children in the developing countries were dying each day.

He attended an AA meeting. One of the speakers mentioned that he had lived on skid row for eight years. He talked of the terror and the fear. Somehow he was able to sober up to find work again. His name was John Marcoz. He attended AA often, but at this meeting, his mind drifted to Sheila's fate - a young Metis woman with two children living in Regina. She had phoned claiming she had been evicted and was in the park with the two babies, as at last the weather was warm.

John wanted to be like Jesus. He wanted to love the Father with all his heart and soul - to do his will and love his fellow man like Jesus loved him. He was able to sleep somewhere and eat due to a gift from God - a military pension and an income from his earthly father.

He also pondered how fortunate he was because he regarded the world of the 21st century to be, by and large, a pagan civilization, where every opportunity for pleasure and personal gain was taken advantage of, regardless of any moral issue. Indeed, he felt humbled by his own shortcomings, although he still had a sense of morality and a knowledge of right and wrong.

When having coffee at his favorite coffee shop, he talked with a Canadian from Morocco. The thought went through his mind that ᶜᵏhe would kill me in the name of Allah, but I will die for him in the name of Christ."

John flew to Palm Desert, California on the 1st of October. He rented a place for the winter. Lazarus wasn't too evident here - it was a playground for the Rich.

One morning, he drove over to San Diego. It was about 6 a.m. when he arrived - downtown.

The street people were waking up on the sidewalk. He saw a dog eating something. Here was Lazarus. These people would be lifted up to heaven by the angels when they die - and the rest of us - who knows what will happen to us.

Christmas has passed. I'm where I grew up- Regina, Saskatchewan - city of infinite thinking - like the horizon. I would rather be here than in Paris or Madrid - a nicer all night coffee shop.

I thought about Emily. I didn't want her begging me all the time for money. She does not act like a human being. I mean with love and normal feedback. My mind is tired - probably from all the whiskey I've drank in my life.

When I was younger, I thought it was simple to make a lot of money. Every once in a while I think of an imaginary blackjack hand.

I was sitting in the Husky House. Two city policemen walked in for coffee. They did not look like pigs. I thought of leading them on a police chase through the city as an expression of my individuality.

Last year, I also made a trip to Lourdes, France. I imagined that the young Karol Cardinal Woytyla, if he had visited there, that he would be happy.

The town buses sold by the restaurant I was in - pilgrims hoping for everything that one could imagine.

The Sartre gift shops stands in contract the great meaning God had ordained for life,

I stayed at the Hotel Christina which reminded me of a lusty woman in Indio, Ca. - but thank God I never saw between her legs. Did the young cardinal ever see a woman like that?

There were small green mountains surrounding Lourdes and a rushing river. The people seemed honest, friendly and full of joy.

My early novels sensed a despair felt by a whole generation, at mainly materialism and war.

They found no alternatives other than the sexual revolution which took the beauty and dignity out of even that.

I sense the 60's generation is frustrated today - the world did not change no matter how hard they tried to change it - still wars, still starving people, still hunger in America.

I am a humble man in a world peopled with greatness. What were the communists so determined about? What were they trying to free us from? Is this so bad - what we have in the western world - something that all people on earth want, except the Muslims.

Lourdes, from Canada, was less expensive than 3 days in Banff including the airfare.

Oh, Lord, don't you love Emily the way I do - she's had nothing in life - she said the bank made her feel dirty when she tried to open an account - because of the color of her skin. But she had French blood in her and someone that made her special and beautiful.

I wonder of people come here before they die - and will I die. In my mind, I have Jesus and angels, little cherubim kissing me up to the father - a kind father.I saw Rick today down on Granville Street in Vancouver. I also ran into Mickey whom I hadn't seen in 12 years. Welfare was paying his rent. He said he was too old to go back to being an ironworker.

"Quite a guy," Mickey said as I walked away.


The devil wants my liver and kidneys. I can't drink or I would die - but I want to drink every night - to lose consciousness and to savor the moment.

I wanted to feel that everything was all right so on Thursday, I went to a massage parlor and got a hand job. It depressed me and I thought of the women in Regina who used to give me hand jobs. Three of them later hung themselves and one of them is blackmailing me to this day because she was only 17 years old when I became involved. Of course, her name was Emily and she's 29 years old now.

The priest in a confession said that this involvement at the parlor was a serious matter — even that my salvation could be in danger.

The church has always said that life was a dramatic struggle between good and evil. Now we say that evil isn't evil.

I thought after the massage worker that I'd like to ask her what her long-term goals were. Maybe she wanted to save enough to start a small business.

Later at night, I was sitting in my apartment watching T.V. and listening to the radio. Something came on referring to "YOU CAN'T TAKE IT WITH YOU." I immediately thought that I'd like to take my 24 thousand with me or at least have 20 dollar gold coin in my pocket to handle cigarettes and coffee once I get to heaven.

It was like the kind of night where I needed a bottle of rum and a woman - but I could have neither. The rum would kill me and the woman would assault my soul. I had been away from Vancouver for a couple of weeks. Earlier in the day, a street person, Evan, told me that Rick had gotten drunk. Evan, himself, was no angel. Anyway, Rick did call me and I said, -

"Did you get drunk?"

"Yes," he said.

"Are you going to meetings," I said.

He said, "I have to - maybe even treatment because I'm tired of this shit."

I said, "Well, Rick, I don't want to be to involved but I know where you have coffee and maybe I'll see you there."

"Okay," he said and hung up.

Over the past 3 years, I had supported Rick because he was a Lazarus - but he wouldn't do anything to help himself and was often away and out of sorts. For my own emotional health, I had to withdraw.

Thinking of people who beg, I don't know how we can hold anything against them because if we were starving we would do the same thing.

Some time has passed now and Rick is still sober. He claims to working at the hot dog stand.

There were other Lazarus. I talk to an AIDS sufferer on West Broadway. I usually give him $10.00 - and of course Evan. Tonight I gave him $70.00 to get into the Jerico Hostel for a week. Rick said to me, "He's a crackhead, wondering around full of delusions." But I had seen no evidence that this was true. The AIDS sufferer said it as well. The AIDS person, Guy, had missed a welfare appointment and had been cut off.

Rick showed up at a coffee shop last week at Bute and Davie Streets in the west end. Angel was with him and I wondered if he was going to try to pimp her to me. But he didn't - she was in inspiration. She claimed that she had been off drugs for almost a year.

# WINDOW TO HEAVEN
## *Novel by T.F. Hill*

What does it all mean? Why did I self-destruct? The paranoid delusions would have in themselves been enough, but alcohol added to that meant a double whammy.

I flew to Paris and was picked up in a bar by an attractive woman who ran an antique store and asked me to move in with her. Following a trip to the Atlantic coast by myself I discovered that, in Paris, she had closed down her store and vacated her apartment. I was by then, flat broke. I ate in a restaurant and couldn't get credit after I had finished the meal. The owner called the police and I went to jail, Happy to have a bed and three meals a day I didn't cause any trouble. I was sentenced to 8 days in prison. By the eighth day I was happy to be released. The prison was on the outskirts of Paris and they handed me a subway token plus ten francs and I returned to the centre of Paris after saying to the judge "was it a crime to be hungry in France?"

I later found a quiet spot to pray. I didn't know what was going on. I was part of a generation that was hoping for a better world.

One phone call to my father and I would have been out of this situation. But I thought he was involved with an international conspiracy to have me put away in a mental asylum.

I took my ten francs and my suitcase around town drinking beer on the bum. The next night I went to a hotel and convinced the manager to give me three nights on credit. But the following day he had me arrested. I received another 8 day sentence at the prison outside of Paris. The reason the manager had me arrested was that I had convinced the desk clerk to advance me 200 francs.

This time I wrote to the Canadian Consul and he contacted my father who was on business in London. He showed up at the train station outside of Paris. At first it looked deserted and he was about to go but then he saw a dark figure a long way down the platform. It was me and he came to greet me.

We took a car, he had waiting, back into Paris and as we were walking down the Champs Clesai I said to him that at the hotel they were putting LSD in the water. He didn't say anything but thought to himself that he had to get me some medical help. To that end we flew to New York and then to Toronto. He had the limousine take us to the Clark Institute of Psychiatry. The doctors came out to the car and asked me how they could help. I said I was fine but needed

$5,000.00 to cany on with my writing career. My father insisted that I needed medical help. So I got my suitcase and walked down College Avenue to the Four Seasons Hotel where I knew we had reservations. I said a prayer and checked into the hotel.

I was phoning trying to make a film deal with a local producer when the door of the room opened and my father and brother walked in with two policemen. They forcibly took me to the psychiatric ward at the General Hospital. There, people held me down and gave me an injection.

The following morning I was free to leave, but I was flat broke. I had been known to the president of a national bank when he was general manager in western Canada. I head to his office with the intention of borrowing $50,000.00. I was well treated at his office and they said I could see him the following morning.

I know Toronto well because I had been a university student there so I went to the rooming house area near the University of Toronto. I managed to get a room for a week on credit. I thanked God.

I was very ill with delusions and anxiety. The only thing I knew to calm me down was alcohol. So I went to the roof garden bar at the Park Plaza Hotel. I thought they would let me drink on credit. Apparently not for as I prepared to sign the bill they called the police. I was taken to the Don jail. This meant that I would miss my appointment with the bank.

The following morning they let me consult with a lawyer. I would have to stay in jail until I came up before a judge.

Somehow my father found out I was in jail and came to see me offering help if I would agree to medical treatment. I said no because I knew nothing about the mental health system except what I had seen in the movies and I dreaded being diagnosed a schizophrenic.

After 4 or 5 days I was led into a courtroom. My father was there and through his influence the prosecutor obtained a psychiatric evaluation for 30 days.

The only problem with that turned out to be that it was in a place for the criminally insane. It was kind of funny because I had often thought that all I needed was to meet the right people and now I ended up with the criminally insane.

Later in my life I found that I had met the right people from the start - they were my own family who incidentally were not the cause of my troubles. I was responsible for it all.

Anyway after the evaluation by a team of doctors and psychologist I was released. They had told myself and the judge that I suffered from paranoid schizophrenia.

Shortly after I was released I went to a French restaurant in the hope they would extend credit to me. After I had eaten and couldn't pay they called the police. It was back to the Don jail in downtown Toronto. I got beat up in the holding cell. The police asked me what I wanted to do about it. I think I might have to live in harmony with these people -1 said, do nothing.

It was 1974 and most of my generation was hoping for an end to the Vietnam war. I privately wondered whether it would ever end for me. I had spent 7 months there in combat. We have to be willing to fight for freedom everywhere or we'll lose it.

But back to the Don jail. My father came to see me and said if I would agree to medical treatment he would bail me out. I refused fearing a sort of "One Flew Over the Coo Coo Nest"

sort of thing - or what I had seen on TV about the mentally ill. This, of course, wasn't true and this was about the time that because of modem medications most of the mentally ill were being released from institutions around the western world.

Another psychiatric evaluation was ordered. This time I went to the Clark Institute. I sat around for a couple of months and was released under the care of a doctor. My father sent me $80.00 a week to live on. I got a room in the student area. But I seemed to have lost my dreams and I gravitated back to my university haunts - the taverns around Bay and Bloor.

All that had happened was a tremendous blow to my confidence, dignity and my belief in myself as an independent thinker and writer.

I spent most of my evenings in the Embassy tavern trying to figure out what had happened to me and engaged in telepathic communication with my father and Prime Minister Trudeau. Of course, this was imaginary but it seemed real. I prayed that God would deliver me from these circumstances. What happened in Toronto was like a crucifixion - like being raped. It was as if life itself were a sin and I was being punished for it.

When I came to Madrid 32 years ago it was a dream - to write and live in Spain, something like Hemmingway had. Now I was back in November of 2002.

We all die some day and did we really live our dreams?

We wade deep in water and then shallow as we come ashore. The water trail is blown away by the wind and we stand on land again, ready to swim again in the vast ocean of our dreams. I was on firm ground again, ready to write the new held meaning of life - willing to fight for it, for it was after all worth fighting for.

They're still fighting wars around the world - would it ever stop? My war ended in 1975 Vietnam.

I was in Madrid because I was an American, although I was educated in Canada and held Canadian citizenship. I was here as an expression of freedom to live and choose my own life.

I woke up at 3:30 a.m. my first morning. I couldn't find an open café, but there was a coffee machine in the lobby of the hotel.

I watched the news until the cafeteria opened at 7:30 a.m. i went down and had fresh orange juice and café con leche'.

We seem to be just here, Rich and poor, trying to live. We aren't necessarily friendly but we are after all in this together. I don't feel the degree of tension and trauma that I used to feel 32 years ago in Toledo where I wrote my first novel.

I thought about 1967 in Toronto when I took LSD. I would see the leaves falling slowly from the trees and would acutely hear every sound.

My story was a human rights story - my existence, my cultural identity was that of an artist. Where could I live and breathe.

The thought of alcohol repelled me. It would ruin my consciousness and my life. Street drugs would do the same thing.

The main reason I'm where I'm at today is the great love my father and mother showed to me.

In looking at the waiter here my thought is - the whole world belongs to him.

We have to compromise in life - even part of our hearts and souls - in order to live.

There are so many interesting cafés and restaurants in Madrid - a coffee drinker's dream, f decided to go to church to pray for my own life.

While there, I felt called to be a Franciscan brother at that church by the Palace Hotel - but it also seemed God inspired to come to Madrid and become a writer 32 years ago.

It seemed that, in Toronto, they raped and crucified me - my mind, my soul, everything.

A business associate of my father said that I was an extension of my father's imagination. He never understood or accepted my life in Madrid.

But do I sit here, my thoughts answering themselves as if I was communicating with both God and other people.

My wife eventually became unfaithful and stopped believing in the dream of my life. She divorced me in 1976 after 3 years - but we hadn't married in the church so I was a single man again with every possibility of working out my salvation.

I've been in A.A. for a long time - without a drink for 6 1/2 years. I thought about going to Ivan Bravo for a meeting but I remembered that the people there were in early sobriety and quite a mess.

I would remember when Heidi and I didn't know where our next meal was coming from or where we were going to sleep. That was when we arrived in Madrid in 1970 - but we made it, eventually living in a beautiful apartment looking at the Quatamera Mountains.

This is when I need a woman - late in the day - to love and be with. It was 5 p.m. and I was sitting in the cafeteria again - and it had to be Madrid or Toledo. There are those that would abuse love, such as John in Vancouver - he tried to get my bank account from me because I was a loving person. He tried to take advantage of that.

I thought to myself "I've come to Madrid to die here - to cap off my life" - and it is as if 32 years have not passed - I'm the same except for the lack of a woman.

One can't be off this world - but we live in it. We need money to live - some type of compromise has to be made, but not like Madonna, a total sell-out to the world - and for what.

I was never an Allemenia person - the bar where Hemmingway drank. I preferred cafés and cafeterias.

Divine providence has carried me a long way - but even Linda would be a comfort now - the Indian woman in Regina that I supported, even while here. To bring her here with her two children would be the end of a movie. After what I've been through, it's amazing that I can still think clearly about my life. I woke up at 6 a.m. on my second day in Madrid. I thought of my arrest in Paris 28 years ago for not being able to pay my restaurant bill.

I fetched the Herald Tribune to see if the Oakland Raiders had won - they did. I also thought of my arrest in Toronto - not being able to get credit for my restaurant bill. It was like the waiter was taking it out on my whole generation.

I had money coming to me and could have paid the bill in a matter of days.

I thought of buying a cafeteria in Madrid -1 had a $43,000 credit line back in Vancouver, as well as $24,000 U.S. on hand in bank accounts. Plus I owned a diamond stock that could come through for me.

The worst that could happen is that, as far as my writing is concerned, I end up as sort of a Don Quixote.

But whatever happens, I take the advise of my father - because my family loves me.

Poor Annette back in Regina -1 loved her, but she hung herself and so did Linda, another one I was fond of - but all God wants is for us to love him and let Him love us.

I didn't realize what a marine was until I became one back in 1968 - and it was a big deal -1 feared nothing.

But now in Madrid, 2002 I was up late at night and found a bar/restaurant open until 5 a.m. A guitar and piano player were there. If there were drugs in Madrid, surely they would be here - but I didn't notice anything. This would be a great place to fall in love.

A tarnished picture of Jesus and my lotion spilled - that I masturbate with. I had my girlfriend in a magazine to look at.

The restaurant was La Recoba on Magdelena Street, not far from the Hotel El Prado. If I can't be a writer I'll gas myself in my condo in Vancouver.

Earlier in the day, I had lunch with a family that we know in Madrid. I gave Jose' a copy of my poem, "Soldier," He was nearly blind and asked me to read it to him.

Soldier etc.

He marveled at its greatness. My mind talks to itself and I think of mental images that I sense are communicated to others, all over the world. - a delusion of an artist trying to communicate with the world.

I thought about a joint or a beer. But I realized that for me they would only lead to tremendous suffering - the relief has to come from the writing.

There were reasons why I couldn't write in Toronto - but maybe they were just internal to my own imagination.

A black woman walking into the café. She ordered a drink and then said hello to virtually every one in the place.

I left shortly after and returned to my hotel and later, while drinking coffee and eating jambón Serrano, the thought crossed my mind "I don't care whether I live or die because my dreams seem impossible." Anyway - this was what was going on in Madrid for me.

I thought back 32 years and how I regarded the making of money as nearly a sin.

It was a wet rainy night in Madrid. I woke up about 10:30 p.m. and eventually made my way to the Plaza de Santona for coffee. I went into one place and met a Russian woman who had been living in Spain for 10 years. She agreed to meet for dinner tomorrow night. God has a plan for each life.

I'm never going home.

The reason I came to Madrid was that I searched for something more in life than a row of Burger Kings. Actually, I had a nightmare that I bought a Burger King Restaurant with my American Express card - it was a nightmare.

Last night, I met with an expatriate American and his wife. She talked of having Franco and the Catholic Church jammed down her throat - of the Rich coming across the border with France after France had won, and the poor going the other way starving.

A voice in my head was saying, "Now Terry take your medication" -1 survived on antipsychotic medication.

I thought of Linda in Regina - how she would come up to my apartment and take her clothes off quickly because her husband was waiting downstairs.

It was always like coming face to face with God through my own inadequacies. It was an ongoing and daily struggle.

With Linda, it was something close to being extortion. I never felt better afterwards. It left me with a malaise of the spirit and Jenny was worse - it became the parting of my body and soul.

She was also married. Her husband would sit in the living room while she jerked me off. He wanted money for drugs. It would always start with her asking me - "Can I help you out?"

I thought of Vancouver. I really didn't have a social life there. There was only 2 hang outs that I knew - Joe Fortie and the arts ciub. Maybe when I go back, I should try to meet some people there.

I knew I thought of the advance of 200 francs i got from the garcon at the Odeon Hotel in Paris.

It got me kicked out of the hotel.

Earlier in the day, a young man approached me for coffee money. He said he had been on the street for a long time. I gave him 10 euros. I thought later, "I hope he doesn't drink beer with it."

My brother and his wife came down from London. We hired a car and went to Toledo for the day. He told me some things Reagan had said, that he was not a great man but he was a man who had fought for great ideas - the dignity and freedom of the individual over the state and that he was an idealist which was another way of saying that he was an American.

We went to the cathedral which had taken 300 years to build. We saw Greco's original Jesus and also St. Peter.

The traditional Spanish music was full of the passion for life. It reminded me of losing two great loves - Heidi and Sharon.

The next day in the evening, I said to the man behind the hotel desk - "There will be a woman asking for me at 9 p.m. Tell her that I'm in the cafeteria."

She came out and we went to the café central to hear jazz.

The following night, we met at the Café de España with my American friend of 32 years. He was a marine in Vietnam like myself. We talked of many things including the Spanish blue division that fought for Hitler against the Russians. I was going to daily mass and communion at a church close by "Toda para Jesus."

I was trying to find the dreams of my youth - at least I had dreams. Maybe I was not a great writer — but there were my dreams!

I ate some chocolate and thought of the chocolate farmers. If only they could be paid more money - but it would be impossible without taking the freedom out of the society.

I was sitting in my hotel room thinking about love. Tina Turner seemed to best represent the world's love — and it is enticing and tempting - most pursue this. I was on a different path - the path of the sorrow of the world - its broken dreams - carrying my cross - the trauma of Vietnam and lost love - the difficult future that God has planned - but the moments of peace coming from the cross of Jesus.

We have got to love one another and love the people of the world. The poor are the people of the world - the rest of us with money are sort of the rulers.

I had two whisk last night - the first drink in over 6 years. It felt great and I woke up energized.

I went to the church for mass and communion, then sat at Starbucks with an Americano coffee, really savoring the moment - being back in Madrid and flush with cash.

Later, I had a salad and some flan at the Café Miau and then went for coffee at the Café Central.

It was late in the afternoon that I appreciated having Heidi the most - because as the sun sets, it cools down and gets lonely.

From time to time, I thought back about Toronto - my great misfortune there. Nothing could really be said about it other than that certain individuals decided to make my life a tragedy - because I was put under a doctor's care and could not leave Toronto, and Toronto was like a death to my spirit and soul - way worse than the Vietnam war. They treated me as if I was only a sick monkey, rather than a human being.

Anyway, at café they were going to have a concert of some sad Portuguese music from 10 to 12 p.m. - then I returned to my hotel hoping Linda would phone from Regina.

I woke up the next day, went for coffee at 3 different places and prayed at the church. Later, I said the living rosary.

After dinner, I went to a desert café. It was there that I thought of the Amtract employee who said at the end of the Seattle to Los Angeles train run, "thank you for letting me be of service to you,"

I was trying to be of service to God and humanity with my writing.

fit ' 0

I remember being at Sacred Heart Church in Palm Desert, California. There was a 50 wedding anniversary taking place. It was a very wealthy family. A working class Latino came over to congratulate the man and the man sort of dismissed him as if he were nothing.

To sum it up, that is what is wrong with America today. In Paris, the street people like to sleepover the sewer grates where there is warm air. It is a cost of freedom.

I had some whisky and went to bed. I awoke at noon the following day and picked up a newspaper and went to Starbucks for coffee. To drink alcohol during the day is a malaise for me.

I thought of Pierre Trudeau. It seemed that he was the only one who could be an individual in Canada. That there was Pierre and then the rest of Canada.

Later, I met an American woman from Iowa. She was a nice one but we just talked and I went to bed, alone. Lazarus was also in Spain. After I left Vietnam, I felt like the morning after a bad drunk, with a dirty whore.

Anyway, I ended up back in my condo in Vancouver, Canada.

I knew this other street woman back in Regina. Little Emily on a street corner at might - she liked that street life. She liked to hug the bottom of society even when you show her the way up to the light — she goes back down - a love of the gutter - a real life — all the issues played out like a tragic play - the starts in school - the treatment centers - the jobs ~ the babies and through it all, she just cannot manage. I sent her $400 a week and I don't care what she does any more. She was what I called a Lazarus after the biblical story of the beggar Lazarus being lifted up to heaven by the angels and the Rich man went to hell for not providing even the dog scraps to feed Lazarus.

There was this other Lazarus - Rich Love. He lived at the Park Street Hotel where welfare paid his rent of $400 a month. He got $ 100 to eat for the month. So he had to do something else in that money did not grow on trees.

So he set up and tore down the hot dog stand in front of the Commodore on Granville Street in downtown Vancouver. For this, he would get some money and a hot dog. He would call me in the evenings for coffee. But I wondered if it was my friendship he craved or my wallet. Probably, a little of both.

I gave Rich some art supplies and he created a couple of abstract masterpieces. I will be very interested in what the galleries have to say.

I was down for a couple of weeks and thought of smoking crack or doing.heroine - but all the drug users I saw in my 56 years of life were very unhappy people.

I don't think that I am through as a writer. I started a new novel - it went asfollows playing on the Lazarus theme.

# A LITTLE SPANISH VILLAGE

*A Short Story*
*Written by T.F. Hill*

A street with stones looking at each other in the dark shadows of night:
Marbeiia to some. To others a little bar adrift - somewhere away - away from
police - away from arrest warrants - dying in dark alleys - feet echoing up little
walkways underneath rose bushes pushing up the sides of walks - wails that
have listened to tears and laughter and even murder. Murder for money - for
hate - for revenge. Cuddled beside the sea, hovered over by mountains,
Marbeiia hid the expatriates of the world - bank robbers, jewel thieves, killers,
thieves, worn out millionaires, actors, writers - the cream and the mud of
civilization. It was a space that battered away at brain cells with *** and rusty
talk at the edge of time. On that night - as the light flickered dangerously close
to the left side of his face - a face that had been hidden for over 25 years along
a narrow street unmoved by the ocean slapping against the rocks. A determined
mind that had been unmoved by anything for a quarter of a century except -
except for one small matter - the murder of one man.The moon crested to the
east - the man stopped and listened - a fishing boat shoving against the water -
a Spanish woman scratching the back of her husband. A bird banging into a
wall - he moved on, seeing the light, eyeing the doorway, noticing the figure
looming at the bar. He stopped - watching. His hands reached inside his
buckled sailing jacket - the fingers cooled against the metal, angling for the
trigger.

His body slid against the wall. The man at the bar shifted nervously - the light
hitting his face. How long could he go on? Another five years? Ten maybe?
How many men were in the unit? How many had he caused to be captured?
How many had lived? How many were after him? Their lives destroyed,
weeping in their sleep, hoping, hating! When would they find him? Would they
simply kill him or would they torture him? His face moved away from the light
He listened to the bushes brushing the wall and then he jerked - a black mass
against the wall - maybe two lovers? Maybe a drunk pausing before he
stumbled into his casa? Maybe? He looked straight ahead his back
straightening, his hands grasping the bar, his soul bleeding above a haze of fire.
His eyes searched the bar for another exit - the eyes of a man who slept and ate
in a state of shock every day of his life. The walls had no openings - the street

poured in from one direction. His arm suddenly smashed upwards shattering the light across the broken bottles of his hell - lunging forward - banging up the street - a shot through the blackness, he rounded a corner. Heaving in pain he could hear the feet coming behind him. He had heard them before. He rounded another corner and another until all that could be heard was the pathetic wheezing of a man driven half out of his mind with fear. The night welcomed no one and it cast out all that welcomed it. It would shake to ashes the flushing puke of life until a disease would tell you more - until in the thunder of buzzing echoes you would stop breaking amidst a mass of swords, all slashing at you above your breaking point. That's how he felt as he fell on the beach - his face landing in the water - his lungs stopped forever. The small man, his body floating in satisfaction moved off the beach onto the street. A knife sliced open his back and he crashed to the pavement. Marbella fell silent for another night.

He stood alone on the edge of the cliff peering down at the dark water and what he imagined to be rocks. They prodded him with a bayonet.

"Where is your unit?" the German officer asked in harsh English.

He looked out into the night - his mind banged against the rocks - he felt the pain - the horror.

'They're 5 kilometers from here", he blurted.

To be a traitor or a dead man. Would they hold to their word and set him free?

"Where?" the voice demanded.

They would be.asleep by now. Would the Germans slaughter them or take them prisoner.

"The first farmhouse outside of the village".

Many of them would be drunk on French wine - or asleep with women. Could he ever learn to live with himself again? Would it haunt him for the rest of his life? Would the survivors come after him? Would they throw him off the cliff anyway?

They pushed at his back. He began to scream. Then they caught him - laughing. He stood there watching them walk across the field. Would it be a visual nightmare that he would remember even in oblivion?

Their weapons banged in the distance an hour later. Were they all dead? Were some of them taken prisoner? Would they know that he had sold them out?

He began walking. He had his life - that was important. First to Paris, and then to Switzerland to wait for the war to end - and then a new life somewhere in the world.

He wondered who had been taken prisoner and who had been killed. How long would the war go on? It was 1940.

# "BURNING COAL"
# A SHORT AND HOT NOVEL
## By Terrence F. HILL

I wondered why I came to Marbella. It was certainly to continue writing, but in sense it was also to alter the horizons of my life. I had found myself, after a time overpowered by the head spaces of some very ignorant people. I had lost my buoyancy and sense of self. The openness of life had temporarily escaped me. It was mostly the story of a very dumb chick who I suppose didn't really appreciate what she had. Anyway, one moves on.

One can dip into a very narrow corridor sometimes - not seeing the large expanse of life and not noticing anything really, except one's own absurd experiences.

I suppose I had spent too much time with people who lived in sub-spaces - vacant little corners of little cities and still tittler life attitudes. Somehow or other they would grow off of one - off any energy and then type one away in some negative ,to justify their unkindness to me, if you hung around long enough, just get to believing them. Then you would think yourself lucky that they would give you the opportunity to be a dishwasher or an alcoholic car salesman - or maybe, if one was lucky, a shoeshine stand. One had to emotionally grow beyond the frames of reference that bound one.

Money laying on the floor and someone banging a drum below my window. That was how I woke up - stretching my mind beyond yesterday - beyond sinks and wastepaper baskets - into bullfights and fishing boats - Swedish woman with legs and ssess as finely woven as a Venus. They were almost too perfect to be attractive. I found myself looking for something more human - more vulnerable or perhaps something that required less effort tograb.

I had a naked lunch sitting on my bed pushing a bottle of cognac up some bird's vagina - or maybe it was just in my imagination. It doesn't matter = nothing really matters anymore. When you've spent half your life doing hard labor in the Sahara Desert and the other half doing hard labor in civilization and all of a sudden you're 50 years old - believe me, nothing matters anymore.

When I was in the Sahara, we built roads - roads that didn't lead anywhere. It was the same thing in civilization. In the Sahara we didn't have women, so we fucked the donkeys. In civilization, we didn't have donkeys so we fucked the women. When you're my age, it's all the same.

The only thing I really wanted to do was to kill the people responsible for the injustices that happened to me. But where would I start - with the little girl in pigtails who I used to give a ride to on my bicycle when we were 6 years old - and in love. I asked her to marry me when she was 7, and she said no. Or should I start with the nun who was always slapping my fingers with a ruler - or maybe that weird kid who kept following me home from school telling me he loved me - or that fat kid with thick glasses who used to make funny faces at me until I beat him half to death with a baseball bat. Or maybe the girl who used to call at my house to get me to go into the garage with her so she could pull my trousers down and suck my one inch penis.

Or maybe I should start with the bully down the block who used to wait for me to get my allowance and then beat me up and take it as I was on my way to buy some ice cream. Or maybe that little girl who was always asking me to go to church with her - the guilt trips that came out of that certainly hung me up for a while, especially when I saw her twenty years later fucking two guys in a car on a quiet street in Paris - somewhere near the Notre Dame Cathedral.

Or maybe I should start with the coach who cut me from the football team because he didn't think 9 year old kids should drink beer. Or maybe the music teacher who used to keep me after school telling me I had talent while he ejaculated I his trousers from holding his hand on my leg.

Or maybe I should just forget about my childhood and move on to my early adulthood - to that lieutenant in the British Army who saw me coming into the barracks late for an inspection. "Where have you been, Private?" he asked.

Tve been to headquarters to take the morning mail to the Captain." I said.

"You're a liar!" he said loudly.

"It's one of my duties in the morning, Sir."

"You're a liar!" he said again.

"I'm telling you the truth, Sir."

"Arrest this man and throw him in the guard house". Which they did.

Or maybe I should start with the military police sergeant in Egypt. I was guarding a wire perimeter in the Canal Zone and he came up wanting to get through. I told him he had to use the gate

"Do you know who you're talking to?" he asked.

'I say, do you know who you're talking to." I said.

"What do you mean?" he asked.

61

I shot off a volley of rounds over his head.

"You must be half crazy. I'm going to report you to your officer".

"This is my officer!" I said as I shot off the rest of the magazine. The next day they made me a private again.

Or maybe I should start with that Lebanese whore who tried to bite my dick off while she was giving me a blow job. I had to bang her on the head with the end of my rifle - I then threw her off a balcony, 20 feet down to the street. I didn't even look to see what happened to her. She could still be laying there for al! I care - the crazy bitch.

Or maybe the Turkish police who threw me in jail for 6 years because they suspected me of opium running. Of course if it hadn't been for them I would probably never have started writing. I had to do something in the cell besides masturbate.

Or maybe I should forget my early adulthood and move ahead to the time when I was 38 and trying to join the Spanish Foreign Legion, i went into their headquarters in Madrid. They said I had to wait for the Colonel and they threw me into the guard house. 1 woke up in Cento washing dishes for an entire regiment. That's how I ended up in the Sahara doing hard labor. One day I had had enough and broke four thousand plates, six thousand cups and assorted thousands of other things such as glasses, bottle of wine, etc. It took 8 of them to control me. In the trial, the prosecutor asked for the death penalty. I thought I was lucky to get off with a 5 year sentence in the penal battalion building roads just for something to do in the middle of the desert. He would stand over us with fan belts and beat us to keep us working. I thought I was back in the 14th century for a while. I thought about escaping until I observed what happened to 5 men who tried. You must remember that you have to go across 2,000 miles of desert. On the first day, 4 of them beat one fellow to death with stone - to conserve water. Thereafter one of them was found dead each day until they all died - the last one of exhaustion. They had only managed to go a hundred miles.

But, maybe I should forget that period of my life and move ahead to when I was 45. I was on my way to Indo China to work for a civilian air company doing cargo work for the Americans. They were going to pay me $50,000 a year. But on the plane I met a CIA operative who was looking for a pigeon to hang a drug charge on. He needed a promotion to support his 3 mistresses in Rome. He set me up in Karachi and the Pakistani authorities gave me a 5 year hard labor sentence building airport runways - with our hands. Well, that was 5 years ago - I've just got out and, as I said, I'm here in Marbella - and I don't care about anything - except maybe killing some of those people. But not for revenge, just for something to do.

Well, that's what I was thinking until this fellow from Ireland began talking to me about writing a novel on the I.R.A. It came down to doing that or going to South America to start a revolution. I was getting tired of the Mediterranean anyway - although the ocean was good for my hangovers and I heard that there were a lot of donkeys in Ireland.

I needed a beer, but I thought I'd wait until 1 got to thebull ring. My seat was in the sun and by the time I lifted the beer to my mouth 1 would have guzzled anything to ease my thirst. I looked around the arena and noticed that most of the people were tourists. The first matador was terrible, but a man named Galloso made up for it. He walked toward his bull, throwing his shoulders back and pushing his pelvis out - he believed in himself. He took command of the entire corridor for the rest of the afternoon.

There was a British girl sitting beside me and around the time of the third bull she put her hand on my knee. She had long legs that kept twisting over towards me. Finally I said "Let's go."

She smiled and we walked back to my hotel room. After dropping her clothes off and kneeling in the dog position she said, Tm ready."

I surprised her by fucking her in the asse. But she liked it.

When we had finished she picked up a book I was reading and began paging through it. It was called "Welcome to the Monkey House".

I took the horse down the steep hills behind Marbella. She was riding behind me, naked. The IRA thing petered out and I was getting too old for revolutions. "Get off, Joan" I said as we arrived back in the clump of trees from which we had departed. She leaned up against a tree with her ass sticking out at me. I got off one horse and onto another. She was so wet it was running down her legs. As we got going she started to tear the bark off the tree and she began to shine as I kept pumping it in harder and harder. In a sense I felt sorry for her - like most women after they've been turned on by sex, they are as helpless as drug addict. I had her so turned on that if we had been in the right position she probably would have given the horse a blow job. The poor animal needed it.

It was an insane moment - the ocean was ebbing out into a haze -bulls were running feely in the mountains and some Spaniard below the hill we were on was beating his wife. ( would hear a donkey "hee-ing" on the road and I wondered if it was one of my girlfriends from the Sahara.

Finally Joan collapsed, moaning in pleasure and I sat down and drank a bottle of wine. The rest of the day passed easily and I ended up in a disco drinking by myself. I kept drinking for about two years. I don't remember much about it other than the fact that I had had started this book. I was sitting in jail in Marbella- that was what sobered me up and started me writing again. I had been accused of fucking a girl on one of the crowded beaches - against her will, apparently. All I had to say was, "Did she enjoy it?" They were not amused.

I used to watch him come down on the beach everyday by himself. He didn't seem to have any friends. He would lay there for a few hours and then take a swim. Sometimes he read but mostly he just smoked - cigarette after cigarette. He appeared to be very powerful but I sensed that it was only nerves and the emotional recovery process of a child. It caused me to think of one old Mexican movie I had seen. A Mexican and an American were waiting in a jail cell together just prior to being executed by a firing squad. They had both been involved in revolutionary activities. The Mexican looked at the American and spit on the floor. He said, "Gringo, in a few minutes you and I are going to die - apparently for the same reason."

He paused and spit on the floor again.

"But no," he said. "You have lived not for love - not for women - not for an ideal - not for nothing but

yourself."

He spit on the floor again. The American said nothing. After a few minutes they were led out and executed.

It also reminded me of an Irish friend of mine during the Spanish Civil War. He was working on a ship loading oranges out of Barcelona and due to an old whore and four bottles of wine the ship left without him. He wandered around for a few days until they marshaled him into the Republican forces. He didn't know anything about the war and really, he could care less. So he deserted and headed for Cadiz hoping to get a ship out. He got lost out in the country and ended up running into a patrol from the Legion who were fighting with Franco. There happened to be an Irishman in the unit who listened sympathetically to his story and the relayed it to the major. The major listened and agreed that it was unfortunate but he would have to be shot. He then ordered the Irishman to take a squad of me and execute him. So they marched the man out of the camp. The man who was going to be shot said to his fellow countryman.

"They're going to shoot me, aren't they?"

"Yes" the other fellow said.

"Well, Jesus Christ man, can't you do anything? "

They then looked behind them and noticed that another firing squad was following the first one. The Irishman in the Legion said "That one's for me if I don't carry this out".

"God damn it" the other fellow said. "Have you got a cigarette?" He gave him a cigarette and then halted the squad.

"Do you want to cover your eyes?" The Legionnaire asked.

"Oh, well.... What's the difference?" the fellow to be shot said. And then they shot him.

He was getting up to go for his swim. I don't know why I thought of these things when I looked at this fellow, but somehow I knew that he had had a lot of bad luck - a bit like myself. But if you hung in at the roulette wheel long enough, your luck was bound to change. I picked up the book I was reading, "Welcome to the Monkey House".

I ate a hot dog, a hamburger, a plate of chips and drank 2 bottles of Coke. Then I walked by the ferris wheel wondering when it was going to collapse. I stopped by a stand with machine guns and won a miniature bull. That was when I noticed her. She was leaning over a food counter talking to an Arab. Her dress was up over her ass and I felt like fucking her right on the spot. Bu I waited until she came my way and then invited her for a drink in my hotel. She took her panties off and laid down on the bed. I jumped on her like a madman biting the back of her neck, pulling her hair and pounding so hard at her ass that the bed boards broke.

"You should really be in England" she said later.

"Why?" I asked.

"How can you write for a people if you don't live among them?"

"It's bad enough trying to write for normal people - let alone having to live amongst them."

She laughed as she rolled over and picked up the book ! was reading,

"Welcome to the Monkey House".

The guard brought my food. I was sitting on a cot to one side of the cell. The waiters were a bit slow in the Marbella Hilton. He uncovered the Cardura Asadecand. I nodded my approval. As he was walking towards the cell door, I got up and grabbed him and began beating him after I had finished, he said, "What's wrong, Sir" (you'll get another year added onto your sentence for this). "You didn't let me inspect the wine" I replied.

"Oh, I'm sorry, Sir. It isn't the policy of the Marbella Hilton when we are serving guests in their rooms" {you crazy son-of-a-bitch. You're in a jail cell, not a hotel), he said.

"This is the last time I'll stay here -1 can assure you of that", I replied.

"Well, I'm sorry to hear that, Sir" (at the rate you're going, you'll be here for the rest of your bloody life).

I was so disgusted with the service that I decided not to eat. I picked up the book I was reading, "Welcome to the Monkey House".

"Get up!" he screamed at me. He was on a horse, the bastard. I had fallen to the rear of the platoon. We were on a 15 mile route march in the desert to wake us up before breakfast.

"You're English, aren't you?" he asked.

"Yes, I am" I replied.

"No wonder you can't keep up" he said, laughing as he rode ahead.

I never fell back again, but I always wanted to get that son-of-a-bitch...

A couple of months later, I saw him humiliating a Negro legionnaire.

"Salute" he was saying, "again and again".

After a few minutes, the Negro said to him, "One day you'll salute me!"

"How's that" said the colonel.

"My uncle is Haill Salasy" he said.

And it was true. Some years later the man became a general in the Ethiopian Army and the colonel saluted him on a state visit in Madrid. They say that the colonel resigned from the legion after that and is not writing poetry somewhere in Africa.

The day before I was to leave the penal battalion I was in a tent with two homosexuals. One of them was due to leave. The fellow who was the woman said to the other one, "Will you miss me?"

"Huh...miss you? Not bloody likely".

They were both holding machine guns and they opened fire at the same time. It reminded me of a book I read once, called "Welcome to the Monkey House" After a time I never really moved, I just let my mind wonder on endless moons dripping off the edge of dimming horns east out in deformed toe-nails. They preached to trees of frozen octopus in the center of horizontal lines and time lapses of diseased tables after they had walked for centuries. Talcum powder making its challenge in the vagina of a lunatic.

The light drifted across the valleys into the ocean where I sat perched on a rock drinking French rum and smoking ***. I was waiting for my boat -the one that I had lent a friend in the 16th century. It was bound to show up sometime. But in the interim, I could keep a good lookout for the grasshoppers from 'OAC' - that country the United Nations is keeping hidden from the world because of all the naked women - and I could read my book from time to time, "Welcome to the Monkey House".

They finally let me out of jail and I checked into the Marbeila Hilton. I was sitting in my room drinking scotch when someone knocked at the door.

"Come in", I said.

A man dressed in a banker's suit frothing at the mouth walked in and said, "All right, I want the truth". "What are you talking about"?

He began screaming "I know that for the past week while I've been on the beach you've been sneaking into my wife's room and fucking her"

"You're crazy" I said.

"No", he replied, "I'm not crazy, I'm psychic - I've had visions on the beach. You see f can communicate with electrodes in outer space -1 can gear my seventh cerebral process to a magnate on the planet Mars. My mind is as powerful as an atomic reactor and sometimes I make love to them".

I stared at him for a few minutes and then said, "Listen, let me give you a book I'm reading, it's called "Welcome to the Monkey House".

# CHAPTER 2

The first night I met her I had to take her to the hospital.

She had stomach cramps or, to put it more accurately, she freaked out on me. The intern gave her a tranquilizer and she bounced out of the hospital as if nothing had happened. She was a little girl - an acid

generation little girl, She drew funny faces on scrap pads and wrote

poetry secretely in the shadows of her bedroom. She had fuzzy freaky hair and pimples on her ass. Nothing she said made any sense - it was always a trip. She was afraid, disillusioned - alienated, but bouncy, light and full of romanticism. Catch her on a high - smiling,

babbling, laughing, and one wondered what she would have been like

without the dope * without the bitterness. One wondered what she would have been like if the counter-culture had never happened, She talked of Ginsburg?? and Whitman and of hollow men - of magical mystery tours and phase three of Bob Dylan. Everybody was into a heavy material trip except her, and her friends - most of whom hung around universities pushing dope and uttering continuous monologues of "wow "far out!", and "Man - am 1 going through the change?"

The next night, I took her out to the beach with a sixty year old friend of mine from Switzerland. He had bought a farm in Western Canada many years previous, and 'now that his wife was gone, he was trying to get in on a little life. We started off at a cabin. There were a few other chicks, a nymphomaniac, a manic depressive and a couple of spectators. We blew a lot of dope, drank a lot of booze and competed by laying trips on each other. The old guy started playing with this nympho's tits. He did it in such a manner that he thought nobody saw him.

It was far out to everybody else. Cud, how long had it been since they'd had a party - probably at least 10 hours.

We drove down to a club a couple of miles away. *For this* reason we took three cars. We walked in and made a big scene. One of the guys conned the band into believing he was going to take than to Mew York. - the big time. They fired their manager on the spot. The chicks started dancing - we were dancing too, but they were gone in some

distant mirage - lost in the dope and the music. She,  call her

68

Panic - because that's essentially the way she made everybody/feel - she stood in one spot, looking at the floor. She moved her arms in a sort of ridiculous way and twisted her knees in some absurd manner that I'm sure a gymnast couldn't manage. It was freaky.

I even started to ask the question then - what was going to happen to these people? Where were they going to go? How were they going to fit in? What were they going to do?

The world had changed so much. Morality and ethics appeared to mean nothing. Even marriage seemed to be more of a door-to-door sales job - a bargaining session where two people amalgamated instead of united. The trust, the confidence, the good old 'for better or for worse' was gone. What happened to principles and <u>men</u> - and I mean men - where were they? Or, had this only really been a myth?

Anyway, Panic and the nympho huns in on the dance floor - fluffing their neurotic bodies into the echo of artists far removed from the dim and almost put-on atmosphere of the club. In the course of the evening, tne -wiss guy took over the microphone - he was competing- everybody wanted to be the centre of attention - to draw all the energy vibes in their direction. The spectators sat there drinking - they were along just locking - dulled impulses - indecisive ainds gawking at life. They would be the future lawyers and middle executives. They didn't have the flow, or the puts. I just hovered around the scene - dancing, thinking, dreaming. Where the hell was *I* going?

Anyway, the Swiss guy ended up crashing in a room above the club - the nympho got a double jump back at the cabin, and I grooved it out with panic. What a mistake that was. We woke up the next day and «rove back into town. She quit her job and we were on our way to Athens. When I woke up three years later , exhausted, half-destroyed

?ised - looking, after a child that wasn't mine, 'vowi What happened'"

# CHAPTER 3

In a sense, they were a tired gentle people - paranoid in the middle of their youth - thrust into a pot of boiling water that never seemed to stop bubbling. It could have been boredom that started the whole thing - but in the late fifties and on into the sixties the froth pushed at their heads with such acceleration and change that 'stop the world 1 want to get off became a shallow cry for peace - a raven's madness startled by a treeless world. No place to rest - no place to stop - no way their heads would just fly away.

Speed and permanent erections - hip capitalists and acid art - cybernetic moon hopping - and Eskimo villages- Trucking - panning - the expanding universe. Trout fishing and cool -aid - flying over a coo-coo nest . It had all become radical chic. The eco-freaks, the fucking gurus - the treks to India - sitars - it was either a renaissance or the end of the world.

Panic and I lasted in Athens for two weeks. She became convinced that somebody was after her there and we split to Spain - Alicante first and then Madrid. It took her four months to get over the feeling that we were being followed - the crazy bitch.

We ran into the disenchanted$_3$ over-educated rest of North America - doing their trips to Morocco and Ibitza - collecting their thousand dollar money orders at the American Express - more money than the Spanish tellers would earn in a year.

Casablanca, Tangiers- the who trip. Were you there?

Pamplona, wine - we'll live forever. But the world started to catch up on everybody in the late sixties - Melanie - beautiful people - understanding - "Just call out my name ..." - it started to get heavy.

An international airport started to look like a freak show « a giant circus - a psychiatric ward. Dylan dropped out, the Beatles stopped - Jagger got nostalgic - the bubble broke and it was back to school and heavy, straight professional trips. Woodstock happened - and faded. Cleaver left the country - May Day turned into a big bust. The trials ended - everybody went free and it started to dawn on the spinning  heads of Alantis that maybe the system worked - that maybe organic farming and communes were nice watering holes, but no substitute for life.

The war ended - the straight end of the generation was making 20 grand a year - and all of a sudden it was like the sixties hadn't even happened.. Where have all the flowers gone.

The nymph married a bank executive, Panic became a straight in some social mission echoing the snobbery of the middle class - the spectators ended up being just what I thought they'd be, and the Swiss guy eloped with a nurse - and me, well, I'm still trying to figure out what happened.

Ginsberg was hung up on the CIA, Whitman died a long time ago and Elvis Presley started to come back in. Archie Bunker became a satiric hero and re-runs of SPACE ODYSSEY seemed less far out than a good commercial..

Smack became a business instead of a trip and even Castanada dropped away behind a consensus reality - it didn't really matter whether it was fiction or truth - just blink and jump from 1955 to 1973 and you didn't miss a thing. Brando came back, Tennessee Williams was on the rise and Sinatra was entertaining at the White House.

It was re-build, conform - adapt - shake the dope - the run
was on, money, a house in suburbia, yachts - get with it. The ethics
of survival - Watergate, the Pentagon papers, McGovern - nobody cared - just leave us alone.

But we ended up with a <u>new lost generation</u> - a generation of future Picassos and Hemingways. They were on the fringe - in little attics in Oregon - in small pensions in Madrid - in rusty shacks in England. Their hands trembling - their minds walking between
insanity and genius ~ their bodies shaking with an energy and insight
that could alter the destiny of man.


Preface:

Beyond, " All Quiet on the Western Front," and Hemingway's,

"The Sun Also Rises", little has "been done since Homer on representing the realities of war, in literature or in audio-visio art*

Incidents, or rather particular dimensions of war have always been portrayed either in the exaggerated humor of "Catch *22*" or the contemporary irrelever.ee of "Mash". War is a word and a thought rational man has still not been able to unravel.

It is a phenomena few understand and it is a phenomena still
occurring in the affairs and relations of man.

It .ever before have so many individuals in varying- societies struck out in a

71

struggle to question the morality of this phenomena. Similarily, never before, has a nation been at war when a large segment of its population disagrees with it or, at least brings it into question.

. Viet Nam has died from the headlines but it has not died in the minds of millions around the world who are still trying to fathom the enigma of it all. Therefore, as well, man has put forth a question that for the first time in history has re1evenee, "Can the species survive ? 20 Century? and a secondary and larger question, "Can a civilization survive its own technology?"

I have refrained from answering any of these questions in the following script because I do not have the answers. But have "out forward the objective reality of war in 1971 .? as well as reflected the dominating sociological questions of 20 Century life in 2-Torth America. I am convinced that this flash of realism about Han's present drama will provoke thoughts that may lead to the solution of some of the major contemporary problems. Vietnam may end up to be the least of these problems—but it initiated most of them, either directly or indirectly. Therefore, Vietnam is the major question of the script.

But how does one go about effectively dealing with such subjects in a script that will be understood by and provocative to the minds of average men? I think for one to do so one must unfold a real and interesting story that has obvious factual basis and simultaneously brings profound questions out in simple dialogue* This, I believe, I. have done. For, fortunately I was able to draw on the experiences of many men associated with Viet Nam as well as my own.

I nave not written this for commercial purposes, although I have every reason to believe it may be one of the most successfull films commercially ever produced. My intention is to bring home to the conscience of man the reality of war. I do not judge or  make Rides in the script, I merely present war's unfolding reality, when the ending is open to any interpretation. It is therefore in keeping with my intentions, for I am not God  if you accept this script you must not be either.

 I, therefore, place one beginning condition on any production of "Here and After"and that is; that I have to approve any deviations from my original

There were a number of espresso coffee shops around a large bookstore on the fashionable west side of

Vancouver. Young professionals frequented the area during the day and in the evening. Many of these had known each other. There was one very attractive woman who worked in public relations. Most of the men spent their time chatting her up and dreaming of being on a date with her. Her name was Ann Bentley, and she a background in sociology and journalism.

Bill Brady was a part of the group. He had been nicknamed the Christian because he often quoted the bible in conversations and discussions that took place over coffee. He was in his early thirties and worked for an internet company. He was in good shape and, along with the rest of the crowd, was attractive.

One afternoon in October he was talking to Ann and asked her to dinner that night. She accepted, and, true to form, Bill quoted the bible in parting company. "But remember "he Said, "that man does not live by bread alone." She smiled, being used to this sort of thing. It was more of an amusement to the affluent void.

He met her at around 8: PM at the Cactus clap on West Broadway. They were led to a table by a young yuppie and left menus

Bill had accepted his single status in life due to the absence of Christian women.

"So Anne, did you ever think of where you might go when you die?" he said.

"I'm not worried about it." She replied.

"Did you ever hear of the sheep and the goats?" he said.

"Ok, do we have to discuss this?" she said.

He laughed and she chuckled. It was sort of an amusement to both of them. But Bill was digging for the Christian truth.

He noticed her legs. He was certainly attracted.

He went on/Christ will separate the secular humanists from the Christians. They all thought that they were good people, but the inconvenient pregnancy that ended in abortion, and the protecting of children from religion in schools to avoid giving them hang-ups, and the use of birth control to avoid upsetting a career, and the premarital and the extramarital sex even though we think of ourselves as good and caring people - these things are not what a Christian does."

"I'm saying this Ann, because I would like you to be different -1 like you."

"Well" she said, I'm self supporting, independent, and free, and I don't believe you have to go to church to be a good person. I go to the cancer walk each year and contribute to three or four charities. I consider myself a loving, kind person."

"Yes you are, as most of the people are, but you're not Christians. I hope by quoting the bible that I can bring Christ into this milieu. If you only knew, Ann, how exciting it is to believe in Jesus and to discount the world which he has overcome."

"Well," said Ann, I don't think there is anything wrong with sex between consenting adults. The marriage thing was only because they didn't have birth control and didn't want orphaned children."

Bill finished his dinner and said, *The only thing important to me is my conscious relation with God - even if I had nothing, if I had that and usually am, I would be one of the happiest men on earth. You may have love for your fellow man, but the Christian cares about the spiritual and the physical - the soul of a person even more than the physical needs. St. Thomas swore off wealth and privilege for a greater intimacy with Christ, which he found."

She nodded and crossed her legs again. Bill noticed but did not lust after her.

He had made his point and he hoped that a seed had been sown in the obviously unfulfilled woman. She was a good person, but so were the secretaries who worked in Berlin during the war.

Bill thought before leaving the restaurant, "There would be weeping and mashing of teeth."

# ESSAY ON WAR
## *by Terrence F. Hill*

When all else fails in representing the war suppose national interests of a country, is war in this age means of solution - or is it in actuality, even when you are the victors, a disruptive and masochistic effort within which and through which you not only give the possibilities of re-birth to your enemy but also destroy yourself in the process. Is it possible that the dramatic character of war as a solution to conflict, and the thereby moral crisis (particularly given the consciousness of man in this ) is so disruptive to the superstructure strength of a society
and indeed its convention it's wisdom-produced harmony at the sub space level that in reality it becomes a catalyst for a neurotic and almost psychotic speeding up of the life of a modern industrial 'techno-structure.

Is it possible that war presents itself as the only rational grand art form to an otherwise displaced set of intellectuals who have been unable to discern the realities of their own lives and as a further consequence have been unable to invent within the society another impetus to courage, genius and national identity. Have we been so sold on action, that we deem it an a priori value that is above that which appeals to reason, and to calm thought - is it above the basic love and *goodness* of man. Will we fight a war just because the military is bored?

When the structure of a super power such as the United States has to occupy itself with maintaining a superiority in military technology and organization, does this imply relative to the experiences of Viet Nam a loss of perspective and the possibility of indirect self destruction
through the demoralization and disillusionment of an increasingly humanistic affluent society. Can war be an instrument of foreign policy to a nation of people grappling with what it is to have a soul - and to love - and to be decent. Is it any wonder that in such a contradiction the U.S. is teetering on the verge of historical suicide*

Given a technology that can destroy the world, are we not signing our own epitaph when we continue to view war as a rational instrument of foreign policy. This is not the 19th Century.

The greatest dreams[1] of man become absurd nightmares when they are finalized in the moving machinery of human conflict resolved by war. Everything we have ever attempted to achieve in terms of a better world is jolted in a ridiculous historical moment to becoming all that we have consistently fought against for all the years..that civilization has prospered anywhere on this planet. A.-e we so proud, and so short sighted, and so stupid that we need to destroy ourselves to prove that we are still a part of an historical legacy. Can we not unhinge ourselves and arrive in our own age, dealing with the parameters and possibilities of life in our time - given that we can, and freedom to be doing, the utmost to refrain from altering our attitudes in regards to dealing with the conflicts of a multi-national world that has the capacity to build a nirvana or create an oblivion.

Will Vietnam be the last note on the trumpet of the egoist consciousness interplaying within the anachronistic self-interest psychology of a head strong military industrial complex - or will it be the beginning concerto to a symphony of unending madness?

# THE CREATIVE PORCH OF OPTIMISM
## *Terry Hill*

What is Optimism? Is it something we wear that keeps warmth in and cold out? Is it something we eat, that nourishes us? Or is it like the sun, as we move toward it, it casts our shadow behind us?

Twenty years ago our country was coming out of a great depression, only to meet a world war which racked the globe for six years* The youth of that day had little to look forward to. Many bankrupt from the depression had to go to war, giving up their schooling, their jobs, their families, and some gave their lives that this nation might live*

All lived in fear that the Nazis regime would dominate the world, Then what made people drive on? It was a force that is in the hearts of all waiting to be fertilized by the example of others, that doing good and helping others will prevail over evil. It is something that keeps the warmth of life in and the cold out, something that nourishes us, keeps us from giving up, something that as we journey toward it, it casts the shadow of our burdens behind us* This is optimism*, And those people were optimists in the word's deepest meaning, they were driven by a force that is the pulse of our very democracy*

They never gave up, They fought for what they knew was right and would in the end triumph* I call them the salt of the earth. For it is their example that lives on today, it is their example that never lets us give up and it is their example that the youth of today must live and Terry Hill

Then it is no wonder that optimism lives on today, and drives people to do greater things, for but a week ago John Glenn showed the world that Russian propagandists were wrong, he did not let what he read make him give up. He went on and his country went on because they knew that they would reach their goal, With the exajnple of Glenn and many more like him in this world today, how can we fail, how can communism take over the world, how can liberty be lost. We will never lose because we all have a goal, and we all strive toward our goal never losing hope,

We know that good will prevail over evil, and by our example we can show the communists, yes them too, that this world was made for the honorable, the just and the good, not the wicked, the cursed, and the bad, that peoples can get along with one another, that arguments can be settled by conference, not by the hot breath of bombs, that there is a seed in every man* s heart, to help his neighbor, waiting to be brought to life by the good example of others, that people were made to know right from wrong and to strive to be good, and that this world will eventually end and the good alone will attain salvation.

Optimism will save the world because there is an optimist in every crowd, showing and helping others to do good and keep hope. And this hope, this force that drives people to live their daily lives as God intended them to, spreads from person to person, from family to family, from city to city, from nation to nation, as quickly as the winter turns to spring* Then, this force will rid the world of the misery of despair, of the fear of our enemies and of the impending doom of an atomic war, Then, this world will be as God in the beginning created it to be, to resemble heaven itself, and can you tell me what greater goal to strive for than the perfection of heaven

# THE CHRISTIAN

### *A short story by*
### *Terrence Hill*

There were a number of espresso coffee shops around a large bookstore on the fashionable west side of Vancouver. Young professionals frequented the area during the day and in the evening. Many of these had known each other. There was one very attractive woman who worked in public relations. Most of the men spent their time chatting her up and dreaming of being on a date with her. Her name was Ann Bentley, and she a background in sociology and journalism. Bill Brady was a part of the group. He had been nicknamed the Christian because he often quoted the bible in conversations and discussions that took place over coffee. He was in his early thirties and worked for an internet company. He was in good shape and, along with the rest of the crowd, was attractive.

One afternoon in October he was talking to Ann and asked her to dinner that night. She accepted, and, true to form, Bill quoted the bible in parting company. "But remember "he Said, "that man does not live by bread alone." She smiled, being used to this sort of thing. It was more of an amusement to the affluent void.

He met her at around 8: PM at the Cactus clap on West Broadway. They were led to a table by a young yuppie and left menus

Bill had accepted his single status in life due to the absence of Christian women.

"So Anne, did you ever think of where you might go when you die?" he said.

Tm not worried about it." She replied.

"Did you ever hear of the sheep and the goats?" he said.

"Ok, do we have to discuss this?" she said.

He laughed and she chuckled. It was sort of an amusement to both of them. But Bill was digging for the Christian truth.

He noticed her legs. He was certainly attracted.

He went on "Christ will separate the secular humanists from the Christians. They all thought that they were good people, but the inconvenient pregnancy that ended in abortion, and the protecting of children from religion in schools to avoid giving them hang-ups, and the use of birth control to avoid upsetting a career, and the premarital and the extramarital sex even though we think of

80

ourselves as good and caring people - these things are not what a Christian does."

I'm saying this Ann, because I would like you to be different -I like you."

"Well" she said, I'm self supporting, independent, and free, and I don't believe you have to go to church to be a good person. I go to the cancer walk each year and contribute to three or four charities. I consider myself a loving, kind person."

"Yes you are, as most of the people are, but you're not Christian. I hope by quoting the bible that I can bring Christ into this milieu. If you only knew, Ann, how exciting it is to believe in Jesus and to discount the world which he has overcome."

"Well," said Ann, I don't think there is anything wrong with sex between consenting adults. The marriage thing was only because they didn't have birth control and didn't want orphaned children."

Bill finished his dinner and said, "The only thing important to me is my conscious relation with God - even if I had nothing, if I had that and usually am, I would be one of the happiest men on earth. You may have love for your fellow man, but the Christian cares about the spiritual and the physical - the soul of a person even more than the physical needs. St. Thomas swore off wealth and privilege for a greater intimacy with Christ, which he found."

She nodded and crossed her legs again. Bill noticed but did not lust after her.

He had made his point and he hoped that a seed had been sown In the obviously unfulfilled woman. She was a good person, but so were the secretaries who worked in Berlin during the war.

Bill thought before leaving the restaurant, "There would be weeping and mashing of teeth."

# PAIN

Pain - just being alive and the antidote - booze, therapy, dope, drugs, sex jogging and many more out of mind experiences

Are we out of our mind sitting on a jet as it lifts off - with no fear as it tilts up and becomes airborne from marble to trees this pain lives on - under the universe, shredded between the stars

High on a galaxy - distant from earth - all aboard a destiny of fire - fire in the hearth - a ride down sunset strip - or over to San Diego - pick up some women - party time - but oh this pain as we barely stay sane

What is the truth - we live for now - the hell with tomorrow or consequences or responsibilities. We knew no God when we were that young and all would be forgotten when we sang that song

Just stop the killing and brothers will live - with the pain

# LOVE & FREEDOM

Love sleeps on freedom Tender, nurtured and Finally expressed - not just To one person, but to all Of humanity - who seek in Their Hearts the glaze Of freedom - beholden to Many dreams of love

And the world spins with their Struggle while many die neither Knowing freedom or love Riding on a cigar in Cuba Aborting a female child in China When will it end - for many Only in jail and we tell Their tale and none waste Their lives in this struggle It's all documented in heaven - Carried by the wind Slow breeze over Vietnam and .Korea - will this one or that one Ever live as a free person Longer than history - man is free And he knows that this is precious He loves, he cares, he fondles The heart of the young as if To say - stay free - it's the greatest Love of all

Out there begging for love, again Who am I I need to find out from you Looking - hoping That someone will notice me

I'm a cross between a Woman and a man - like everyone But oh, that marble falls Hard on my feet - the water Gusts up into the wind And drips down on my soul.

## CANADA                    Poem by Terry Hill

THIS LOVELY LAND, CANADA
CRIES OUT TO ME
SING MY SONG
NOBODY HAS HEARD IT YET
LIKE A BASKETBALL IN THE NET
WE PRAY FOR YOU, O CANADA
TO BE THE LAND OF LA, LA, LA
HOME TO MANY LOST DREAMS
WE ARE ALONE, SO IT SEEMS
DEAR CANADA
ANSWER ME BACK, FROM
YOUR GREAT PROSPERITY
TO US WITHOUT A FEE
O CANADA, WE LOVE YOU
SING YOUR SONG, FOR US TO
LIVE YOUR LIFE
BY YOURSELF
LIKE A WINDOW ABOVE A SHELF
YOU LONG TO BE
SO WE CAN BE FREE
HERE, NOW, WE ARE
A PART OF YOUR GRAND DESTINY
LONGING TO BE
THIS SONG, THIS DREAM
LIKE A LIGHT BEAM
TO THE STARS
WE SEE WHAT IS OURS
THIS COLD GREAT LAND
WE WILL BE IT'S DESTINY
LIKE RAIN AND FIRE
WE BREATHE OUT HOPE
SO YOU CAN FIND US
WORTHY OF YOUR GRAND DESIGN
OH NOW WE TALK OF THIS
AND MORE BECAUSE
WE KNOW THAT HERE, THERE IS NO WAR.

THINKING OF YOU

Mr. Terrence Hill
112 Castellana W.
Palm Desert, CA 92260

# LETTER TO ROLAND
### *by Terrence F. Hill*

I loved you, Roland, and I considered you the greatest man living in Vancouver - because of your love for all - your patience and understanding - and your cheerfulness in the face of greatest and tragic circumstances.

The first time I passed you when you were begging in front of the drug store, I gave you two dollars, and we talked briefly. You told me that you had to quit drinking because of your liver, and that you hadn't eaten in 15 days. You were everything I wanted to be, because you were like Jesus.

Dignity has become so associated with material goods - but you had dignity - more than any person living in Vancouver - and all you owned was in two shopping carts. The love and humility of God flowed through you.

# SEPTEMBER/2001

### *A Poem by T. Hill*

We died together We cried together All of us on Sept 11th

We picked ourselves up We looked to the morning sun We slept in the dawn We woke in the night

All of us have changed Life has changed Civilization has enemies But we will bare any burden Pay any price To secure the worlds freedom

This is not a time to doubt Not a time to not care We have come close to God He will see us through

From dawn to dusk We do our Presidents bidding To live our lives In confidence - Like the Confidence that the first snow will come And we will know that God is with us

**'I want to be like Jesus'**

*A poem by T.F. Hill*

I want to be like Jesus

I want to love my Father

I want to love everyone

I want to heal the sick through Him

I want to walk from desert town to desert town

I want to proclaim the Kingdom of God

I want to invite the wretched back to God

I want to wash the homeless

I want to pray all night in a garden

I want to stand with Moses in Elijah

I want to be like Jesus

I want to be pure

I want to not slander or gossip

I want to give up the world for the truth

I want to give up my life for my brothers and sisters

I want to suffer so that others may see God

I want to rise up after death into paradise

I want to fast for forty days

I want to do the will of the Father

I want to die for Him.

# <u>CHARLEY</u>
## *a play by Terrence F. H*

OTHER WORKS BY TERRENCE HILL:
"War and After" - a novel
"Until You Win Or Until You Die" - a novel
"No Es Amigo" - a novel
"11 Minutes to 11" - a screenplay

Setting: A private sportsman's club. It is shoddy. There are pictures of hockey
teams on the wall. Charley, who is about 4.5, unshaven , wearing old clothes,
is sitting at a table. A large bottle of beer is In front of him.
CHARLEY
I'm playing myself although I need these lines in front, of me
uh because, you know I've never been myself in front of anybody
else,
(Takes a drink from the beer,)
Uh   I've been to all kinds of doctors you know, about my nerves
(he holds his hand up. It is shaking) well, they don't know what's
wrong with me. Uh   but hell, doctors only judge symptoms, not
causes - not perspectives - not whole lives . Huh I (pausing and then adding)
Whole lives Manifest the right symptoms and I suppose one is all right.
But what are the symptoms of being alive?
(Another man walks in the door - about the same age and appearance. His name
is Ted.)
TED
Oh shut-up Charley. I'm tired of listening to you talk to yourself

Char ley Ted A*)*
Pas i !
Paco
E a r b a r a
Psychiatrist
Two Canadian Policemen
Two Spanish Policemen
Crowd •- Northern European

about all that bullshit, (He walks behind the bar and Helps himself to a beer) (and then says laughing) The symptoms of being alive --- huh you God-darnned fool (walks over to a table adjacent to Charley's) You see that picture up there   do you

remember Charley   when we won the championship   yah, well

That was being alive.

CHARLEY

So we only lived for those few seconds, eh?

TED

Oh don't start in on all your philosophical crap   a lot a good

those God damned degrees did you. You're still sitting here in this God damned dive like the rest of us,

CHARLEY

Yah, but I'm here because I thought about it all, and destroyed my

bloody mind   and that's the big difference (sarcas I. i ca 1 ly) old

buddy. You're here because you never thought about a damn thing In your entire miserable life,

TED

So now it's my miserable life is it? You don't hear me complaining.

CHARLEY

Mo, you've never had the bloody guts to complain.

TED

(Getting mad) So now f don't have any guts   huh   I've had the

guts to face reality, that's more than you've ever done.


It doesn't take any guts to face reality   it takes guts to try and

do something about it.

TED

And you're doing a lot about it aren't you Charley (He laughs sarcastically)

CHARLEY

Well I didn't throw my wife off a balcony like you did   you're the

person who did   you're ther person who couldn't handle it any more.

(Ted turns slowly and glares at Charley. Then says calmly.)

TED

The inquest called it suicide.

CHARLEY

Yah, I know about the bloody inquest   your old buddy the *coroner.*

Huh (Laughing) (He then turns and looks at the door as a man of similar age, but well dressed, walks in.)

CHARLEY

I guess it's time for me to leave. I'm sure as hell not going to listen to you and that coroner bullshit. (He gets up and walks out.) (The coroner gets himself a beer and sits down with Ted.)

AL

'What was he muttering about?


TED

Ah   he's still talking about my wife --- you'd think he loved her
or something. (then getting mad) well I'm the one who had to listen to her bitching insanity day and night until ! was half out of my mind until I until [ uh.

AL

Until you threw her off the balcony and she deserved it.

TED

Shush you fool   what if somebody heard you.

AL

Ah! There's no one around. (A man's head appears in the doorway and then receedes./ He is about 60.)

/

TED

Look you idiot   I payed with half my life living with that neurotic slut   I'm not planning on going to jail for her,

AL

Don't worry   we covered it up (then chuckling) nobody would dare
question my word You know, there are other people in Vancouver who
have done this kind of thing   in different ways, but essentially
the same thing.

(The 60ish man walks in. His name is Basil. He's a bit scruffy looking, with a moustache and grey hair. He has a British accent.)

BASIL

Hello there   (smiling) how are we all this evening,

TED

Just fine Basil,
BASIL
(As he gets a beer.) Good, good. Have you seen Charley tonight?
(Ted and A1 look at each other.)
AL
Uh   yah   he left a short while ago.
BASIL
Well, that's odd.
TED
What is?
BASIL
Charley leaving   you see, he phoned me this afternoon and said to
meet him here   that there was something important he wanted to talk
to me about. (He pauses in thought. Ted and Al look at each other soberly.) Oh
well.  (smiling) I guess it wasn't that important,
TED
\Isuppose you've heard that Charley's losing his mind,
(Basil looks at him for a second and then says nonchalantly)
BASIL
No I hadn't.
AL
Oh yes, he's going right off his rocker. Something is going to have
to be done   I mean, we're his friends (smiles at Ted) we owe it
to the guy to see that he gets some help,
TED
Yes , you're quite right Al it's awful to see one of your old
buddies disintegrating right before your eyes.
BASIL
He seems well enough to me.
AL
Oh, you haven't seen him lately - he sits in here drinking, talking to himself.
(just then Charley walks in. He goes behind the bar to get a beer.
As lie comes abreast of Basil, Basil whispers
Watch yourself. (Charley looks at him for a second, and then nods.) (Ted leans
across the table and whispers to Al)
Let's get him going. If we can get him raving, we can call the police and have

him put away. Uh   I mean you've got a lot of pull. (Al
nods).
TED
well Charley old boy, what was that (winks at Al) you were saying earlier about
the symptoms of BEING ALIVE?
(Charley looks at him for a second , then smiles and says)
CHARLEY
Yes, the symptoms of being alive   I've seen fishermen in the south of Spain
who can't read or write and who just scrape by from day
to day   but they're alive   I mean really alive and excited a-
hout it. (Then pausing, and saying sadly)   and I've seen people
in this city who have made enough money to feed themselves for a 1000 life
times   sitting - hollow eyed - unmoved by anything.
AL
Oh for Christ's sake -- don't start that stuff again. God, if you
don't like it around here why the hell don't you leave   (then
laughing) go visit your bloody fishermen.
CHARLEY
I probably will   but there's something I have to straighten up
around here first.
(Ted and Al look at each other.)
AL
Oh? And what would that be Charley?
CHARLEY
You'll find out soon enough (and then turns to Basil) how were the ho li days
?
BASIL
Well England's still there. I ran into an old friend I hadn't seen in years and it
was kind of funny.
CHARLEY
What was?
BAS1L
Well, he went on and on about how the bloody Taxi Drivers are making as
much as the business executives these days.
CHARLEY
What's wrong with that

BASIL

(Sternly) What's wrong with that? You don't put money in the hands of commoners old boy.

CHARLEY

Well what do you think this rif-raf is (holding his hand out towards Al and Ted.)

BASIL

Oh yes, but this is Canada   everybody's a bloody commoner here, 1 mean, you don't have a culture   you people just exist. (chuckling)
But I'm sure you'll get over it one day.

CHARLEY

We all agree with you there.

AL

Well, I don't, bloody well agree with you you snotty old bastard.
I mean, who the hell are you? Beyond your accent and phony airs, you're just another old drunk.

BASIL

(Sternly) I'd watch myself if I were you.


AL

Huh (laughing) you slob, 1 don't have to watch myself.

BAS I L

There are certain matters pertaining to Al's wife that I just happen to know about.
(Ted and AI are stunned. They look at each other, not knowing what to say.)
But then again, people are always making up nasty rumors. I don't place much stalk in such things.
(Ted and A1 smile in relief. Charley is hunched over the bar, and this causes him to sit up and look at Basil.)

AL

Yes, isn't it terrible how people play on the misery of others. As if poor Ted hasn't been through enough in this past month.

CHARLEY

He a good fellow Basil, and hand me another beer.

BASIL

Certainly. (Hands him a beer.)

(The lights dim)(End of Scene i)

SCENE I!

(Same setting)

(Charley is sitting alone drinking by himself» Off to the side and behind Charley,

Ted, Al, two policemen, and a psychiatrist are hiding inside the door of the washroom.

They are watching Charley.)

CHARLEY

Yah   (drinks some beer) I never asked much of life   S just

wanted a role that would allow me to be myself. (Pauses for a

minute) ! never found it   there were always compromises and sell

outs cheap smiles and phoney charades. [ guess it. finally took

the spirit right out of me. Now I'm just like the rest of them

going through the motions   uh   (shaking his head) living it out,

not knowing why. (Then getting mad) Jesus! What it could have been. (Ted, Al etc come out of the washroom. The two policemen grab Charley by the arms).

ONE POLICEMAN

You'll have to sign this doctor. He hands him a piece of paper, (doctor looks at Al. Al nods his head)

DOCTOR

Okay(He signs it)

CHARLEY

Hey   what the hell is going on!?

POLICEMAN

"omo o.' old boy   nobody's going to hurt you. We¹ re going to give you the kind of help you need.

CHARLEY

What?   help? (He looks at Al and Ted) (Then screaming) Look these two have murdered a woman they've

POLICEMAN

Sure they have (smiling at the other policeman as they drag him out the door.)

AL

Well, let's have a drink.

DOCTOR

No, no   I've got to be going, but there's just one thing Al.
AL
Yes, what's that?
DOCTOR
You're sure about this violence business?
AL
Oh yes, ask Ted,   Charley would go beserk, threaten to blow the
world up.
TED
That's righ doc. he was out of his mind. and you know Al and I
are his friends   1 mean we just want to do what's best for him
before he really hurts somebody.
DOCTOR
Fine (He walks out the door.) (Ted walks over to Al and shakes his hand,
Jauc'h i ng .)
TED
You're a genius Al   That's a load off my shoulders.
AL
Well , I'm in this as far as you are. We had to do ¡t. (Then saying loudly) Charly
was finished anyway.
(Lights dim) - end of Scene II
SCENE 1 I 1
(Same setting. A1 and Ted are sitting at a table.)
TED
Well, it's a couple of years since old Charley was put away,
AL
Yup,
TED
Do you think they'll ever let him out.
AL
Oh sure, someday, but that won't matter, nobody would ever believe what he's
got to say now.
TED
(Laughing) Yah -- once you've been in the looney bin, that is, it.
AL
out you know, I often wondered why old Basil never said anything.

TED

Oh hell, he was just going on gossip  and besides, at his age he
isn't going to get messed up in something that's none of his business. (Charley
walks in the door. He's a changed man. He has a new suit on and is very well
groomed.) (Ted and Al are stunned. Charley is smiling, and he walks over to
the bar and helps himself to a beer.)

TED

Well  uh  Charley --- uh welcome back,

CHARLEY

(Looks strongly at them and then turns away) it's not Charley anymore, it's
Doctor Turner.

AL

(Laughing) DOCTOR TURNER?

CHARLEY

That's right, while I was in the nut house I completed my Ph D and I'm now a
lecturer at the University of British Columbia.

(Ted and Al stare at each other in disbelief) (Charley pauses and then continues
)

you see, I discovered something that night the policeman hauled me off
(pauses). I spent half my life criticising -- blaming, and yes, occasionally
sticking my nose where it didn't belong (be pauses again AS he walks out in
front of the bar and then says lightly) oh — and don't worry about that other
matter, the wife thing  you see, I "am" to realize that no matter how things
appeared, I could not stand  out side of another individual's life, a life that really
I know nothing about  and pass judgement I mean, I don't know all of the little
things that have gone on in your life, Ted, in the past 45 years. If you had to
resolve some situation uh , in a manner I cannot understand, and one that I have
no way of proving, well  it is you who must answer to yourself, and God,  if
he exists.

(Ted stares down at the floor as both Charley and A1 look at him. Slowly, tears
come from his eyes, and he looks up at Charley and says)

TED

To know that someone  uh  understands, even if it is only slightly. means so
much to me Charley  uh  for that to come from you,
whom ! have wronged in the most wretched of ways  well  I uh  if there is
uh (he gets up and walks out the door, unable

to control himself.)

(Charley sits down at the bar with his back to Al, A1 looks over at him and then back at his beer. After a few seconds, Charley sayst

CHARLEY

You were fucking her, weren't you Al. (Al looks over al him, but doesn't say anything) (Charley continues)

and she had threatened to tell Ted, didn't she? (Al continues to

stare at Charley) and you knew that if Ted found out , he'd

kill you instead of her (loudly as he turns around looks Al)

directly in the eyes) isn't that right A1(then he pauses, and turns back to the bar and says quietly) oh you don't have to answer , you see, as I said to Ted, it's really none of mv business  and it's you people who have to live with whatever happened.

(Al gets up and leaves, slowly, his head hanging down) (a couple of seconds after he does Charley gets up. He appears to be loosing his composure as he loosens his tie and throws his suit coat on the floor. He goes behind the bar and opens three bottles of beer. He lifts one

up, and guzzles it down. He then takes the other two bottles and

walks out from behind the bar and goes across the room. He slumps

down on the floor against the wall.)

Dr Turner?  huh   last week I thought I was Napoleon Bonaparte

(looking out at the audience) Oh, I know I'm out of my mind (louder and emphatically) but what is that? (then, enunciating each word as if it stood by itself) liberty stands atop the head of each man (then

louder) for a second in time only   for a crashing wisp of a moment,

it does not hover, or wait -- one grasps it or loses it forever. I

may be insane, but I am free.  I have no guilt  no sin  no

manners  no hell  and no heaven. (Pauses and then says emphatic

 I am a man!

(The lights dim.)

SCENE IV

(Same ¡retting. Ted is seated at a table by himself. Basil is at the bar. They are both quietly sipping their beer.)

TED

You know, it's odd that we haven't seen Charley   he came in one

evening a couple of weeks ago and we haven't seen him since.

BASIL

Yes   I'm looking forward to seeing him.

(at that second, Al walks in.) Ted and Basil look at him.)

AL

Wait till you hear this.

TED

What?

AL

Well , I triad to phone Charley today, out at U.8.C. and they've
never heard of him.

TED

What?!

 AL

They've never heard of him. So I called up that funny farm   and

(he stops talking as he hears somebody behind him at the door. He turns around
as Charley appears in the doorway. Charley just stands there. He is unshaven
and his clothes are filthy, His eyes are a bit beady as if he's been on a toot, (it
is a tense moment) Basil,

 Al and Ted stare at him. Basil looks over at Ted and Al and says jovially)

BASIL

And here we have one of the symptoms of being alive (he laughs very loudly
and Ted and Al join with him. Their tension releases itself in an exaggerated
reaction that is almost a mad kind of laughter.) (Charley walks in slowly,
looking at each of them sternly. They tense up again and watch him go behind
the bar and help himself to a oeer. He opens the beer, takes a drink, and turns,
facing Basil.

He says quietly and sincerely)

CHARLEY

It's good to see you Basil*

BASIL

It's good to see you old boy. (Then pauses and asks quietly) how have you
been Charley?

(Charley looks directly into his eyes for a second, and then turns, as a slow
smile comes onto his face.)

CHARLEY

! haven't been too bad, really. (Then the smile disappears as he stares
at the floor ). No, I'm not going to lie to you Basil  it's been
awful  it's been a bloody nightmare. (Then loudly as he looks up)
my whole life has been a nightmare! (quietly) I really don't know why 1 was
ever born, (Ted and A) down there beers and walk out.) (Curtain falls)
SCENE V
(Setting: the street outside the club. Al is standing on the sidewalk and Ted is
standing on the street beside the curb.)
AL

He escaped, and from what they've told me, they consider him dangerous.
Apparently he doesn't know who he is any more.
(Ted sits down on the curb with his chin in his hands. A1 pauses and then
continues)
AL

They've done everything to him, shock treatment  the works. (pauses
and adds sadly) The poor bastard. (He stands there for a minute and then says.)
We'd better phone somebody.
TED

I have not. phoning anybody. These years have been the worst years of
my life A1  I've violated ever thing I've, ever believed in (then
louder) well it's going to stop, right now! (he stands up, tears
in his eyes.) that man ¡s going to live as he wishes to live  for
once in my life !'m going to do something that I believe is right, (pauses and
then starts to walk back towards the club. He stops and lurns to say to Al.)
I'm going in there and I'm going to give Charley anything he wants
to do what he pleases, to go where he wants (louder) whatever!
AL

Watt a minute you fool. How do you know that he's not going to turn
on us again (getting mad) Don't be a damned idiot  we could be
-.taring at life imprisonment!
(Ted stops in front of the door, turns around and says quietly)
TED

y./e' re not staring at life imprisonment, we are already living in life
imprisonment. (louder) we've built the prison and we've sentenced ourselves!
(he starts to walk in the door but Al screams and stops him.)
AL

V/ait a minute! Let's at least think this over for 5 bloody minutes.

TED

I don't have anything to think over   and if you do, that's your
problem (he starts in the door again,}

AL

(Screaming) Wait! (Ted stops) Look Ted. I've never asked anything
of you   uh   for all the bloody mess   uh   for me, will you
come back here for just 2 minutes. (Ted doesn't move in either direction. He
just stands there.) Please!

(Ted turns around and walks back towards him.

TED:

(Quietly) as if I owed you my soul. (They stand there, shuffling their feet. Al
paces back and forth, perspiration beading from his forehead,

AL

Okay, we won't phone anybody   but we're not going back in there.
We're just going to leave -- he **can** do what be wants, and it has nothing to do
with us. (He looks at Ted for **a** second) we're just going to
walk away Ted it's the .only way.

(Ted looks at Al) and says)

TED

Al, you do whatever you want to do. But I've walked away all of my
life, I've passed starving children on the streets of Calcutta   I've
refused to give even a quarter to a shaking drunk *2k* hours away from death.
I've turned my back on friends, on everybody in some vain pursuit of social
position and power. (quietly) well, **I'm** not walking away this time (louder) I'm
going back there and I'm going to
face Charley   and I'm going to face what we've done (then pausing
as he turns to go back) and let the chips fall where they may.

(As he reaches the door, Basil come out. There are tears in his eyes. Ted stops.)

TED

What's wrong Basil?

BAS I L

He's dead .

TED

What?

BAS IL

(sadly) He just fell over, mumbling something about 'thank God he'd lived for at least a few days of his life.[1] (They all look down at the street. Then Basil adds)

With what has gone on, we'll have to leave him there, else they'll think we've had a hand in it,

(Ted and Al nod sadly as the three of them walk down the street off the stage. A few minutes pass and then, suddenly, Charley appears at the door. Me steps out on the street and looks out at the audience and says quietly and pensively)

CHAR LEY

I think all four of us are free now. (He turns, and wo lks down the street in the opposite direction until he is off slatje. The lights stay on a few minutes and then they dim.

CURTAIN

Scene ! (Setting: A sidewalk cafe beside the beaches and waters of the mediteranean sea in southern Spain. All the tables are occupied by casually dressed, well tanned northern Europeans. Charley is seated at one of the tables by himself. There are 2 empty chairs at his table.. They are the only empty seats. A beautiful you woman walks into the area of the sidewalk cafe. She looks around for a table, and seeing none, walks over to Charley's table. Her name is Barbara, Charley is noticeably older but well groomed,

BARBARA

Would you mind if I joined you.

CHARLEY

(Smiling) No, not at all

(She sits down)

BARBARA

Do you speak Spanish?

CHARLEY

Yes I do.

BARBARA

Oh good. Would you mind ordering me a drink?

CHARLEY

What would you like?

BARBARA

A Gin and Lemon

(The waiter, dressed in a white shirt and tie, and a white linen jacket walks up

100

to the table.)

WAITER

Si señorita?

CHARLEY

Lá señorita egousta Hinebra con limon.

WAITER

Si .

(He walks off stage to the bar)

BARBARA

(Smiling) That's very impressive.

CHARLEY

(Laughing) Really, it's about all I do well in Spanish -- that is, order drinks.

(Barbara laughs and looks off stage at the ocean).

BARBARA

The tide is going out

(Charley follows her *gaze* off stage)

CHARLEY

Do you see that fishing boat coming in.

BARBARA

Yes

CHARLEY

He's a friend of mine. Paco. I've known him off and on for 20 years.

BARBARA

Oh really, do you live here?

CHARLEY

I do now -- but I've been coming here since I was your age, I spent the major part of my life in Vancouver.

BARBARA

Oh, wow, that's where I'm from.

CHARLEY

(Cheerfully) How is it these days.

BARBARA

(Laughing) Oh we still talk about the rain and I suppose its changed very little. But I would love to live here.

CHARLEY

Do it then. I came here as a young man and wished the same thing. Only !

didn't do it. I wasted half my life running somebody else's race. (Then looking off towards the ocean) For what I don't know. (The
waiter returns with the drink and sets it down. Charley reaches into
his pocket) allow me.
BARBARA
No, no, (smiling) I ask no favors and ! expect none to be asked of me.
CHARLEY
(chuckling) okay.
(An old distinguished peasant dressed Spanish man walks into the cafe area. He Is the fisherman Paco. He walks up to Charley's table)
PACO
Comma es ta ami go?

CHARLEY
I am well Paco  uh   this is señorita Barbara.
PACO
(smiling at Barbara) Olah
BARBARA
Hello
(Paco sits down. The waiter comes up,)
PACO
vino tinto for favour
WAITER
Si senor
(Waiter leaves)
CHARLEY
How goes the fishing.
PACO
Not as well as your senor (nodding to Barbara. Charley and Barbara
laugh)
(The curtain falls .)
SCENE II (Setting: The inside of a rustic humble villa. The
ocean can be heard off stage. The waves are gently lapping the shore. It is early morning. Barbara and Charley are asleep in a bed, to the right of the main living area. Barbara wakes up and gets up. She is dressed in a nearly transparent night gown. She walks to the window that looks out on the off stage area

where the sounds of the ocean are coming from. She looks and smiles and then walks into the kitchen. She puts a kettle of water on the stove. Charley lifts his head up and rubs his eyes. Barbara looks back at him and says)

BARBARA

it's a great day Charley,

(He smiles at her)

BARBARA

Paco will be here soon   what should i cook for breakfast.

CHARLEY

Nothing for me, but i'm sure Paco will eat anything in the morning.

BARBARA

(Laughing) How about Cordera Asada and a bottle of wine?

CHARLEY

(Chuckling) Well that might even tempt me.

BARBARA

The wine or the lamb?

(Charley gets up wrapping a sheet around himself and walks off stage to the bathroom. Sounds of running water and gargling are heard.)

CHARLEY

Barbara,   will you hand me something to wear.

(She goes to a closet, picks out some casual clothes and hands them to him. His bare arm is visible coming out from the off stage area. A loud knock is heard at the door, at the back of the stage. Barbara walks over and opens it. Two Spanish Policemen barge in pushing her as i de ,)

(Loudly) Charley!

CHARLEY

Yes (as he comes on stage dressed)

POLICEMAN

Senor, please pardon our intrusion but we have information Lhal the señorita is m possesion of illegal drugs.

CHARLEY

You're out. of your mind.

POLICEMAN

! am sorry senor, but we must search the villa.

CHARLEY

(Madly) Well search then, you're not going to find anything.

103

(The policemen begin searching. Barbara and Charley's eyes meet and tears come rolOing down Barbara's face. They stand there staring at each other while the search goes on.

POLICEMAN

Senor

CHARLEY

(Looking over at him) Yes?

POLICEMAN

Look at this (He is holding a package of something. Charley walks over and looks. The two policeman exchange embarrased glances as Charley walks over to Barbara. He stands in front of her and they look at each other in silence for a few minutes. Then still looking

in to Her eyes Charley says.

CHARLEY

it is mine

POLICEMAN

(startled) Que?

CHARLEY

I said it is mine. (Charley turns around and walks up to the policeman who has found the dope. He stands there looking at the policeman .)

POLICEMAN

No senor, it cannot be yours. You are amigo to us all. It cannot be.

CHARLEY

(nodding his head and saying sternly) It is mine.

POLICEMAN

(Shaking his head) Then you are in much trouble senor. (He motions to Charley to walk out the door. Charley does so, and they follow. Barbara is still standing to one side of the door. Tears arc streaming down her face as she watches them leave.

CURTAIN FALLS .

SCENE I I

Setting: The inside of an old Spanish prison.

Charley and other prisoners are sitting on mattresses laid on the floor. There are bars that open onto a corridor to one side of the stage. Barbara walks up, escorted by a guard.

104

Charley is unshaven and scruffy looking. Upon seeing her he walks over to the bars. They stand there looking at each other. Barbara is cry i ng.

BARBARA

Oh Charley (holding her hands up to her face) I'm sorry.

CHARLEY

Don't be sad. I've been in prison before  not this kind of prison
(then pausing) not prison like this, worse ones *I*  the ones we create
for ourselves.

BARBARA

(A bit more in control of herself) But for 7 years (then breaking down) my God
what fucking justice.

CHARLEY

Barbara, I am an old man  a man who's life has already slipped
through his fingers (then looking away) dashed against a great slab of rock like
the surf pounding a wall. 1 lost a long ! ime ago.
(Then looking at his fellow prisoners) I lost life I lost, what
even these despairing souls still possess, (then louder) hope! courage! dreams'
(then pausing) Go away and live your life Barbara our few moments together
were much more than I deserved.

The lights dim on the prison part of the stage and the guard walks away. Barbara is standing there alone. She lifts her head from her hands and rubs the tears away. The sound of the ocean is heard off stage. She gazes in that direction.

The sound gets louder and louder and then dies away. She turns her back to the audience, and with her head bowed walks slowly down the corridor to the back of the stage. The lights

Scene changes are not used as
setting changes. They are in all
cases a brief interiude that

*2014*
*Re TERRENCE F. HILL*
*E:MAIL HILLTERRENCEF@GMAIL.COM*
*LIVES NOW IN ROME, ITALIA*

This is an earnest request from the Creative Community of Palm Springs to have you consider the works of Humanitarian, Playwright, Poet and Novelist, Terrance Hill. Having read his works over the years I have witnessed his dedication and growth. As a creative individual, his work has been an inspiration. His Humanitarian point of view has continued to inform his Works.

As a retired Navy Veteran of the Iconic Vietnam War, his quest has been, to contribute to the literary conversation.

His published work "War and after" is provocative in it exploration of Contemporary problems initiated by that conflict. He draws from his own experiences, such as his struggles with PTSD and adjustment to civilian Life. His close connection and interview of his creative contemporaries, has enabled him to confront large questions, as "can Civilization survive its own Technology" and "the conscience of man as the Reality of War"

These new works are in touch with the unconventional struggles to explore the contradictions of conscience. For your consideration

*BERNARD HOYES*
*ANTHONY SILVA*
*please*
*Google*

# QUI EST MARCEL

*A two act play for the stage*
*by Terrence Hill*

In place of the avante garde theatre of the

sixties, this is the  theatre of essence

Setting: The setting is the dining room of a large, well fashioned, post-colonial house in north of Terminillo. The time is the present at the rear of the stage, along the back wall of the room

**Scene I:**

are a large English colonial cub board full of dishes and glasses, a stereo, the cabinet of which is made in the style of the same period and a long drawer - cub board for tablecloths and platters. Above the cub board hangs a very good copy, in actual size of the original, of Goya's Maja desnuda. In front of this, stage centre, is a dinner table, set appropriately for a four course meal. Five people are seated, about to begin the first course of smoked salmon and lemon. In front of the dinner table, close to the front of the stage is a small table that has an original replica of the Aztec culture. On it obviously occupies a position of importance in the room. It is a piece of poetry PieiTe, the host is at one end of the dining table , stage left and Anne , his companion, is seated at the other end. Mitchei, John and Otto are seated along the back side of the table facing the audience. Pierre is about so, of slight build and well groomed. John, Otto and Mitchei are about the same age. their appearance is not important. Anne is about 40,very attractive but obviously a woman of depth, character and genuine beauty and charm as the curtain goes up the stage is dark except for a spotlight on Pierre and Anne.

Pierre: (To Anne, calm but with feeling and intensity) All the moments of my life could go away - drift into a moving mist and I would not care for each second with you has, perhaps a tortuous, arduous, sometimes trembling life ( more softly) but nevertheless a life (distantly) a lazy , lost confused dream - a

107

mystery - my Mona Lisa ( pauses, then says more directly ) I could do nothing but sit and watch you breathe and not move except to touch you when you needed touching - to run my hand gently across your face to know your warmth and for you to know mine - a little cloud radiantly, stupidly lost in an infinite static moment of love. I don't care who you are, what you are, where you are, what you've been, what you will be, where you will be - (strongly) nothing! (long pause then Pierre says in est) now look the other way while I throw ( reaches for a bottle of wine in front of him) this bottle of wine at you. (Anne and are about the same age. their appearance is not important. Anne is about 40,very attractive but obviously a woman of depth, character and genuine beauty and charm as the curtain goes up the stage is dark except for a spotlight on Pierre and Anne.

Pierre: (To Anne, calm but with feeling and intensity) All the moments of my life could

go away - drift into a moving mist and I would not care for each second with you has, perhaps a tortuous, arduous, sometimes trembling life ( more softly) but nevertheless a life (distantly) a lazy , lost confused dream - a mystery - my Mona Lisa ( pauses, then says more directly ) I could do nothing but sit and watch you breathe and not move except to touch you when you needed touching - to run my hand gently across your face to know your warmth and for you to know mine - a little cloud radiantly, stupidly lost in an infinite static moment of love. I don't care who you are, what you are, where you are, what you've been, what you will be, where you will be - (strongly) nothing! (long pause then Pierre says in est) now look the other way while I throw ( reaches for a bottle of wine in front of him) this bottle of wine at you. (Anne and Pierre laugh)
Anne: Thank-you Pierre
(The spotlights go off and the lights come on all begin eating the smoked salmon but Pierre and Anne use a small fork to squeeze the lemon over the salmon before beginning eating)
Mitchei: I'll have to apologize for him again tonight. He won't be coming he gave me a reason as usual, and as usual I didn't understand what he meant (Pauses) and of course. I felt it would be rude to ask
Pierre: (Long pause, then says a bit irritated) Who is he? Where is he? I've been hearing about this god-dammed Marcel for five successive dinner parties-

why the hell don't you let the rest of us meet him?

Mitchei . I really don't know who he is (Pauses) sometimes he tells me a bit about himself

John: Yes, so we've heard. What was the latest bit of genius

*Mitchel: Well, nothing really, just a bit about his childhood. I asked him, of course, and he said it had been normal.*

Pierre: Well, he went on to say that he hung around street comers. With leather jacketed companions - Threw wheelbarrows through picture windows - Pulled fire alarms - Stole bricks from construction sights and generally made as large a nuisance of himself as possible (Pauses and looks at Pierre) How about yourself old boy

Anne: (Interrupting, a bit irritated) Why are we always talking about him?

Otto: (Goes into the dry heaves, then says) Oh inflation, bank interest rates

Pierre: Shut-up Otto!

John: Qui est Marcel?

Mitchel: We live together, that's all.

Pierre: Après tout the talk of him. It's getting as if we all live with him (Pauses) Dam it - Where is he? - Where has he been?

Mitchel: It's his business (Pauses) But I will tell you that 8 months ago, before he moved in with me, he—

John: (Interrupting) Before we met you

Mitchel: (Annoyed) Yes (Pauses) He spent a period of time in a psychiatric assessment unit (Anne stares defensively at Mitchel)

Pierre: As a patient?

Mitchel: He said it didn't make any difference.

(The waiter rolls on a dolly with the next course - Spaghetti - And begins clearing away the plates and serving. He begins with Anne. The conversation continues uninterrupted. The waiter's name is José, and after he is finished serving the spaghetti, he opens the wine and pours a small amount for Pierre to sip. Pierre nods and José completes pouring for the guests, beginning with Anne.)

Mitchel : And he did mention that there were six women there with him. - All of whom were murderers.

John: (Smiling) Sounds like a villa in the south of Spain.

(Pierre laughs)

Mitchel: One of whom he apparently became quite enamered with and she was released about the same time he was. (Pauses to sip some wine) He shouts about her occasionally

Pierre: What do you mean shouts Mitehel: I mean (Strongly) Shouts - Quite literally - He screams her name - Wonders why she touched his being so strongly (Pauses) Says openly that it's all quite mad but always adds (Slowly) So is life.

Pierre; And what was her name?

Mitehel: (After a sip of wine) Louise.

John: Didn't you say he was involved with art.

Mitehel: Yes. He shouts about that too. He's always bitching about what's happening to the world of art - The critics - The doddlers - The static, still, stifled minds of those (Strongly) who cannot see the wind (Pauses) He says art doesn't exist in the defined world of behavioural science. There apparently is no place for art except as a symptom of pathology. (Pauses) He said he wouldn't live in a culture where art is viewed, predominately, as a symptom of mental illness.

Anne: Can you blame him?

Mitehel: (Looking directly at her and saying strongly) No! The architecture of this house is by itself a standing comment on that. The very essence - The very expression of what man is, or isn't - Of what a country is or isn't, is its culture - its art; if it has to import it, or doesn't have it at all - It is a vacant; withdrawn scar on civilization (Pauses to sip his wine) A country that cannot produce great artists and a consciousness that amounts to a distinct cultural identity is nothing more than a sad shadow dark and blind beside a booming, blossoming oasis of life and energy - The human saga - The history of man is the history of art. From the discovery of fire to the poetic yearnings of Keats. (Pauses) Without the perspective Shakespeare created for England you would have never heard of the commonwealth. Art is that which refreshes, rekindles, reminds, inspires (Pauses) It's quite simple - Man is a dead fish without it - That's all

John: (Long pause.) Yes, while you were saying that I was thinking about the Concorde - When I saw it chills ran down my spine - It was awesome - Breathtaking

Pierre: Antigone by Sophocles in the theatre of Dyonsys in the year 700 B.C. - Opening night

Mitehel: Exactly

Otto: (Goes into the dry heaves) Oh Inflation, bank interest rates

Pierre: Shut-up Otto!

Lights dim H

## Scene II:

Setting : The same. As the lights come on the characters are eating the main course, cordon bleu. Mitchel is talking.

Mitchel: —The whole world went rushing by - He did nothing, heard nothing - He saw nothing (Pauses) Tumbling along, forlorn, destitute (Pauses) Crying, weeping - Because, for him. It was too late.

Pierre: What was too late?

Mitchel: (Long stare and then says softly) — Life. (Long pause) He stood cornered, crumbling ~ Leaning on a cane that may either have been a prop of justice or a melting candlestick of innocence. (Mitchel cont'd) In either case it was temporary and certainly not remedial - His crisis, his recovery was a momentary absurdity that unfortunately was very real for him, in spits of the humor it evoked in others, and it characteristicly, as he remarked, continued to forget to add <u>him</u> to the daily headcount of humanity (Pauses to sip some wine) Leaving him, as always, a rejected novice dripping from the end of a broken wooden spoon that had somehow escaped a thousand year sentence in a salad bowl. (Pierre and John chuckle softly) This came as a result of a deceptive gesture aided by a napkin and a dinner plate. (Pauses as all smile) This sounds humorous but it is serious - It was all some years ago, and since then he's been stumbling backwards, not knowing where he was going or even from where he had come -1 don't think he really even knew who he was (Pauses) For years - And I'm not sure that he really knows now (Pauses) And you know, I don't think he even cares - (Pauses) You see.

There was a time in his life when he couldn't hear the music - Listen to the echo in the vast chamber of daily re-birth - A lovely, lifted, lighted lampshade - Just a soft moment of meaning somewhere - He was long past the worry of burning out - Of losing what in essence jt is (Pauses) He had both overcome that moment and stood naked on the threshold of another (Strongly) Madness (Pauses)

Pierre: And now?

Mitchel: (Pauses to sip his wine) Oh now NM (Smiles) He talks of this love he

111

had (Strongly) But now it is just a phony, crashing piece of fiction (Pauses) But he shouts on and on as if the love was still real - As if she was still his (Pauses to sip his wine) He says there's a certain aspect of falling in love that makes the rest of the world fade into a vague irrelevent shadow - The petty, paternal, patronage of one's association with culture, slides off a comer somewhere - Saved in some other reality, but lost completely to the surrounding smile of love (Pauses to sip his wine) He said the other day that some of the greatest moments if his life - Those of love, of beauty, were savagely stunned by his own unsorted, blind introversion - A passive pain, pouncing patiently for some ridiculous moment that no doubt came and went - Wanting only the blink of an eye and receiving not even a swallow - (Pauses) - While the sun rose and set, he was, becoming permanently lost - Bent - (Pauses and says in a deeper voice) Tying his shoelaces - And half the time tying them together, so that even if he did stand up he would be immediately making the rest of his decisions from a prostrate position on the floor - That flat surface we use to wear the soles of our galoshes out and sometimes our minds.

Lights dim - End of scene.

## Scene III:

A dark stage is used to signify a flash back to obviously a different time and setting. The characters remain seated on the stage during this scene. The female voices
come from stage left and the male voices come from stage right.

Male voice A: I'm in favor of downstaging for not attending the occupational therapy meetings because without planning the week-ends are a drag.

Male voice B: No, I would discourage the use of downstaging and the taking away of liberties.

Female voice A: Well, I would like to remind everyone that occupational planning is not only for week-ends but for the Monday to Friday period. As well

Male voice C: It's obvious that too much emphasis has been placed on forcing people to occupational therapy meetings rather than iniating gennine interest.

Male voice A: Well, it's the patients' ward

112

Male voice B: Yah, and you can't threaten us to do things

Male voice C: That's right, but I suggest if the patients aren't interested it should be dropped altogether.

Anne: Let's stop talking like little girls and boys - For Christ's sake can we move on to something else.

Male voice A: I agree - We'll now move on to feedback (Pauses) NM. MR Timmins has asked for feedback this week

Anne's voice: (Sarcastically) Why do you want feedback?

Mitchel's voice: Well, my moods have fluctuated since coming back from the hospital and this has effected some people: - Therefore, I would like the differences aired to improve my relations on the ward.

Male voice C: Have you discussed the reasons with your doctor - After all, the usefulness of having the doctors here is to help the patients prior to having to approach the whole group with your problems.

Mitchel's voice: (Loudly with bitterness and hatred) Four sauna baths could quite easily replace the doctors on this floor (Pauses) And it would be less expensive (Pauses) And look motherfucker, I have to live on this ward and get along with these people. (Pauses) -1 want to find out what's happening to me.

Male voice B: (Calmly) Theoretically, one should see the doctor first.

Mitchel's voice: (Angiy) The whole flicking ward can jam it.

Male voice A: (Loudly) I resign (Footsteps are heard)

Female voice A: I don't think a patient should be allowed to leave the meeting.

Male voice B: He's returning (Footsteps are heard)

Male voice A: (Loudly) All right, he's got every right to go for feedback, - For God's sakes he just wants to see how people are relating to him.

Male voice D: Things are becoming progressively more distorted and people are becoming emotional over what is nothing more than a procedural difficulty.

Female voice B: Yes, I agree, and as a result I would discourage MR Timmins from going for feedback at this time.

Male voice B: (Irritated) I resign (Footsteps are heard.)

Male voice D: Well, I would encourage you to go for feedback.

Female voice A: Yes, I agree.

Mitchel's voice: I am ridiculously hurt by all of this, and I decline. (Pauses and says quietly) But I don't know who I am.

End of Scene HI

**Scene IV:**

Setting: The same.

As the lights come on the characters are eating the fourth course - Strawberry shortcake

John: (Points to the piece of pottery in front of the table) I've been looking at that all evening and wondering what the hell it is.

Pierre: Oh yes, I recently acquired it. It's a replica of the Aztec culture. It was used in religious ceremonies as a recepticle for drops of holy water. Today it is just another ashtray.

Otto: (Goes into the dry heaves) Oh Inflation, bank interest rates

Pierre: Shut-up Otto!

Mitchel: Evidence of the advance of civilization I would expect.

(Anne laughs)

John: (Stunned) You mean that's an original

Pierre: All of life is original (Pauses and looks at Mitchel) That's a quote from Marcel I believe - But it seems odd that I'm quoting a man I've never met or read. (Pauses to eat, then says looking at Mitchel) Isn't it something you mentioned that he'd said.

Mitchel: (Pauses) Yes - It was during one of his zealous, bubbling creative moments.

Anne: (Cynically) The ones he doesn't have anymore.

Mitchel: (Looks at her surprisingly, then smiles, and as he is about to begin eating again, says) Exactly.

John: (Long pause) I sit here wondering how he spends his time. I try to imagine him moving in with you - What he would look like - What he would do

Mitchel: He looked out - Always looking out, the fool! - Confused by what everybody else was doing and not seeing any point in it for him. He just sat and watched.

Otto: (Goes into the dry heaves) Oh Inflation, bank interest rates

Pierre: Shut-up Otto!

Mitchel: (Long pause) Oh, and he goes on and on about what he calls the Santa Claus reality - About the glittered neon life - About the clustered 100 hour watt existence that is re-purchased by buying a new employee on the market when the old one has burnt out. (Pauses to sip his wine) He said that when he saw a

114

playground full of kids in grade eight, the thought crossed his mind that they were putting time in (Pauses) And would continue to do so for 40 or 50 years until their allotted bed in some nursing home became available - At a price that would be directly related to diminishing their life long earnings as quickly as possible.

John: That's a fictitious, disgusting sense of reality.

Mitchel: (Pauses and looks at John - Then says intently) The Santa Claus culture - The way he saw it.

Pierre: What does Marcel have against working in some middle income area of the society. (Pauses to sip his wine) It's a good life

Mitchel: (Long pause, then says in a deep voice looking at Anne) He says he doesn't like the ending

John: That's all

Anne: That's enough

Pierre: What a futile, pessimistic, depressing observation

Mitchel: Watch full tolerance unlocked in the midst of ignorance.

Anne: The truth, or a man living in hell.

Mitchel: But he does not ask the rest of us to join him - Or even to listen (Pauses to sip some wine) Actually, for the most part, he lives on bullshit, in it, out of it, off of it.

Anne: (Smiling) But you agree with most of it.

Mitchel: (Surprised - Looks at her then says looking down) Yes (Pauses to sip some wine) Because I'm essentially lazy - I have this tremendous aversion to doing something. (Pauses) I like to sit and ponder moments of near success and near failure. You see Anne (Looks at her) It suits my disposition and attitude towards life to almost arrive - To almost accomplish, to almost fail, because, to me, life is essentially silly.

John: Could I be excused for a few minutes.

Pierre: Certainly - The first door to the left down the hall (Pauses) And don't worry about how you look to yourself in the mirror - It's a bad one - One of those mirrors that somehow always makes you look ugly - It could even give you a case of the uglies if you took it too seriously (Anne laughs, Mitchel, Otto and John smile. John stands up and exits stage left)

Otto: (Goes into the dry heaves, then says) Oh Inflation, bank interest rates

Pierre: Shut-up Otto!

(Long pause then Pierre asks to Mitchel)

Pierre: What was Marcel doing today that kept him from coming?

Mitchel: He was reaching around my philosophy shelf - Trying to draw an historical parallel to today - He moved from Bertrand Russel to Durant and

Pierre: (In jest) That's a long way to move

(John enters laughing stage left, and sits down.)

Anne: (Smiling) On the contrary - That's not moving at all. (Pierre and John laugh)

Mitchel: Well, anyway, he got into Durant and began ranting about the fall of Aristocracy after George HI lost his wits and Louis XIV his head - Sometime after 1789 - And about that period of time, about Shopenhauer writing " The world as will and idea," ' The most powerfull and comprehensive attack ever made upon man's faith in progress and civilization.' He went on about Keats dying of consumption and despair in 1821, after ' Writing perfect poetry scented with the death of autumn leaves and weighted with the tragedy of lost illusions." And of Shelley drowning in 1822, * Perhaps without an effort to save himself; " He had lived long enough " (Pauses) As Caesar had said - And of Byron dying of epilepsy, ' content to disappear from a world which he had described with such acid irony in Don Juan [7] - Of De Musset publishing " Confessions of a child of the century describing ' A ruined world and a people without hope ' - Of Pushkin dying in Russia and Leopard I in Italy ' After phrasing pessimism in such poetry as neither nation has ever equalled since. It was a despondent generation.'

Anne: (Long pause) Yes. But Hugo's Hemani gave birth to the modern drama in 1830 - Ibsen was bom in 1828 - Balzac and Stendhal were perfecting the novel, Heine and Hugo were perfecting the lyric, Sainte-Benue and Taine were perfecting criticism, Tennyson and Browning were publishing their first volumes, Dickens and Thackeray were opening their rivalry, Turgeniev, Dostoiesk, and Tolstoi were growing up in Russia - Turner was flooding England with sunshine; Darwin was gathering material for the most vital achievment in modem science, Spencer was preparing a new philosophy, and Renan was writing " The future of science. " (Pauses for a sip of wine) So you might say (Smiling) That things were picking up a little bit.

Mitchel: (Surprised, says after a long pause) Well Uh I Uh well,

as I've said before, Marcel doesn't' have exactly the best perspective on things. (Pierre laughs)

Pierre: And you?

Mitchel: (Says pensively) To play or not to play - Fve always thought of life that way. Perhaps it's because I'm essentially alone.

John: (Startled) What?

Mitchel: Well, who is Marccl?

Lights dim - End of Act I

ACT H Scene I

Setting: The same. The Warsaw concerto by Aransel is heard faintly in the background. After the curtain rises and the lights come on Mitchel begins speaking. He speaks to eveiyone at the table, looking from one to the other as he talks.

Mitchel: (A bit worked up)

He lived in a - 30 - Cent - Bus - Ticket - Reality (Pauses) A rider in life, who stayed on the same vehicle and never had to upgrade his fare; he thought he stood on the stilting songs of life.

Watching, while the world went bolsteringiy mad around him.

Thus his madness coiled on the wisty pull of wind, and on a crashing breath of ocean acting as his lungless respirator destined to breathe, or destined to die (Pauses)

It was the same stupid train going the same stupid way in the same stupid world. (Pauses, the waiter, José walks on stage left with a tray, holding a pot of coffee.

He begins pouring with Anne. Mitchel continues) " However, I suggest we forget about him - Leave the conversation."

Pierre: (Somewhat irritated) You have captured him, bound him, tom him, ripped away the facades - Humiliated him and then dropped this man you euphemistically call a friend (Pauses) On my dinner table as if he were going to be part of our next meal (Soft, chuckle from all except Mitchel. Pierre takes a sip of coffee. And then says somewhat pensively) And now you have dismissed his struggle as tastelessly irrelevent (Pauses and looks at Mitchel) Mitchel, what do you? What explanation can you offer us? (Pauses) And what of your loneliness.

Mitchel: (Calmly) I don't have to explain anything. My very presence here reflects a

certain answer in itself. (Pauses to sip his coffee as José exits stage left) And yes, I was lonely once, before Marcel, (Pauses) Somewhere. For a foolish folly of time - I saw - I thought - I pondered (Pauses) I stood unbridled by hours or

days - Stuck out of the chaos - The debris - The hatred - The torment - (Pauses)
Stuck out of the silly dizziness of sitting on the boredom and complacency -
On the treacherous treadmill of the exhausting essence - The crashing
confusion of being alive."
(Lights dim except for a spotlight on Pierre)
Pierre: Waiting where we won't wallow itching into infurnoes of injustice
tangling together for two tomorrows
Lifted lightly like lost laughter and after an announced answer we wait, -
Wanton,
- Watch full (Pause) Of onerous old oaks owned on top -
Teatering trecherousiy - A silent softness, - Sapped sorrowfully - Sent swiftly
-
Saundering savegly - And finally sinking sadly.
(Long pause. Then says in jest looking around) Where am I, in the 17 cent
(Stage lights up. José is pouring cognac)
Mitchel: (To José) Qu'est ce que c'est José?
José: C'est Napoleon, monsieur.
(José continues pouring and then exits stage left)
Anne: (Sips her cognac, then says) To objectify this conversation I want to ask
why?
Otto: (Quickly) What?
Anne: Did anyone in history ever come up with a satisfactory answer to the
question why? (Pauses for more cognac) For instance, Buckle spent 20 years
reading the finest minds in human history while learning French, German,
Danish, Italian, Spanish, Portuguese, Dutch, Walloon, Flemish, Swedish,
Icelandic, Frisiac,
Maori an, Russian, Hebrew, Latin and Greek - Then, spent the next 20 years
trying to write an explanation of human history (Pauses to sip cognac) In all
that time, he managed only an introduction - Of course, it filled four volumes,
but it did not contain an answer. (Pauses to sip some cognac) Thousands of
years of thinking and writing - And what really, do we know?
Pierre: (First sipping his cognac) We know that we listen, laugh, nod and peer
about - Sometimes like idiots and sometimes as inside, we held a pole - A mast
that could topple in the wind or sandpaper the edges of our minds and remind
us of such verbal bullets as * I love you' - (Pauses) The boastful! bantery of
beasts reduced to bones - And quite often it is also the expression that says au

118

revoir (Pauses and says as he lifts his cognac glass up) A final trite irony - An example of it all.

Anne: Um - Well (Long pause) I'm still thinking about him, about Marcel - Être he is our answer (Pauses) Pu être he was an added angel angered by time itself - That tempered tea tattler tying all of us to trapped tomorrow - Tightening, twisting, tormenting this day, (Strongly) Today * Etching it as a tombstone, tumbling - Tattooed with our silly names, and even sillier life spans (Pauses) Are we merely spoons, pieces of dated cutlery

Otto:, (Confused) What?

Pierre: (In jest) Stainless steel I hope (Soft chuckle from John and Mitchel)

Mitchel: (In jest) Aluminium probably (Pierre and John laugh)

Anne: (Upset) Don't invite poets to dinner if you can't respect (Pauses and then says smiling) Their babbling.

(Lights dim. End of scene.)


## Scene V:

Setting: Same. As the lights come on José his clearing the table. All are sipping their coffee and cognac, which has obviously been refreshed. As the last plate is put on the tray, which is on a small rolling table behind Pierre, Pierre says.

Pierre: Merci José

José: Bienvenue monsieur. (He rolls the table out stage left)

Anne: You're very quiet Mitchel, pourquoi?

Mitchel: AH of life stands still at some moment of time (Pauses) For all of us.

(Lights dim except for spotlight on Mitchel for solhque)

Mitchel: Unconjured, unconquered unbridled

A man with a regiment, a barracks, a mistress - A man casting anchor sometime after an iceburg has pushed its rude presence upon him (Pause) A reference to an ocean - Too deep to give grounded root - Running sound echos by merely sighting the taughtness of rope - Signaling rootlessness, but honest unfrenzied rootiessness.

Simple, stretched, unleashing of that which is real in life - The continuing exploration of who we are, and where we are going - And a further enquiry as well into the bold truth - (Pauses) Whatever the hell that is (Pauses) Perhaps the sloping roof of a church - A ski slope - That either obscures life, or invites us to explore, re-use and to re-design (Pauses)

Realizing that the flexibility of life is fundamentally restricted, not by science or the limitations of technology but by men who to a large extent construct their own barriers and prisons"

(The spotlight goes out and the lights come back on)

Anne: Thank God for the music

Mitchel: (Smiling) Well. *T* m not so sure of that.

Anne: What do you mean?

Mitchel: (Smiling) We're getting too serious (Pauses to sip some wine) Tolstoi said to Gorky that where you want to have slaves (Looks around at the other guests)

There you should have as much music as possible.

Music dulls the mind.

Anne: And you're startled by the significant when you're mind isn't dulled - (Smiles) Mitchel, I would suppose that this music keeps you're sanity from being challenged.

Pierre: (In jest) That implies quite a presumption

John: (Laughing) Yes, that he is sane.

(Anne and Pierre join the laughter)

Mitchel: Being stunned by significant elements of the human drama has always challenged my sanity.

Anne: But you're not an artist

Mitchel: What diffence does that make?

Anne: It makes a hell of lot - Fm only a poet but if you have the responsibility of recreating - Or better creating from what you have been stunned by - Or even further creating anew in an art from - Mastering the conceptual framework and building in it, significantly, a view, a vision, an understanding - Concretely - A real story - A plausible perspective on life (Pauses) And when it is upwardly streaming, sublimely racing, running out of you as if the acropolis and all that mattered since Athens would anaestfaize itself into a silent, dead stupor unless you grabbed onto it and not only placed it somewhere, but gently, and objectively, let it find it's place in a planned Parthenon of art - Whether it be a landscape, a play or an inspired, spirited molding of sculpture. (Pauses)

Don't you see - The moment at which you tangjle with the decision to brush it off - To push it away or to do something about it, is the moment on which your mind totters unmolested on a pioneering flood of explorative creation and peace, or lifelong madness - To have lost that balance - The compensation for released genius is to have lost the sensitive second of overwhelming depth - Of touching the hearth of 10,000 years of the human struggle - To (Pauses) Have lost this to the sad echo of a bantering hush avec no mañana. (Pauses) Once the artist has even allowed himself to breathe this fury - To write his first creative work - To oil his first canvas - To settle his fingers gently over his first piece of clay, he must _ face this decision recumngly for the rest of his life. It is a moment the non-artist never faces - He was gone a different way (Pauses to sip some wine. The others at the table are spellbound by her comment) (Anne then looks intently at Mitchel and says) Have you ever known a moment like that (Pauses) Marcel. (Pierre, John and Otto stare in shock at Mitchel then gaze in amazement at Anne as Mitchel replies)

Mitchel: (Long pause - He looks intently at Anne) I've been very close (Pause) Louise.

There is a long silent moment Then the lights dim. End of Play.

# THE NOBEL PRIZE A Novel

The trees turfed ard sloped upwards into tha green maze that hung below the angelic white frost cloaking the mountain tops. The wind rode down the steep surfaces and then up again as it played with a kind of freedom only it would know,. Amidst this awe, a small wooden cabin puffed out of a quiet hollow in a deep valley. An artist was at work. The glib and the facade of brick skylines and paved valleys could never evolve so that he would fit. The large untamed habitant of God was his home - the mountains, his street corners - the trees, his mail boxes - the birds and wind, his companions - the fresh frisky echo of restless nature, his nightclub - and the springing rush of water and deer, his city hall - his car and whatever else the little superstructures of finite man produced».

An old iron stove drove its intentions upwards - but around it, inside the cabin, a brush touched softly, and moved with flow ard charm.

.Sheila lay spread across the wool on top of the bed. Her softness being overtakin by the innocent divine glow that illuminated the hard brown room.

Sheila had fallowed Boris as a diciple would follow Christ. She had been untouched and unscarred by the brutal egoism of the cultural worlds.

It was this gentleness and beauty that inspired the creative urge of Boris. The long white lines of flesh - the firm but graceful curves of breast and hip were merely the form that held within - merely the window to a sensuality beyond, imagination.

To most men, she would have been a sensual bsast. But to Boris, she was a spirit as fresh and pure as the white froth crashing below a waterfall - clean» new born» never touched, the image of image itself.

Boris put his brush down and walked to the window. It was a moment of frustration - a flashback to his beginnings. As his eyes melted with the gusting blades of grass, flittering within their larger cousins,[1] the trees, his lungs opened - not in a sigh or a gasp; they opened to the pulse and feeling of touching the corner of the universe. She gazed at him, noticing the unique outline of his features - the pleasant flow of his body, and the sparkling intensity of his eyes. She felt the unhinged tremor of his heart, and sensed the vitality of his being.

"Boris, come here" she said gently.

He heard her but didn't look over for a long while. When he did, a rushing roar of sensual emotion moved through him. He moved over to the bed and stood above her. Ha thought of how much he loved' her, of how lucky he was to be able to share his life and love with another.

She watched his hand as it moved down to touch the soft warmth between her thighs* His hands had a unique beauty and strength to them.

He bend down to kiss her softly on the slightly bulging portions of her upper leg. His mount then moved between her legs and she felt the smooth tickling sensation of his tongue licking the opening of her vagina. She reached for his naked body and pulled him beside her, grabbing for his dick as if it was life itself. She pulled it into her mouth, driving it to the base of her throat and reached for the white flesh of his bum to drive it even further. She would swallow him if she could. She felt the

He painted to describe a feeling, an anxiety. He made love to Sheila because he loved her, and he wrote so that his soul., would be able to breathe. The many mediums of art that his being manifested itself in, were, in comparison to writing, tulips in the vast array of infinite life. rbsic; painting and sculpturing, to Boris, were primitive beside the creative beauty of literature. Other art mediums were merely a state of conscieneaness an awareness. Whereas, in order to write, at the level of art Boris prided himself, one had to evolve in every plateau and dimension of being - not just as a state of mind, but as a manifest conscienceness transcending as well as being involved in the absurdity of life. To be crushed, crashing against an infinite wall - to die in the centre of a volcano - to fuck Mount Everest - and to then disperse enough energy to undo it all.

That was being at the level necessary to write.

"Boris, I've brought you some wine".

They didn't hear the car pull up as they normally do, for they were both individually involved in an inner subjective struggle - something to to with their past, and possibly something to do with their future.

"Carlos'* Boris said as he rested his hands on his friends shoulders.

They smiled and even laughed. For each of them to see each other was an uplifting event.

"How are things in Banff?" Boris asked.

"Everybody is getting arrested". Carlos replied.

"Is that still going on... the revolution was six months ago."

"Wow that they've got power, they think everybody is a counter revolutionary".

Sheila had made no attempt to clothe herself. She vas enjoying watching Boris and his friend encounter each other.

"Are they that paranoid?" Boris asked, his face wrinkling in thought.

ⁿf/.ʳell, the new minister of information was on television the other night explaining that there wore still many enemies of the people at large, and that undoubtedly, mistakes would be made, but they would be cleared up.

"How's George and BarryV Boris asked.

"George is super paranoid that he's going to be arrested because of his establishment contacts, and Barry is acting as if nothing has changed. I saw him on the chairlift the other day, stoned out of his mind",

"Well, come on you two... let's have some wine" Sheila interupted as she threw a large blanket over her shoulders. She went to a wooden table by the window and picked up three glasses.

"I see that youᶠve already tasted it" she said to Carlos upon noticing the open bottle. They smiled at each other and Carlos poured the wine.

"Have they sent a people's representative chairman to Banff yet?" asked Boris.

"Oh yes... he*s really into a power trip. The day that they made the declaration that there was no more private property and that everything is free, he took the largest suite at the Banff Springs for his living quarters... and of course, now that everything is free, there never seems to be enough of everything to go around. They explain that as a head transission problem in that people still have to work out their material hang-ups. Surpriseingly, though, everybody is really pitching in to do everything that needs to be done. Most of the people in the larger cities have returned to their regular jobs."

"Well, the old economic systems were merely means of distributing produce anyway... but those systems evolved out of times of scarcity, when their wasn't an abundance of even basic things. Today, there is,,#,, there is no longer any need to promote a competitive man against mans way of life. *Vie* can share and co-operate to produce the things that need to be produced.." said Sheila.

"Man*s sense of justice, dignity and fair play being the distributor of produce... I thing that's the very way the chairman put it." replied Carlos.[1]

"What's happened to the older people... they must be pretty freaked out.ⁿ said Sheila.

ⁿOh man... they don't know what's going on... they're hoarding and saying that at least they own this... it's unbelieveable, they can't understand that man is no

longer defined by his economic function or his accumulation of wealth."
replied Carlos.

"Kow are they going to get people to do the shit jobs, like garbage and so on?"
asked Sheila.

[11]A referendum was taken and it was agreed that all 18 year olds would spend
one year of limited freedom so as to be directed to those work areas.
Surpriseingly. enough, the younger people thought it was a great idea - after
all, what's a year at that age." replied Carlos.

"What about immigration, our international monetary relations and all the
maze of other areas that were natural extensions of the other system?
I mean we do have to import mar$r products - how are we going to pay for
them?" asked Sheila.

Do you forget that we also export many products? We,, are a wealthy nation
and enjoy a favourable balance of trade. Our exports more than off-set our
imports." replied Carlos. He looked over at Boris who was standing gazing out
the window.

"And people feel good about being alive now... I mean man, now we[T]re into
life for something larger than ourselves. We are part of an historical experiment
that could change the destiny of man." added Carlos.

Boris replied quietly, "some of us are involved in a larger historical experiment
that transcends even this planet." The short term destiny of man is but a flash
in the millenums of time and infinity."

"Yeah, but I'm not going to be around in infinity, man. I want to get it on today,
now." said Carlos with a .'.laugh.

The twenty miles into Banff splintered the space Boris had been in, as he
arrived on the outskirts of town. He parked his bike outside of a chalet-like
hotel on Main Steeet and went in to check the bar. It was quiet. He sat down
and ordered a pitcher of wine.

The fireplace wasn't burning at the end of the narrow room, but it didn[t] matter.
Boris had not come in to watch a fire. He had come in to get his head together
on a number of issues; one of which might involve his life. Drops of wine clung
to the moist skin inside his mouth releasing a certain tension, a particular hold-
on sort of feeling. To be on for a thousand seconds and off for one. One could
lose it all "in that one - or gain it all as one's mind slipped into a diminsion that
would allow a rest, a perspective and possibly a new plateau to settle over one.

He had to remembar at times like this what he was, and what he was about. He had not decided to become a cultural slave * a manager in the process of useury - a parpatuater of discriminate value systems. These were prisions, whether of Ricardian determination or of Marxist. He wished to fly with the birds.

George strolled in. His angular figure and odd face bobbed over to Boris* table. "You're in trouble."

"With whom."

"The new people. They are mad at you for failing to devote your writing abilities to re-indoctrinating the masses."

"I'm an artist, not a propogandist, and if there's no place for art in this society, then I'm not staying."

"It doesn't appear as if you're going to have much of a choice. They're getting ready to arrest youy"

"For what?"

"They are afraid of what you might write about them."

"Then they should have no fear, because they are not worth writing about. It is always the most shallow and empty of our species who must build the largest fortress... to protect nothing."

"Boris, be practical, you must leave Canada. I'll help you."

"When?"

"You better get moving very quickly.

"I got the word from inside."

Across the street, by strange coincidence, the man Bor»is had sought to meet all of his life was engaged in a conversation over a cup of coffee. Taras Molere was a man who had survived the Bolshevik revolution, to become one of the great literary genius' of^his times. His gentle sloping forehead and punchy white hair had been through prisioner of war camps and six different beginnings in six different countries. He had started and failed so many times, that he had learned the universal story ~ that one is always beginning.

Boris had sought this man out many times - in Paris, in Barcelona and in Alexandria. But he had never succeeded. However, now, Taras was only a few feet away from him. It would be unfortunate for their paths to cross and not to recognize each other - for each of them was the universal artist at different stages of his evolution.

For some odd reason, Boris and Taras stepped out on to the street at exactly the same moment. They were directly accross from one another.

As their feet touched the sidewalk respectively, their eyes met.

"Taras! ... Taras Molere" Boris yelled out.

Then Boris stepped back in disbelief of his seeming lack of respect for this man. Taras, however, was not hung up on such petty matters and he beckoned to Boris; to come over and shake his hand.

Taras was along and the thought crossed Boris* mind of how opportune this might be if he could persuade Taras to spend the day at his mountain retreat.

It was quite a day. The sun cuddled the rugged rocky upper slopes and cast a soothing shadow on the gently rising green of the lower valley. Mist-like clouds floated west* high above it all.


An alpha wave calm and understanding reached through their handshade and Boris said very quietly, "Will you come to my cabin for some wine?"

"Are you a writer?"

"I'm an artist." ~ -

Taras melted his spirit with Boris' for a moment as they looked into each other's eyes. ^

"And how do you manifest your being?" asked Taras.

"In absolute art, hopefully... mostly in writing."

"I will cone then" replied Taras,

Taras followed Boris in a small green Alpha-Romeo that a friend had lent him in Calgary.

When they arrived at the cabin*, Sheila was sun bathing in the nude by a large tree that dominated the front landscape of the house. Boris and Taras walked over to her. At first she did not hear them, as if the sun, like a shining 'Budavista had drawn her conscienceness into awareness and sanctity, asking her to be it's sakti, it's goddess.

She reminded Taras of the imagery of the Earth Mother - a vital force in man's world.

"This is Sheila."

"Oh... hello" Sheila replied. She was not able to see to whom she was saying hello, because of the glare of the Budavista. She raised herself on her elvows and her round full breasts leaned outwards.

"Tou are fitting tribute to the sun. Did he just create you?" asked Taras.

She smiled as she realized to whom she was talking.

"iou may create in me anytime you wish, Mr. Mole re."

They laughed as she got up to fetch some wine.

Hours later, when Taras had seen and learned of Boris' work, and had touched his spirit, they calmly moved into a personal dimension in regards to art. Boris was explaining his lack of acceptance in the publishing and art council worlds,

"But Boris" Taras said, " you are- an original - you are the one in a hundred years. The cultural artists attempt to defest any artist who is better than they are in order to retain their own superficial positions. I encourage you to continue. You will eventually break through. But you know, Boris, regardless of how understood one is at a particular time, or how appreciated - no matter what heights of mutual ecstacy or warmth one achieves , you will always end up walking down the beach by yourself - alone and perhaps afraid. But walk with dignity and don't forget to notice the surf smashing on the sand and don't forget to notice the spray touching the stems of the leaves as they rise and fall beneath the descending" sun. And don't forget — you might meet somebodyelse on that beach. Your alonaness exists only as far as you wish it to. Tour fears exist only in as much as you are unwilling to let life take you - only in as much as you resist and want to be a part of death — only in as much as you won't let yourself see and understand."

"I remember" said Boris "what the alter-ego in your novel "THE LAND IS OURS" said to the detractors and critics of artistic freedom and I hope you are not saying it only in that sense. As you recall, he said to them 'when you meet someone and they say, about themselves* about some creative expression - what do you think of this?[1] - and you allow your abstract subjectivism and ego to criticise or diminish, because you have never tried cr grown to the point whereby you could even do what he had done - if you are one of those who does this, remember this - when you think you meet this person you don't- Xou really only meet yourself, and also, remember this. If your life destiny was so blessed so as to bring you into touch, with the soul and spirit of a budding artist, you will have come even closer to heaven than when you touch a new born child - and if you have slapped that child, or put down that artist you have possibly destroyed a beautiful flower, a Froust, a Pasternak, a Hemmingway — yes even an Einstein. You will have dealt a negative blow to possibly another Ghandi. To the great dream of life you will have said, 'I do not care. But even if you do not understand this, you will live long enough - perhaps other life times until you, on your own, in your own way and on your own terms discover what I have just said to you* said Boris.

"Yes, I remember that, but I also mean, when I encourage you, that you are very close to becoming yourself and that will manifest itself in great gifts for mankind[11] replied Taras.

"I am like a prophet moving across a long desert. Occasionally, the heat and the hardship make me delirious and I lose my way - but only momentarily" said Boris.

"Well, if you're not gone in an hour, you're not going to be in the middle of the desert, you're going to be in the middle of a jail cell', said Carlos.

"So they're really coming to take me away, are they?"

Yes, not in a straight-jacket, but in shackles - although I sometimes think the former would be more appropriate." said Carlos as he smiled at Sheila who was sitting on a blue cushioned chair. One leg was lazily stretched out while the other was casually bent outwards at the side of the chair. She was absolutely naked and absolutely beautiful. The soft, short rolls of pubic hair curled around the moisture between her thighs. She was really too much, Carlos thought.

"Okay, I'll split to Vancouver and get a boat to Japan. Sheila, are you coming" said Boris.

"It's better if you go separately and meet in Vancouver. They'll expect you to be travelling together", replied Carlos.

"You're probably right. I suppose the least conspicuous method of travel would be the old box car routine." said Boris.

Three hours later, in an open box car somewhere in the middle of the Rocky Mountains, Boris pondered his future. He remembered what Taras had said to him as they parted company. Taras had said "the process of life involves many periods and phases from birth to death. Live all of them - enjoy all of them. Don't define and judge - allow it to happen - be yourself.

People work through their difficulties whether it takes them years or centuries - every human story has a happy ending."He also remembered what Carlos had said to him. "Boris, if you become unhappy, just think of how much unhappier you could be." Carlos had laughed and patted Sheila's bum saying "I can't force her to meet you but I'm sure she will,'"

''Where did you come from?'' a trainman on the tracks said to Boris as the train stopped at Kamloops,

He had. just jumped out of the box car with the intention of getting something to eat.'

"I rode the train from the crossing a block away - just as a joke." replied Boris. They stood there and stared at each other for a few minutes, and then the trainman said, with an expression on his face as if he had just discivered electricity, "the trains are free - you're running from government. Let's go - you're coming with me.

Boris started running across the tracks as the trainman blew his whistle.

A policeman was close by and started yelling at Boris to stop. Boris was in a state of absolute terror as he ran. He thought of only one thing - freedom - they were going to cage him up - he would go insane. He heard pistol shots behind him but didn't turn around.

Some miles away, he threw himself into some bushes, completely exhausted.

It was Monday afternoon, and he had to be in Vancouver by noon of the following day or he would miss his boat.

Sheila had said, "1 love you Boris and I'll be there, on time."

They has agreed to meet in front of Pier 8 where a German freighter was departing for Japan. Carlos had talked to the captain and made the necessary arrangements. Boris didn't have any doubts about whether she would be there or not. He knew she would be there - hopefully dressed in some clothes, he thought amusingly.

In the mountain cabin, Sheila rolled over on top of him, opening her legs and allowing him to slide up inside of her. She could feel the pulse of his heart as he throbbed up and up. Taras was really not old. The spirit of an artist took a long time to die. His hands moved down her back and up on the clean white flesh of her ass. He pulled and pushed until in an unbelievable scream, they both shook and banged themselves into non-time.

"Wow," said Sheila as she slid down his body and let her tongue touch the moisture 'she had left on his still hard penis.

When he was leaving, he said the only words that were spoken between them that afternoon, and it was almost as an after thought. He turned around as he was going out the door and said, "life is so small, so little without direct love. I mean you can love mankind and Christ, but somehow that demands a direct manifestation - a woman, a human being in which all of the ideals and enlightenment of history are symbolized in the simple act of putting yourself inside of her and saying we are one - in laying there, as we did, panting and saying the hell with the cultural, one-second prisons - you know - the prisons of competative man, the obsession with material definitions. Well, we know God in that moment - maybe in the second before or after we describe or think of it in a selfish or cultural way - but in that second of orgasm there are no props - there are no phony smiles - there are no spologies.

Think of that *my* friend until I see you again."

His only move now, he concluded was to wait until nightfall and get out on the highway. If he got a ride without being spotted, he could make it.

Later that night, he stood on the highway as car after car passed him.

He began to feel insecure about everything. It was night. He was alone and he was a fugitive.

Eventually, a girl pulled up in a blue hardtop,

"Where are you going?" she asked,

"To Vancouver."

"So am I, Know how to drive,"

"Xes"

"Take over" she said as she slid over. He walked around the car and got behind the wheel. They smiled at each other as he noticed her beauty. They both felt an immediate warmth for each other.

About an hour later, as he was driving, she leaned over and undid his trousers. She pulled them down and began breathing heavily as she saw hisH dick jutting out at her. She put her lips over it and began moving up and down. Boris was really enjoying it. She began to move faster and finally with a quick jerk, he blew it all out inside her mouth. She loved it and moved away even more sexually satisfied than Boris. But this wasn't enough for Boris. He pulled the car over and changed places with her. As she was driving along, Boris unfastened her skirt and took her panties off. She opened her legs to receive his tongue. In a very short time she was gasping, well on her way to orgasm. She finally hit the high note and zlmost put the car over a mountain ridge.

"Beautiful" she lamented later to Boris as she let him off on Robson Street in downtown Vancouver.

It was nine o'clock in the morning. The mountains were visible across the water as Boris walked down towards the wharf. He was stopped on the street by a Zen Buddhist passing out pamphlets. After listening patiently to this yound gentleman, Boris interrupted and said, "Listen to me for a minute. The Bhudda would have you rid yourself of all desire in order to eliminate pain.

131

But the American would have you produce all that was necessary to satisfy your desires in order to eliminate pain. I would have you understand your being, its physical nature and its spiritual nature. Do not deny either. Live in harmony with yourself and your environment. If your body needs food* feed it. If your soul needs nourishment, seek it out. But do not say that one is higher than the other, for both are, in this life - and, you will only eliminate suffering and pain by recognizing both. When your spirit leaves your body for good, at your physical death, then forget your body. But not now, or else you will end up fostering a nation of poverty, ignorance, and suffering - such as India.
Don't forget, when Buddha pronounced his first sermon, .he ended it with this;
'Destroy your passions as the elephant would trample down a reed hut; but I would have you know that it is a mistaken idea to believe that one can escape from one*s passions by taking shelter in hermitages. The only remedy •against evil is healty reality* . "T
''But¹'* the young gentleman answered, "the way of the physical, the way of the Americans has not eliminated human suffering."
"Yes, but at least they have the means to do so - the physical means." said Boris.
"Yes, but what is it to hold five loaves of bread in your hands, with twenty-five starving people standing around you, and then to eat it all yourself. Is it a higher state to have this means and use it as such - or is it a lower state" replied the young Zen,
"it is neither higher nor lower, or anything inbetween - and it is not any opposite to any of these things" said Boris.
"Right on" replied the Zen as Boris walked on down the street.. He turned the corner into Gastown and walked by the European Hotel, then across the street
and into a pub. There were only three other people in the place, so he walked up and joined them.
"Hello" he said.
The two women nodded to him and the guy just kept on talking.
"Uh.ₑ, two draft please" he said to the bar maid.
He turned to one of the women and said, "what are you into?"
"I'm .independently wealthy, so I don't have to do anything" she responded rather defensively.

What a bitch, thought Boris. He got up and moved his beer over to another table.

A thirty-fiveish man in a suit came in and sat down at the table next to Boris. "Why don't you join me?" Boris asked.

The man hesitated for a minute and then came over. Boris was looking for an argument and after he had learned that the man was an American Business dude on a trip to Canada, he knew something could be started.

"All you people are prostituteing yourselves" said Boris.

The remark caught the man off guard. After a momentary pause, he replied, "What do you mean? I provide a vital necessity to human life by building houses and developing real estate."

"Well, let me put it this way, when a woman sells herself sexually for money - that is called prostitution, but when she does it for nothing, freely giving of herself - that is called love. Right?"

"Right."

"Okay, when a man builds houses and sells them for money - that is prostitution. When a man builds houses and then gives them away ~ that is love, for he gives of himself and his talents - and, if everybody gave of themselves,

as they are now here in Canada, you wouldn't need to sell because whatever you earned from the sale would be useless. There would be nothing to buy.''

Boris finished the last bit of beer in his glass and wandered out on the street, Sheila would be arriving soon. It was almost eleven o'clock. They were supposed to meat in front of the big statue of Jack. Boris leaned against the building and waited. About a quarter past eleven he began to become apprehensive. Where to hell was she, he thought. His stomach started to pull a bot and mausea overcame him as he thought of the possibility that she wouldn't show. She was a vital part of his life. He loved her,

eleven thirty, he was really in trouble. He had to get down to the pier to catch the boat. But what meaning did the boat and his freedom have if he couldn't share it with Sheila, he thought. *My* god, what was life without love. He paced back and forth. Finally he started towards the pier trying to pull himself together.

What could have happened? he thought. Should he miss the boat and risk going to jail. He was very confused.

When he arrived on the pier, they were just pulling up the gangplank. He ran

up to it and then stopped, looking back down the street for some sign of her.
He then moved up onto the ship, looked out towards the open sea, and began
to cry.

The freighter was making a stop in San Francisco before goint across the
Pacific and by the time the waters under the Golden Gate were smashing over
the hull, Boris had regained his perspective.

Looking at the city as it gently curled and flowed over a maze of rolling hills,
Boris knew he was staying. The bay worked its way around Telegraph hill and
yielded only to the sun in its unquestionable power and beauty. A soul could
fc© reborn here, thought Boris as the ship pulled and gushed up against the
pier.

"Thanks for taking me this far[11] he said to the captain as he slung his
handbag over his shoulder and walked down the gangplank.

He walked by the warehouses and over the railroad tracks towards Fisherman's
Wharf. The small of fish, a couple of guitarists playing on the sidewalk, and
the general diverse color of people and shops reminded him that he had been
away from San Francisco for too long. He boarded a cable car and rode up the
hill towards Broadway. The car banged and riveted up as Boris stood holding
a post and leaning out against the wind. He got off a few stops up the way and
walked towards Columbus.

It was 4 o'clock in the afternoon and Boris noted a few of the North Beach
entertainers and dancers on their way to a first cup of coffee and also a few of
the permanently rich trying to make it to a hairdresser or restaurant in order to
fully wake up. Boris supposed that there were enough Hiltons and St. Moritzs
to hide them from life forever, if they wished. But they didn't have the same
tingle and thrust in their faces as the people who were banging it out from day
to day. All the health clubs in the world couldn't produce the vitality and
rejuvination inherent In every day life in this beautiful city.

Boris found himself a cheap room and dropped down to a bar called the
Camels just above Columbus. He sipped chaples the rest of the afternoon, not
really noticing the sun setting behind the hills to the West of San Francisco.
The bartender was a bit drunk and for some reason seemed overly friendly.
He had just come over from Italy and didn't speak English very well. The bar
itself was an antique from the old golden age of the late nineteenth century.
Two middle aged ladies were sitting a couple of stools down from Boris and
for some reason they were engaging the bartender in an argument,as only an

American can."So, you stand back there and get drunk. What kind of person are you?" one lady said.

"You've got a big mouth lady."

"You gamble away half the till,"

"I said you've got a big mouth,"

"Hey" said Boris, "this guy's a friend of mine. Leave him alone.'"

"Hey^ man" boomed a voice from a large afro-American at the end of the bar, "You're out of it. This is between they and him,"

Boris then realized what was going. The two ladies owned the bar and the black guy was hoping to get the bartender's job.

He turned away and minded his own business. In America, you minded your own business and that was all there was to it. In England, you might be told you were being rude, but in the United States somebody was just as likely to hit you over the head with a bottle if you pryéd into anybody else's private life or personal affairs,

Boris walked out of the Camels and headed towards Broadway. When he was about half way down the street, he noticed Karcel, It couldn't be he thought, but it was. Fortunately for Boris Karcel hadn't seen him.

They had met in Calgary a couple of years back. Boris had agreed to write a screen play based on Marcel's life. Karcel had spent eight years in prison and had made a good try at living a straight life for seven years until, due to his record, his employer and the banks closed in on him, Boris had written the screen play and circulated it. But there were no buyers, and in some way Karcel blamed Boris; as if Boris was responsible for the irrelevent life Karcel had lived.

Marcel just couldn't accept the fact that his life wasn't interesting enough to be written about. Possibly he was right, but Boris didn't control the selection mechanisms within the motion picture industry. All he could do was to present a reasonable product and hope for the best.

At any rate, Marcel had vowed that he was going to kill Boris, What a heavy to be running into at this time, thought Boris.

He turned around and walked back towards Washington Square. If Marcel was here, Boris concluded, he must get moving. He had been planning on going to Los Angeles anyway to meet with a publisher concerning his last novel. This seemed to be a good time to do it."It's provocative» interesting, veil written and very unique. How much do you want for it?'" the Los Angeles publisher asked Boris.

"Nothing."

"What?"

"I said, nothing - I give it to you and to all who can usa it and benefit by it."

"Okay.[11]

"But - if I find an offering from you of say $50,000 and a healthy royalty share in what I have given you - I won't refuse it - because I know it will be given in the same spirit of love that I give you this work of art.

"Well - vie were thinking of $25,000 - would that be a suitable offering?" "The amount of your offering makes no difference because I know that you give what you can afford to give. But the more your offering, the less of my people go hungry."

"Who are your people?" '

"The people of the world."

"Uh..,," they looked around at each other not knowing what to say or do. The built in mechanisms of capitalism somehow couldn't relate to this drama. Finally, one of them said,

"Thank you for giving us this book. We also wish to make you an offering." He picked up a pen and wrote out a note on a piece of paper and then wrote out a cheque. When he had finished he handed them to Boris. The note read,

I HAVE THREE LEGAL WITNESSES THAT YOU HAVE GIVEN ME THIS BOOK FOR NOTHING. THANK-YOU'

and the cheque read ƒ

PAY TO THE ORDER OF BORIS ANDRE

ONE DOLLAR 00_ CENTS

100

He then said, "Have you ever heard of where the buck stops?" and they all laughed - except Boris, who had become very pensive and very angry.

Boris moved very quickly and grabbed the manuscript. He caught theia by surprise. He pulled a lighter from his pocket and set it on fire. They chased him as he ran with the burning manuscript out through the offices. By the time they caught him, it was just ashes.

''We'll sue you, you bastard. That is now our property."

"Well take it" Boris said as he looked down at the ashes, and you can sue me for its total value. I have the check right here - one dollar."

He stuffed it in his pocket and walked into the hallway. They didn't follow.

fen always get caught by the limitations of their own values, thought Boris.

As Boris walked out into the sunlight, his mind flittered back into his past, and for some reason stopped at his grandfather's funeral. It was the last time he had seen his family and he recalled what he had said to Sheila upon returning to the mountains.

She asked him about the event, and he became very distant, looking off at the sky as if he was reading something written up on a cloud. He said:

"Standing there amongst them, the creatures of culture, the caretakers of my youth, I could not help but think that in regards to myself, they had also been caretakers of an historical process, and that now our beings were as separate and apart as two universes might be. I was no longer a planet revolving around their sun. I was my own sun and my own future and in that, something larger, for my life was not an (ego-1) thing. It is a larger universal phenomena - the phenomena of the universal being - the peasant, the light, the atom, the essence. I was in some way the manifestation of these things. My destiny - my fate, was never more clear - and never more certain." "Well, what is it that motivates you Boris?" Sheila had asked.

"To end up having lived, having participated in the great drama of life in these times - to have a say in what is happening, I suppose that is what motivates me. To be a part of the age in which I live - to fulfill myself relative to these times,and if I can, relative to all times. But, I'm not really afraid or overcome by guilt. I know that I am what I am and that I do and will do whatever is a manifestation of what I am."

"What are you?"

"Well, I was in Los Angeles, and I was thinking about my other lifetimes, and I had a feeling that my name used to be Cervantes and that I used to live here somewhere, so I've returned" said Boris to the amusement of his listeners. He v/as in a meson, near the Plaza de Santana in Madred, having a gin and lemon and sort of introducing himself to some of the artistic community that frequented the area. He had decided to fly to Spain and continue his writing there.

He had been fortunate in running into a very interesting group of people.

One of the people he was talking to, Ramon, a Mexican American, had the same

level of talent Boris did, but he lacked to te energy and discipline to make use of it. The tv/o people with Ramon, Bob and Tom reflected a different kind of talent. But they a!! shared a sense of freedom and life - a sense of courage and spirit.that made them good friends and fun people to be with.

"What are we going to do Ramon'?'Tina asked.

"Well, it's a sinch my acting career will be over when your father finds out we're married. I'll be blackballed by everybody in the Hollywood film industry. This is supposed to be an enlightened age. It's 1956, not the 17th century. So what if I'm Mexican?" said Ramon.

He had a lot of fire in his face, and a subtle kindness that would make one v/onder how this man could have enemies.

"We I I have to leave" Ramon continued "to South America, to somewhere, where we can be happy. I've got forty thousand dollars - it could last us for a long time."

They left for Bagota the following day and after six months of touring South America, decided that it wasn't their rainbow. Ramon still had about twenty thousand dollars left and they decided to make a go of it in Mallorca, off the Mediterranean cost of Spain.

They settled into a small villa on the ocean and Ramon later managed to lease a small bar in Patina.

They would walk for long hours on the beach, dreaming and loving.

Ramon's bar soon became the rage of Palina and Tina began to develop her writing abilities. Ramon would write as well, but at this time, most of his work was merely ridding hem self of the cultural reactions and the logical vertical thinking of robot life in North America.

But suddenly tragedy struck. Tina had a still birth and had to return to America and later, the women who leased the bar to Ramon refused to renew it. It was rumored that she turned it over to one of her young lovers in order to keep him.

Ramon, thirty-five years old by this time, was left almost broke and very alone. He went to Madrid to attempt to begin his acting career again. In the next five years he managed to do well, landing small parts and meeting the right people. But he was getting old and he knew that any real chance of success for him was almost gone. Fortunately he always had beautiful and young mistresses, two of whom went on to become stars in England. They wouid send him money occasionally and they left a door open for Ramon if things didn't go too well in Madrid. He v/as attempting to write screen plays, but the wine and the v/omen took their toll on his time-

Bob had grown up in a very straight business fami Iy, pursued his business degree and even gave the old family firm in Los Angeles a bit of a go. But the rigid orthodoxy and narrowness of Sparta could hardly appeal to an Athenian. He left for England, studied acting for two years, landed a few parts and eventually ended up in Spain where the living v/as cheap and where life seemed to be always bubbling over. He would land a part occasionally, and it provided him with enough income to carry on.

Tom had been on a Mediterranean cruise with the Marine Corps, and at one of their ports of call, Barcelona, had fallen in love with all that was Spain.

When he got out of the Marine Corps, he returned. He wandered around at first until his money had gone. His friends carried him for a time after that unti I he landed a teaching position at one of the many language institutes in Madrid. He moved from that into advertising and sales, but what really characterized this fellow was his fascination with courage and his great interest in the vibrant life and history of Spain, and it was this about him that brought him into contact with free spirits like Ramon and Bob. Not thaf Tom had to take a back seat to Ramon or Bob in terms of art or understanding of life. He was just a bit more pragmatic about it.

"I'm going to Spain" Tom said to his parents one night after he had been home for a few days following his release from active duty.

"You're going where?" responded his mother.

"Mm going to Spain and I'm going to live there."

"But where - and what are you going to do?" said his father.

"1 don't know - but that's where ! want to live. ! don't dig this Kentucky Fried Chicken trip."

"But Tom" advised his mother, what about Nancy and the job you've got wait ing for you?"

"She'll still be eating Kentucky Fried Chicken and so on thirty years from now and that just isn't me, and as far as the job goes, where would I spend the money - on Kentucky Fried Chicken? Well big deal." said Tom.

"What's with this Kentucky Fried Chicken business?" asked his father.

"You tell me - it's your trip not mine. Mine is out there in the world."

"... and why did they arrest her?" asked Boris of one of the turned on chics sitting next to Ramon in the meson.

"Well, because she was in the car when the hash was found. The Turkish authorities held her responsible and being a former Playmate in Playboy doesn't carry very much weight in a country in which the women habe yet to unveil their faces let alone anything else." replied Joan in an amusing way.

"If she can get some publicity out of it, it wil I probably help her acting career" said Bob.

The mixture of conversations shredded the buoyancy of social life in Madrid. The singing and musing, the bulls and Torreros fought with each
other in the constant inter-play of the subline and the brutal. The tapestries
of courage displayed but plagued the real end and nirvana to all struggle - the end of the beautiful - the end of sanctity and artistic dignity. Without this halo, Madrid would be nothing.

Boris flittered with the toys that ebbed from the bar until in a mistic haze of intoxication he walked past the blurs of human cells out onto the streets.

A dog v/as waddling gently along below the sometimes moving leaves in the plaza. Taxis would spur up and down the narrow streets, some coming from the Palace and others going down past the fish and frolic to the roadsters center of it ail, the Puerto del Sol - the door of the sun - the opening to the universe - the gate to paradise. It was where all miles to and from points in Spain were measured from. It was really the beginning of Iberia.

But not too far away, in the direction Boris was walking, the bulls had made their first historic stand over 400 years ago, and Spanish rob Inhoods had hidden themselves in caves that still dripped of the dew that sparked the folding ripple of paper with pen under the art movement called Hemmingway.

Dark skinned mustaches leaped to the call of the stopping footsteps.

" A gin and lemon, per favor" said Boris.

Boris gazed around him. Long white red strands of hung
on the walls above huge wooden barrels of wine. A door arched through to a dim but gay cellar where a caballero was singing about La Vida and groups of people were sitting on small two foot hight stools around hundred year old tables that still had the names of the son's of the Grand Tour on them. Today, it seemed, that everybody made the grand tour, thought Boris. It was the age of the common man.

Boris had to leave Madrid two months later - it was an intuitive thing. He just had to get moving. But he had made some good friends and they would keep in touch, their lives now being interwoven and somehow interchangeable.

Their respective evolutions dealt with the same mystic yearnings. They would all succeed or none would. It was a parable
dilating in the rain before it touched the earth. If one drop, if one frag
ment of moisture dried up on its alpha free fall, they would all dry up.
It was the test of how high the cloud was and of how saturated its being had become in the uninhibited flow of nature. They were all the same cloud, and now it had broken - whatever happened was unchangeable. Not even the wind,the pressures of the sub-spaces of dulled life, would be able to stop this flow.
It was Los Angeles again, and even if Boris hadn't noticed,.the chantings of an odd man on Wilshire would have reminded him that he was somewhere in North America. This hniddle aged, self-called prophet was giving his own interpretation of the bible.
"But know this," he was saying, "that in the last days, critical and hard to deal with times will be here." His sermon from the mount of blurring
sidewalks was catching a few listeners, for the U. S.and Russia were on the brink of world war over Viet Nam.
"For men will be" he continued, "lovers of themselves, lovers of money, self-assuming, haughty, blasphemous, disobedient to parents, unthankful, disloyal, having no natural affection, not open to any agreement, slanderers, without self-control, fierce, without love of goodness, betrayers, headstrong, puffed up (with pride) lovers of pleasure rather than lovers of God."
"Wow, man, you're pretty heavy" one of his listeners tailed out.
"This is all in the bible" he replied, " and we are approaching the end
of the world. Forget your vanities and make your peach with God. I beg you to I i sten to me."
The people just moved on as if whatever happened they could not control.
Boris took the whole scene in, but Boris was a man always at peace
with the infinite. He hadn't given his life over to the short-term
processes of time. Boris had never become what he did not want to become.
His being had stumbled and played with other dimensions but he had always re-centered his spirit before it turned upside down.
Later that night, as he was coming out of a bar, somebody grabbed him
on the shoulder.
"Turn around man" a voice said. He turned around and as he did a large
black fist smacked him and as he went down a boot to the face finished him

off.

When he regained conscienceness, he was strapped to a chair in the middle of the sitting room of a large old house. A group of blacks were standing around drinking wine and laughing. When they noticed him come to, one of them said, "Surprise" and they all laughed.

"You'figured we wanted your money, but man, we v/ant you - for kicks, you know - can you dig that?" another one said.

One of them, who obviously had the respect of the rest of the group, started walking slowly and musically around the chair, the others stood back in silence. He was looking the other way, and with a rhythmic bounce and a yell, he planted both feet in the middle of Boris's face. But Boris, a split second before the boots landed, had slipped up to a level of conscienceness in which he had blotted out all physical pain. In essence, his spirit had left

his body. Therefore, beyond the blood streaming from his eyes and nose, and the ripped flesh around his mouth - beyond this sight, there was no evidence that Boris was in pain. He was conscience but he was not groaning. This startled his tormentors.

"Hey baby, we're going to make you scream - yah" one of them said as he nodded to the big guy they caI led Marvin.

"Get some, Marvin I"

Marvin lumbered over to the chair, turned around as if he was going to walk away, and let his heel fly up and into Boris's balls. Boris sucked some air in, but did not scream.

"Wow baby, you're too much." Marvin said as he let a volley of counter punches go up and down Boris's face. Boris remained alert, but unphased by the pun i s h ment.

The blacks were really v/orking themselves up. it was obvious, that the climax was going to be Boris's death. But they were confused about the courage Boris was showing.

"Okay baby - are we ready for the operation" Marvin said laughing.

"Maybe a little amputation - a little plastic surgery". The others were getting off on this as they drank and hee-hawed around the chair.

Marvin pulled a long razor blade out of his pocket and waved it in front of Boris's face. Boris looked at it and then at Marvin saying,

"Big deal - you black animal"

"Wow - did you hear the man rap" said Marvin. His face took on a kind of twisted crazy look and he moved the blade down ina quick jerk cutting Boris's head open.

"Now what you got to say baby?"

Boris was barely conscience, but he managed to say,

"You ain't anywhere man, and you know it."

The blacks started to move away from the chair. Some were a bit disgusted. The wedding v/as turning into a funeral. They huddled together on the other side of the room and Boris overheard one of them say,

"This guy has got jam, man, he deserves to live."

As if in concurrence with this thought, a couple of them moved over the the chair and untied 8oris. They picked him up and carried him out onto the street. Marvin came out and said,

"Let's drop him off in front of a hospital."

And so they did, but just as Marvin was walking away, he turned around and came back. He looked at Boris, who was near death laying on the sidewalk bleeding and said,

"Just one more baby" and kicked Boris in the ribs, sort of grinning as he did it. Boris was soon found and taken into the hospital. He fought for his life most of the night, and he pulled through.

"You hand out with the wrong kind of people".the nurse said smiling at Boris' bandaged face. He could only sort of mumble and he said,

"They're really very nice people, they just drink too much occasionally."

She laughed as she walked around the bed to check his intervenus feeding line. Boris pulled the covers down, revealing a hard and still potent penis. The nurse took a deep breath in excitement at seeing It. It was as If all of her emotions were somehow drawn out by Boris laying there In the condition he was in.

" I'd like to find out if it still works" he mumbled. She walked over to the door, locked it, and returned to the side of the bed. She then leaned over and put her lips around it. After sucking on it for a few minutes, she pulled away. Boris groaned,

"More".

She lifted up her v/hite skirt and took off her panties. Her long, well formed legs fitted easily over Boris as she spread herself on top of him. in a sitting position. His prick slipped up Inside of her and she felt the completeness of her

143

body as she moved up and down. She bounced and bounced, her face wrinkling in pleasure as they both moved into orgasm. It was as if her legs were screaming as she finally jerked them both to the final moment. Boris almost had a brain hemorrage as her soft white ass slammed down against his dick.
"1 made it" he said, gasping.

Her face was flushed as she wondered what had overtaken her. A smile was all Boris needed to know that his stay inthe hospital was goint to continue to be eventful - and she did smile as she realized that what had taken place was probably the most exciting moment in her l i f e - as if in that second,

her individuality had triumphed over all the prisons of cultrual conditioning.

It was like screaming at the top of her lungs, "f am alive, and free, and I don't feel ashamed about it. This is me. This is life. I'm going to live you bastards."

When Boris was finally released from the hospital, his being, his mood and his entire disposition towards life had substantially altered. Perhaps it was the many hours of quiet meditation and reflection or possibly the

recurring dilemma of the relevance of life. Whatever, he needed a cultural change - a head clearing episode with some opposites.

For this, he chose Mexico, although the province of Baja, California was more American Mexico than anything else. He split to Ensenada. An intuitive power led him on, as if something else was directing his life and evolution. Being an artist, Boris has developed a tremendous confidence in his feelings and intuition.

He moved to the side of the curved barrier -around its fading yellow edge into a Mexican tequiila hall called Hussongs. Violins and music stomped its way through the young around the country peasants

for whom this trough had been built. It was a screaming, shoving space - a fight against obscurity, against not having been around in 1892 when men were tough. The youth of a new lost generation were attempting to ply the doors of solid, no-nonsense reality open - even if the brown wrinkled face of an old man selling peanuts reminded them of what their civilization had done to the creatures of the earth and sun. Los Angeles and Laguna Beach would feel less tension after this flying start to stop what one had to do to live in Southern California.

Boris found an opening against a back jerking on the bar. He reached over her hair and ordered a tequiila. Someone fell against him as he did and when he turned around, an unshaven dark face looked up at him and in a brown eyed factory worker way, said,

"It's all right to be Mexican isn't it sir?"

It was an intensity, a reminder of life's vibrancy totally inclusive, up the ladder from tragedy to freedom and transcendence. A cantina, a bar,' a place for people to meet, a creator of stories, of legends of now, and now people. So much repression had perhaps walked Into that place, but so much

freedom had walked out. People pouring through doors and windows, corner people, outfront people - Mexicans watching - drunks, smiles, belches, gasping - toothless grins lighting up life hardened faces.

A knarled hand reached in front of Boris, grabbing the loose breast of a young woman. She smiled and pushed it away. It was a Mexican ranch hand trying to imagine himself as part of the 20th century.

Later that night, Boris was in a darker, more Spanish place, sitting at the bar observing an American salesman trying to pick up a Mexican chic. The girl had a pleasant, non-hustling aura about her - it was as if she was the lover of some great and idealistic revo 1 ut ionary who lived in the mountains. Boris wouldn't believe, at first that she was selling herself. She was seated at a table, drinking alone, close to the bar.' The American kept jabbing her and making rude remarks but she paid no attention to him. Finally a Mexican gentleman approached her and led her over to his table.

'ʳ I told you she was a good girl" said Boris in mild triumph to the American.

"No, no, the bartender told me she was a hooker. This fellow she*s with is a lawyer here in town and is in love with her" said the American.

Boris watched the couple as they nuzzled each other and looked with love into each other's eyes.

"Well, if she is, she isn't tonight. You've lost man" said Boris. "Don't worry, money talks - 1 make fifty thousand dollars a year" the fellow said laughing.

What a tragedy thought Boris. He hoped she would tell him to go to

He! I.

The fellow got up and went to the back of the bar to talk to the owner. He returned a few minutes later grinning.

"He ¡s going to set it up for me - twenty-five bucks."

"1 still don't believe it" said Boris.

A few minutes later the girl got up and walked back to the washroom.

The owner stopped her and talked to her for a few minutes. He then walked up to the bar and said,

"Okay, but she has to get rid of this other guy first. Meet her out on the street when she walks out."

"Cool man" the idiot replied.

And so it went. Boris tryed to rationalize it. She needed the money for this or that humanitarian reason, but he finally had to admit, that it just wasn't any fun to be poor. In Mexico, unless you had a family or knew people, you couldn't get a job. This girl was surviving, that's all there was to it.

The white washed brick climbed up in angles to bel I towers and red clay tile. The sand hills rolled down to the salt water and curved around the bay of the harbour. The clams and aba lone boats drifted unnoticeably beside the over five hundred yachts and sailboats that had come down from Newport Beach to Ensenada for the annual regatta. it was a fiesta with every dimension.

Boris had moved out of the Bahia to escape the noise and had launched himself at a quiet old Catholic mission - turned motel in the centre of town.

The streets and bars were crowded with youth and age trudging hand in hand to the unknown bedrooms of stort-term happiness. Every gir! was
destined to be toved that night - by someone, somewhere, in whatever state
she was in - nude or fully clothed. There was a point in time, a gesture of tequilia processes, in which it didn't really matter. The uptight
became the loose, and the loose became the tormentors and the tormentors became the heros in the struggle to grasp some ass. But hero's corns and go and it was the uptight playing an opposite who would endure the stretch of bravery to be a bit more forward - a bit more foolish.

"I was on the ship Hope, I'm a doctor. We travelled around giving free med i cal attent ion to th\rd world countri es. 11 was rea My fulf i I li ng."

"It wasn't satisfying..." "Did you see..." "Why don't we go..." "Oh David..." "You're a bastard."

Boris was walking through the bar at the Bahia, overhearing' bits and pieces of conversation - the most prevelent being "Give me another Margueritta."

There were the spectators and the participants - the jumping, sexy, long legged blondes grabbing the hardest dickand the subtle, not too sure of themselves, freckled brunettes who were merely satisfied at being there.

Boris found hemself a beer and a vantage point close to the dance floor.

Some slender, well moving skin was bouncing in reasonable pace with the music. Most of the wiped out people sitting around the area, were watching the lust. But it didn't seem very important to Boris. It was just another movie in a series called 'The Great Escape.'

What attracted Boris' attention, had probably not been noticed by anybodyelse. There were two things about the scene that stood out to him.

The first was an old Mexican woman, dressed in black cloth, standing out on the street looking In the window. Her nose was up against the glass, and she had been standing there for over an hour, fascinated and probably confused by what she was observing. She had lived most of her life without paved roads, electricity and even radio. Television was stiii something of the future to her. The rosary and Our Lady of Quadalupa were her frame of reference. She had lived a simple and tough life - gave birth to many children - had seen many revolutions and political changes, but her life had not been affected very much by any of these things. She remembered, however, that most of the changes were supposed to be about improving things for people like her. But this scene she was gazing in on - what was this, Hell or Heaven. Somehow she knew that whatever was

taking place inside that hotel would change life more than any of the political or economic movements of her times. It dawned on her that the only way change happened was when the people themselves changed and caused it.

It could not be leg!I sated. She could also see in the uninhibited freedom of this party a certain essence necessary to cause a people's world to happen.

This was all in spite of her moral shock at the undulating sparsely clothed women moving about the bar. It wasn't really that shocking to her although, for she had seen much In her lifetime that v/as much more profoundly shocking - the starvation of a six month old child, the killing and oppression of her people; the de-humanization of life by economic separation of the few from the many. No, a healthy, flush woman's body starving for sex on a dance floor really wasn't anything to her other than fantastic and in some ways beautiful. She felt like saying to one of them,

"Don't feel sorry for me - your sorrow will only increase the sorrow of the world. If you have a chance to live, do it - take it. Celebrate it for all of us v/ho never have had the chance, and never will."

Sitting on a chair beside the bank, was a young Mexican girl, staring at it all - disoriented, seIf-conscience and alone. Boris looked at her.

She was not beautiful* Her feet were twisted awkwardly underneath the chair. She wore a gray skirt and a black sweater beneath an unattractive middle length

147

hair-do that was a take-off on something somebody had done in 1925. Maybe it was Gretta Garbo.

But her innocence, the startled and unsure flicker of her eyes - the obvious purity of her soul. What beauty, in the midst of these animals

thought Boris. He walked up to her, took her hand and kissed it. A few people stared at him as if there was something wrong. He said to her in flawless Spanish,

"Don't be awed by these barbarians. You have about as much to tearn from them as a rose would have to learn from a group of prickled twigs. You are the beautiful flower, do not annoint their ignorance."

She looked into his eyes and began to smile radiantly. But he said,

"and don't be impressed with me, I am not Don Quiote."

They both laughed. He let go of her hand and walked out of the bar into the sunlight and said to the old lady against the window,

"You have always lived in the sunlight - you have been honest and brave. Your life has been simple and beautiful - I can see it in your face. Please, do not pay heed to these fools."

She looked at him, a bit puzzled at first - but then she returned his smile and said in English "you are a good man."

The bright blue sky was fading in the light dusk of evening as Boris walked down the street and into La Laberna. It was a step into one of time's cancellations.

Boris walked over to a tabie in the corner and ordered'a sagritta. He was soon joined by an American who happened to be sitting by himself and felt like talking to someone.

"Excuse me i f i seem a little drunk. Mexico always seems to do that to me" he saii·d.

[11] I'm trying to forget a few things myself -. including a woman I loved very much" replied Boris.

"Yeah, some affairs just don't work out."

"Well, I feel that all relationships are destined to be unsuccessful - and it seems that the more intimate they are, the more tragically unsuccessful they become. But for the few brief moments."

Boris paused in thought about Sheila and then went on.

"Yes, for the few brief moments of high fleeting ecstasy, most endure

148

the tragedy and are alive in those moments. Before them they live on hope, and after, they live on hope's death - memory! But I'm only talking about life that is the way it is.

"You must be a writer or something. Man, you've got a heavy rap. You should get loose, get into some good form."

"What you really mean is that I should get into your space, or into some definitive front of the culture - but look man, I'm searching for my own style - my own form and my ov/n hang-ups. Most people in all areas of life model themselves after accepted forms. I'm not trying to do that.

I'm attempting to evolve something totally unique and original - and 1 suppose the struggle to do that sometimes manifests itself in moods and presences of being that cannot be understood by others. So don't react towards me - just accept me as an unknown entity and carry on. We might have some fun'ᵣ said Boris.

" Okay", the other man said smiling, "I'm interested in you and I'll like to ask you a question. What was your father like?" He said the question in a kind of a quick jesting way. But Boris paid no attention to that and answered the question spontaneously.

"He became very wealthy and successful - and that helped some of the other members of the family. But you know, I've never known a man who suffered as much as he did. This guy suffered every day of his life - as if he was in purgatory for the rest of the human race - and the thought did cross my mind that not only did he make it for the rest of the family in this world, but possibly also the next. I think he was the guy braking trail and in a way he probably suffered enough to get them all into Heaven."

"Why don't you include yourself in that group - he was your father wasn't he?"

"Yes - but you see, I am also a trai I breaker - his life has really nothing to do with mine. In a sense, we are sort of equals although most of my trials are ahead of me - his are behind him. I'm in that sense, going to

have to make it for a whole new group of people. I think it happens to be the fate of a few people in each generation. But my road is far different - and 1 think, much less glorious than his. It is the road of the soul.

He was in the picture of my life just long enough to undo the damage he had done to me - but don't misunderstand that - anything he ever did for or against me was out of love and good intentions. But the best one can do for a young man destined for greatness is to set him free. To others one must maintain dependence kinds of things - but to an original these things only obscure and delay his life for he above all others is capable of standing alone, unafraid."

The other man just nodded his head over and over again not knowing what to reply.

"What was your childhood like?" he finally asked.

"Well when I was younger, I used to think that the destiny of the world was on. my shoulders. But now, I realize that it is on al l of our shoulders - and I was probably just one of the first to realize it."

"What a heavy thought. But I suppose the world would be a better place if we all thought like that."

"Yes, I used to tremble with terror that such a fate had befallen me,

but now I think of it completely differently - for even if it Is true,

I can only do what I am doing and I can only make decisions as best I can - if .they're wrong or right -well, I can't be any more than myself at any given moment."

"Wow", the other guy said "when other kids were playing In sand boxes and thinking of being firemen, you were into all that. What kind of toys did you play with - encyclopedias? he said laughing.

Boris laughed as well. It seemed that his evolution had been very

different, In a healthy way, than that of others.

They both turned as a girl fell down on their table. The bar was packed and she had obviously ,ere;u lost her balance. But Boris said joke IngIy,

"What's wrong, are your breats too heavy?"

"Not when they're being held" she said with a wink as she pulled herself up. She v/as wearing a low riding pair of white jeans that revealed the top portion of her ass, and most of her back except where a cotton halter strapped back to hold her breasts. Boris stood up and whispered in her ear.

"I want to fuck you."

She turned her head and looked at him for a minute, and then whispered back,

"Okay"

Boris led her out and back to his cabin. They didn't speak another word to each other. When they walked inside the door, she began unfastening her halter. It fell to the floor revealing a round set of beautifully bulging breasts. By this

time, Boris had removed all of his clothing. He layed down on the bed. She stared at his huge red penis as she slipped off her jeans and panties. As If unable to control herself, she leaned down rebbing her tits on his penis. They were both very aroused and became even more so as she slid down to swallow his penis. Her eyes were closed tightly as if she was trying to hang onto a great moment in her life. Her mouth seemed to open wider and wider as her lips moved up and down. Finally,he pulled her up on top of him and she spread her long legs out to the edtes of the bed on either side. She felt his penis slip up, gushing into her now-moist vagina. They went off almost Immediately, grabbing and scratching at each other like two animals in a cage. She jerked forward and up trying to catch his strong quick movements. His penis pulsated at Its end as he went off and she could feel It way up, close to her stomach. His hands were dug into the
flesh on her bum and he pulled and pushed as he felt her going off. She
jerked and jumped, saliva running from her young fresh mouth, as she finally shook and trembled her way into the ultimate moment.
They layed there for a few moments, gasping and catching their breath.
Then Boris rooled her off of him. But as he did he rolled sideways with her,
keeping his penis inside of her. He pulled her leg up over his to retain a free area of movement as he began banging into her again. She started to throb as the motion picked her up and pulled her into another orgasm. But, just before they were about to go off, she jumped up and leaned with her
legs apart, against the dresser. Boris came in from behind in a hard crashing move that sent shudders of sensuous excitement up and down her lithe naked body. Boris bent his legs and pounded them both into another orgasm. She screamed as she felt the last rush to through her.
Catching their breath again, they parted. Boris sat down on the chair and watched her walk over to the bed. But, before she could lay down, however, he notjoned to her to come back. She started to pant a b it as she noticed his penis rise to a hard. She opened her legs around the chair, and sat down on it, feeling the skin being pushed aside as it moved up inside of her.
With her legs arched a bit, she was able to bounce up and down. In a quick splash and with loud groans, they went off again. They they just sat there, in a daze, too exhausted to move.
After about twenty minutes, she got up, put her clothes on and left - not saying a word. She didn't have to. It was understood that somehow in time their paths

151

had crossed and an electric charge was there. They had made the most of it, not wasting energy and time on ridiculous game playing conversations or on symbolic cultural identification processes. They trusted their intuition because their intuitions had become their beings. They were both artists - no definitions or v/ords were necessary.

Somehow, all of Boris' intimate sexual encounters were acts of love for Sheila. She had personified and symbolized to Boris the purity and refreshing surge of womanhood.

Boris would stomp on horseback, his shoulders back and'his long hair playing with the wind into the rough, edgy Mexican countryside. It relieved him from the four or five hours of writing he would do each day. At night, he would roam the streets and bars meeting people, dancing and moving away from the intense introspective space of writing great literature. He would venture into conversations and sometimes stun his listeners with statements such as "we are the originals of our way and that is our contribution to infinity." or, in reply to one yound lady who was rather puffed up about the motion picture industry and the death of the novel, he said one night, "audio-visual art is merely techno-sculpture. It is merely an awareness of the tools and a manifestation of that awareness. Whereas literature is total originality. It is the basis of all norms and revolutions. It is the

fire of the historical process as well as Its ashes. It is the dream of whatever can be."

One night, on a dark road he v/as attacked by four hoodlums With knives.

He struggled with them for a few minutes and then yelled,

"Stop you fools - I am one of you."

They responded as if their own brother was talking to them.

"Behind those twisted, ignorant seemingly vulgar faces are the hearts and minds of children. They could just as easily cry over you as kill you." Boris said to them in English that they could not understand. It was a quote from Cortes.

But one day Ensenada came to an end for Boris. The steep cliffs and rocky shores drifted behind him, but he had completed two novels before leaving. He had sent them In to publishers without leaving a forwarding address. After all, thought Boris, when a wave has crashed against the sand one can't stop it from slipping away into the ocean to rise again on another shore - and who would want to, thought Boris. To call attention, or to stop on one wave was to deny

152

the flow and beauty of all waves, and was to trample into dust the other possibilities for life.

The piane broke down in Karachi Pakistan. Boris and the rest of the passengers boarded small buses to go into the city. Each bus left for a particular hotel, and the bus Boris took had only one other passenger, because Boris had said,
"Take me to where the people stay."
The rest had gone on to lavish replicas of their own cultures. It was interesting however, that somebodyelse had thought in the same manner.
"So what takes you to the National Pakistani Hotel" asked Boris.
"I'm one of the people, man, and 1 don't live above them" the black man said smiling.
Boris later learned that this man had spent nine years in the Arab world arranging international hash runs at two hundred and fifty thousand dollars a crack. He had married a girl from Sweden and had deposited her in a seventy-five thousand dollar pad in Torremo1inos, Spain. But, through it all, he had not lost his affinity with the people of the world.
They blew some dope together under a gently turning fan in stone room
of the hotel - but stoned would probably fit better with the music that floated in from the crowded market place.
The plane found its bearings the following day and managed to make it to New DeIhi.
Boris settled into a humble hotel in Old Delhi and made his way to an Indian coffee house. He noticed a North American couple sitting a few tables away from him, and let his mind play with the question of whether they were Canadians or Americans. They were sort of staring blankly into their coffee - occasionally looking around in a somewhat disoriented manner - a bit hesitant and apprehensive - obviously not open. Their faces had a kind of withdrawn character to them and they seemed bored and unable to see the beauty around them. They had to be Canadians concluded Boris. He remembered when he was younger, when he first travelled outside of Canada on a two year sojourn, he was asked in the Montreal airport why he was leaving. He had said,
"The overriding probeIm of this culture is guilt - because it has never fought a revolution - it has never strived for its own identity; it has borrowed its technology, its arts, its language and its culture. It therefore has no spirit and no individuality. It is like the rich adolescent who inherits his wealth and walks

through life sulking and bending because his spirit has never lived. My spirit is going to live."

Boris looked over at them, almost in sympathy. They were obviously modern-day Loyalists who had sided with the crown. The Canadian foreigner embassies had all sided with the pre-revolutionary government and had carried on an absentee administration, supported by Britain. Tens of thousands of Canadians had left Canada after the revolutionary government. The only foreign power to recognize the new regime, was China.

Boris later joined the two Canadians and found out that the deposed Prime Minister was residing at the High Commission in New Delhi. There were rumors that a counter-revolution was being planned with the aid of the Royal Indian Army. The possibility of Indian troops launching an assault from American soil had apparently been shoved aside by the U.S. Government as too risky to their sensitive internationsl position. It therefore appears that little could be done without a strong counter-revolutionary movement inside Canada.


Boris also learned that facts had come out proving that the revolution had been planned by a group of Americans.

"A revolutionary consulting firm in New York, probably." joked Boris.

He moved out onto the crowded street and was stopped by Indian officials.

"Are your Boris Andre?"

"Yes I am."

"I have a message here from your Prime Minister."

"Which one?" mused Boris.

The Indian official was not amused. He handed Boris the envelope and moved on. Boris opened it. It has the official sea! of the crown on it and the slogan, "Her Majesty's Official Business""at the top. Where are these people's heads at, thought Boris. The note was an invitation to have tea with the deposed Prime Minister.

"Half the world is crumbling in corruption and poverty, and we're going to have tea together" said Boris aloud to himself. It was a humorous enigma.

He signaled a three wheeled taxi and rode out of Old Delhi and into the new section that housed the foreign embassies and the affluent Indians. It looked like Palm Springs next to a migrant workers camp.. In India, ninety-nine percent of the people were sort of migrant workers.

As he drove by the lavish Intercontinental Hotel, he wondered why these people didn't get up off the streets and either take control of these places or burn them down. The British influence had obviously left an intangible social system that repressed and subjugated the masses. Surely they would rise up one day as they had in Canada* thought Boris.

He got out in front of the Canadian High Commission and walked across the well-kept lawn and Into a large arched doorway. A trim smiling woman greeted him and led him to the back lawn where the Prime Minister was seated, sipptng tea and reading the New York Times. They said hello and Boris sat down.

The Prime Minister was an angular stiff faced man who had grown up in an elite family in the Maritime region of Canada. He was a good example of the Eastern Canadian crud game - whereby men attempted to imitate nineteenth British lords. But they did a poor job of it, and it was a hundred years too late. "Boris, it's nice to see you" he said.

"Don't waste my time with correct social conventionalities - what do you want to talk about?" replied Boris.

The Prime Minister closed his mouth and twisted it in a kind of *now- don't-be-naughty$^T$ look. Finally he said.

"Boris, I'm aware of your talents and as you probably know we are planning to regain control. But it has become apparent that we can not do so without spurning internal unrest and an internal counter-revolutlonary movement. You could help us do that through your writing."

He stopped talking for a minute to assess Boris' reaction. But Boris just looked at him, not revealing any reaction. After a few seconds, the Prime Minister continued, in a sort of 'we-are~good-friends$^T$ manner.

"As we both realize, the values and morals of a society are either reinforced or town down by the creative arts, not by politicians, not by businessmen - but by artists - and Boris, you have a responsibility to the people of Canada to do something." he concluded.

"Responsibility was a word invented to keep people in serfdom - along with guilt and a lot of other words." replied Boris.

"Listen to me, Boris" the Prime Minister said intently," you must help us. I know that you were forced to leave Canada by these - these - whatever you want to call them. That must mean you stand to gain by helping us."

$^M$No, it doesn't" said Boris. "You see, i am an artist, and that means that I've

155

had to fight and revolt against all cultures and mores in order to become culture free and value free. I've had to fight my own revolution against the conditioned being I had become within institutional society. One cannot become an artist until one goes through a process such as that - and one cannot become itself until it does that, and until we in the world become ourselves there is no sense to anything. What is going on today, has nothing to do with man. He is a pawn in a vast chaotic nightmare and he can only emerge if he achieves a level of consciousness whereby he understands this. Then he can make his world and his life work.

And don$^T$t misunderstand me when I refer to art or artists, because those who create before they achieve the sort of rebirth I am talking about, only create affirmations and supportive reflections - whether they be positive or negative - which serve to perpetuate the existing order. It all feeds on itself at that level of art. Even the frontal assaults against the establishment to this, because they serve as contructive outlets and escape valves for the frustrations of living within a structured rigid society. Reactive art is a kind of abstractive big brother saying $^T$now, v/atch this play and when it is over we wil I a I I return to our neat Iittle cel Is Ii ke good boys and girls.$^f$

My dream has always been for a world where every citizen is an artist - or has achieved that state of consciousness. But in order to do that, an individual, a nation, or the world must revolt against everything it has heretofor been to emerge on a new plateau and on a new non-thesis. It may then use some of the things of the old order, such as technology and so on, but it won$^T$t matter because the people will have arrived at a state of awareness whereby they - and I mean they - are controlling and using these things towards collective and individual ends that they - and I emphasize they, again- that they choose to pursue.

This is, of course, not the state of affairs today. Man is merely another variable in a large techno-maze, in a large prison farm that spreads out over the entire planet.

Now, you are seriously asking me," Boris said, strongly emphasizing $^1$ rne$^T$ to contribute to the suppression of a revolution, when I believe that revolution is the only pre-requisite to achieving the state of awareness of an artist. No, there is no way I will help you. Maybe Canada will become the first of the Nations of artists that I envision v/iI I cover this planet one day.

But, don't mlsunderstand me. I'm not talking about a world whereby

156

everybody would be painting or writing - one could express his awareness and artistic inclinations through making shoes just as easily as through writing if we lived in a balanced world v/here everything was produced out of a collective awareness and a sense of relativeness of everything to everything - and if we were conscious of the variables needed to effect harmony. Nothing is more obvious than the fact that this world, today, is not in harmony.

Any your political system Is not the answer because you cannot regiment harmony by political or economic repression - for, just as the waves continue to hit the shore, man will continue to struggle to be free and to become himself - and becoming himself is achieving the level of consciousness of the artist - and, concluded Boris, to do that he must revolt. So you see, I cannot help you."

The Prime Minister sat there for a minute without saying anything. Then, In an indifferent manner he asked Boris,

"Would you like some more tea?"

"Would I like some more tea!" Boris said loudly, "Christ - you haven't understood a thing I've said. You sorry son-of-a-bitch sitting there in your smug, closed, psuedo pomp and ignorance. The whole superstructure of the world is about to take a new breath or crumble and you've put a wall of glass around your empty head that won't allow even one new thought to penetrate Her Majesty's cunt - and that's what you are."

Boris got up and started to leave, but as he did, he turned and yelled, "well keep fucking you bastard - maybe the royal mint will put your dick on its next issue of nickels."

On his way through the arched doorway, the Prime Minister's wife grabbed Boris' arm and stopped him. He looked into her pleading eyes for a few seconds and then she said,

"You must understand that it is hard for us to change. I'll admit that I liked the old Canada, the church, my car, but I wasn't that happy. But Boris," she continued, "I felt we were getting somewhere."

"Well, all 1 can say," said Boris in low, understanding voice," is that more and more cars aren't going to make anybody free or happy - they may soothe things for' a while, but that's all - and more and more Christ escapism is going to make you free. You are not going to become free until you become Christ, and become aware of what he was aware of - and this is what he asked you to do - to join in union with Him. He is real, and he is God, but you have not found

157

Him. You cannot find himuuntil you find yourself. But you v/i I i not do that unless you revolt and achieve the awareness of the artist. Christ led a revolution in trying to liberate Israel from Egypt. It has taken him almost 2,000 years to succeed - but he has done it. Israel is now free. The odd thing about it, is that it is the Israelites who do not recognize their own Savior, for it is the Christian world that spawned the seed of a free Israel. But it doesn't matter. What is happening today in Israel is the birth of the new covenent - and it is possibly the beginning of a new world. In consciousness, because of their self-less collective awareness, they as a nation, have come closer to the level of consciousness of the artist than any other. Canada, as usual, is in the wings of time, moving in the right direction but without a historical significance.

"Mrs. Adrian," continued Boris, "I do understand. I only wish that you did."

Boris moved out on the lawn and down the driveway, brushing aside the offer of a limousine ride back to the square. He set out on the sidewalk, walking. After a short distance, he took off his shoes and gave them to a desperate beggar on the road - who looked like he had been on the road a I I of his life. Boris left the sidewalk and took to the road as v/ell - as if saying "in a city where two million people sleep outside, with blankets wrapped around them, you shouldn't build sidewalks before you build houses." The long corridors of cells and bars stretched up in tiers inside the Federal penitentiary Carlos was inspecting- The twelve years that had passed since thé revolution seemed to have aged Carlos considerably. He had risen up in government ranks to become the chairman of the Canadian penal system.

It was a high rank in what had turned out to be almost a police state.

The prison warden made occasional remarks in pointing out improvements since Carlos' lasf inspection.

They moved through a large steel door into the psychiatric wing of the prison. As they were walking by one of the cells, they overheard a voice saying,

"I got you Boris - I told you I'd kill you."

Carlos stopped as if a flashback of his entire life had overtaken him.

He looked at the warden and asked,

"Who is that man?"

"His name is Marcel Lamont. He's in here for armed robbery although he keeps telling the doctors that he has killed a man. . Sometimes he claims it was Boris Andre, the writer who disappeared before his works became famous.

158

Carlos acknowledged the reply without giving away his personal alarm and emotional reaction to what had taken place. But he later asked to speak with the prisoner privately, using as an excuse, that it was part of new inspection procedures. When he and Marcel were alone, he began guesfioning him.

"Are you being treated fairly?"

"No, they have not convicted me of all my crimes. 1 have killed a man and I must be convicted for it." Marcel replied.

"Are you sure that you have killed a man - or do you wish that you would have killed a man" said Carlos.

"I should have, I mean I have killed that bastard."

Carlos got up and went to the door.

"You can return the prisoner to the cell now" he said to the guard.

After a chat with the prison psychiatrist, Carlos left the penitentiary unsure of whether Marcel's ranttngs v/ere imaginary or real. It somehow seemed impossible to imagine Boris dead. If it were true, Carlos thought, a small vibration or the bending of a flower as he was passing a garden,[1]would have In some way, let him know. An emptiness v/ou I d have occurred regardless of how far away Boris was. If Boris had been killed there would have been some indication that something wasn't quite right somewhere in the universe.

As the plane lifted up in a more even arc on its Toronto-Vancouver flight, Carlos pondered what he would say to Taras and Sheila about the Marcel incident. He knew of the great personal love they had for Boris as v/ell as the guilt they felt about not communicating to Boris In Vancouver when he v/as leav:igg the country.

Later in the day, Carlos was sitting around a fireplace with Sheila and Taras sipping cognac trying to displace the damp coldness of December.

After relating the incident to them, he added,

"Marcel's disorder may have caused him to substitute the real world for a v/orld of fantasy In which everything appeared exactly as he wished it to. One of the major things about the real world that disturbed him was his desire to kill Boris as both retribution for the lack of success of the screenplay they had worked on, and for the lack of success and relevence of his own life. He blamed Boris for both according to the prison psychiatrist. The psychiatrist also said that he didn't know where to draw the line between Marcel's real and imaginery world so that he couldn't say what v/as true and what wasn't. Marcel and Boris are the only one's who know."

159

Sheila had become very upset during the course of the conversation, but she was controlling herself extremely well.

''When I was in England last year, Carlos, I met, quite by chance, someone Boris had known in Spain. He v/as a fellow named Ramon, who was a very successful writer in London. Boris and he had apparently been very close in Madrid and shared some mutual friends. They had also worked together on a screenplay called 'The Circus'. Ramon told me that Boris just disappeared one day." said Sheila.

"Who were his other friends?" asked Carlos.

"A man named Tom Atfwater who apparently is a very v/ealthy businessman now in Madrid - and Bob Seaver, the producer in Los Angeles." replied Sheila.

"Well, one of us should see if v/e can trace Boris down. I don't think any of us will be at peace until we find out what has happened." said Taras.

''Okay, said Sheila" I'll go, as I should have in the first place, twelve years ago, and besides it isn't possible for either of you to get away for the length of time that might be necessary."

Taras and Carlos concurred on the decision and she was off for Los Angeles the following day.

"That's odd that you should be asking about Boris at this time." said Bob.

"Why is that?" asked Sheila.

" A couple of months ago I ran into a psychologist named George Masdane. Do you know him?"

"Yes, as a matter of fact I do. But I haven't seen him for years." rep li ed She il a.

"He was looking for Boris as we! I, but two days after i had talked to him, I read in the newspapers that he had been accidentally killed in a freak snowmobile accident at Tahoe." he said.

Shei la was a bit shocked but concentrated on what she had come down to find out.

"Could you tell me about your contact with Boris?" she said.

"I am as interested in finding out what happened to Boris as you are, and if I can give you any information that would be of help, I'll do so." he replied as he walked over to the bar in his lavish apartment that overlooked Los Angeles.

"Boris never really talked about his future plans when I knew him in Madrid" Bob said as he poured them both a drink.

"But" he continued, "about a year after he disappeared from Spain, I ran into him on Revolution Avenue in Tijuana. We laughed a bit, at the coincidence of it, but he refused to say what he was doing. I talked him into coming to watch Jai AI i games and we started betting. Boris picked eight out of twelve winners. I could hardly believe it. But the only thing he said to me during the games was something about an old woman who looked like she was penniless walking up to the cashier's window with a winning ticket. He
really thought it was beautiful and he went into quite a description of it.
Her arms were shaking and so on. Boris was so overcome by compassion that he gave her every cent he had on him. At the end of the evening, I invited him up to Los Angeles but he wouldn't come although he borrowed fifty dollars from me. That was the last time I saw him."
"Did he ever pay the money back?" asked Sheila.
"Yes he did" replied Bob. "I got a money order from him about six
months later, but there wasn't any note or return address.'"[1] However, I do recall that the letter was from somewhere in Spain."
Sheila arrived in Spain armed with the hope that she was moving in the
right direction. The openness and vibrancy of Spain picked her up as she
drifted through the marble dominated airport. Her taxi fought its way down the Avenue of the Americans, past the Plaza Casti 1 la and into the heart of a romantic mist. Caesar had never touched.
She called Tom, introducing herself as a former mistress of Boris'. He
was intrigued and invited her out for drinks and pinchatos.
"So it's Boris you're looking for and not me." Tom said smiling. He had become even more impressive with age.
"Have you seen him since he disappeared from Madrid?" Sheila asked.
"Yes I did" said Tom "about two years later I was on a business trip to
Tangiers and I saw Boris on the street walking with a well-known guide named Akmint. Boris was dressed In a loin cloth. He had changed a lot. His face wasn't as full and beaming as it used to be - it was sort of sullen and determined. I said hello and he merely nodded to me and then he moved off the street into the crowded Casba. I never saw him again.'[1]
Sheiia stared out the door of the meson trying to imagine what kind of
a trip Boris was moving In. She remembered a letter she had once written Boris after his first book was turned down. He was so depressed and dejected that he turned away from art and writing and told everybody he was going to become

a banker. It v/ent on for about six months until the letter from Sheiia shocked him out of it. She had written:

Dear Boris,

Anyway you look at It, this world is about people. This is a world you understand - you who have graduated from the great school of life in one of man hardest tasks - the task of asking why, and finding out.

Your mind has interacted v/ith the principle thinkers of all ages and all nations. You have walked down the streets talking v/ith Homer - you have discovered Rome - you have toasted Athens with Plato and Socrates - you have strolled In the Parisian countryside with Rousseau and Voltaire - you have been re-born sipping beer with Kant, Freud and Hegel - you have touched the earth that Marx and Engels changed the destiny of man from - you have breathed the clouds of Laotse and Confucious and you have trembled with the spirit of Mohammed Ghandl. You have travelled the world and met its challenges, and succeeded more than most. You have opened your heart to the great suffering of mankind. You have starved with him and suffered for him - you have given of yourself as much as you could, and more.

Boris, you don't have to prove anything to anybody. The beautiful people of the world are waiting for you - not inside banks where all problems are fantasies - but out here, where the soul breathes and lives.

You have artist's hands and an artist's spirit. Why don't you start using those hands again and start letting that spirit fulfill itself. «...

Love Sheila

Sheila's memory moved over an entire range of events in their love. Perhaps she would at least still have Boris if she hadn't prodded him to continue. But what had he continued into, she wondered.


Tangiers began, for Sheila, on a blue warm morning that vibrated in her ovary, inviting her to fall in love but warning her that beyond the rolling coast and history enamored harbour were other things, not so lovable - and many that would make her wish that women didn't have ovaries at all, at least, in this portion of the Garden of Eden. Inside and around the mysticism of biblical, whîte-flowing robes and turbans and behind the unshaven, determined faces, was a life process and social structure at v/ar with the human spirit and the desire to live at all.

The days were long gone since Tangiers was an international port and the ships and traders from everywhere would blend into the daily affairs of this now fading city of the Koran and Isaac.

Akmint was always on the streets and Sheila met him easily." But she said nothing of Boris, sensing that she must win him over before he would release any information.

Akmint had. been born on thé -streets^ fatherless and motherless. But meshed in the cerebral fluid and nerve endings of this composition of cells was every vice and virtue, every mannerism and gesture of western man in the twentieth century.

She allowed Akmint to act as her guide and by the end of the day, she had seen his Tangiers - she had eaten in the Casba, smoked grass with the fish mongers - watched the families of the prisoners bring them food - prodded a snake charmer to.do his thing - paid respects at the grave of the Tangerian Marco Polo - bought black market cigarettes and thoroughly destroyed any Santa Claus that might have existed in her mind. The sky no longer looked blue, it looked gray. The ocean was no longer emerald, it was black and filthy. Her eyes were no longer twinkling. They were tv/itching from the thought of the abundance elsewhere. She detected a latent disgust and immorality about it all. But, however discouraged she was, she was determined to continue 7 to eat on the ground - to do everything to find 8oris. She felt that if she could unravel the reality of this humanly conceived Hell, she would also solve the mystery of Boris.

That night, Akmint took her into a dark cafe, where they sat on the floor passing around a giant peace pipe, and wandering off into their own worlds.

The stoned - brown-black-glazed faces around her seemed to be in a quest for forgiveness. Perhaps it was for being alive. It was a twelve thousand year old opium den pushing its way around Christ like figures - Christ like, not only because of their appearance, but also because of their suffering. Of all things, there was a television set, high in one corner. To the others, it was something from Allah, whereas to Sheila, it was a mid-twentieth century wrought by the neurotic energies of men floating in green paper clouds.

Akmint interrupted the space by saying "Miss Sheila, you seem to have come here in quest of more than most. I knew a man once, who talked of a Sheila like you. I taught him Arabic and the Koran and he taught me what it meant'[1] he said laughing a bit.

"Was his name Boris?" she asked.

"Yes" he said sadly "we miss him here in Tangiers. But if you are looking for him, I cannot tell you where he is - he didn't say where he was going. But when he left he gave me letter and told me to give it to you if you ever came looking for him."

He pulled a letter out of his robe and handed it to her. She opened it and read it aloud.

"Up here you can exist forever and see it all ~ each must find his own way up. I've left a well-cut path but unless it is used, the jungle will grow over it as it has to other paths - and then we'll have to wait until either by chance or perception someone else cuts another path and ends up at the end of the jungle, sees the mountain and climbs it.

Maybe v/e'll only have to wait ten years, or maybe a thousand - or maybe never. We might be the last to make It out."

She dropped the paper and wept, and in a faint whisper said,

"Boris I'm coming - lease leave the way open."

The following day as Akmint was seeing Sheila off on the boat to Algeceris he remembered something that he had forgotten to tell her.

"When Boris first came down here" he said "he mentioned that he had been living with a woman named Martha in Toledo."

Sheila reacted with a double emotion but was generally excited at finding a new piece of the puzzle.

The Rio Tajo wound its way around the steep stone walls that had protected the dreams of the men who had woven Spanish History. The Alcazar loomed up on the large hill that Toledo was built on. Sheila noticed the castle-like town jump up in front of her as the train from Madrid rattled around a bend.

She didn't know where to go to look for Martha and what might be her last remaining clue. A taxi took her from the old rail station to the Carlos V hotel.

" I n a town with twenty-two cathedrals, where yould you go if I wanted to swing?" she asked the desk clerk.

"Well, he said, "there are three disco here. They are all very nice. Perhaps you would like to Elfin. It is across the piaza and the first street to the right."

She got settled in her room and headed out in search of something more important than El Greco - at least to her. The Elfin was a sm31 I club with the Intimacy of a scholar's study. Scarlet rugs dominated the inner sanctum immediately below the l adder-l ike stairs. A small boy greeted her at the landing. She smiled and moved onto a stool ordering a Cuba Libra. Far out sounds bounced into a light show in a small room adjacent to the bar. A few people were dancing and others were getting intimate in the dimness of the shadowed corners. Four other people were sitting at the bar - Denny, the fellow who played the music; Antonio, an off-duty bartender; Paco, the owner; and young English speaking women. They were all on the ladder of life that all must progress on before they can truly live and before they can die. They were all struggling - as all life struggled. Even the caterpillar was moving; struggling; emerging; glowing in the twilight.. The fire fly was laughing and the earth was breathing.

"Did a man named Boris ever come in here?" she asked the bartender.

Denny, Antonio, Paco and the girl all jolted their heads towards her as if she had spoken the name of a favorite saint, or a lost lover.

Nobody said anything as if stunned by a large shock wave that riveted them to some moment in tne past. Finally Paco got up and moved over beside Sheila. He said

"We ail knew Boris - you must be Sheila. He used to talk about you when he got drunk. Boris was our friend - he was an artist, a fine man."

"Have you seen him since he left Toledo?" Sheila asked.

The girl got up and came over, stopping in front of. Sheila's stool and staring at her.

"i've always hated you. There was something of you in Boris that he could never let go of - something intangible and beautiful. I was never able to replace it. You should have come years ago - now we've both lost him." sai d Martha.

Sheila stared into her eyes flashing through the intimate moments Boris must have spent with her. She put her head in her hands and started to sob. Martha put her arms around her and said

"Come on, we'll go to my apartment and cry together." She began to cry a bit as we I I. The small I boy at the door was also crying and the rest seemed about to.

It was Christmas Eve. People were singing and dancing in the plaza and travellers were looking for inns in which to spend the night. There were real shepherds in the countryside watching the sky and real beils ringing from the large cathedral where the pontiff of Spain would celebrate midnight mass.

Martha moved over in the bed, crawling on top of Sheila's naked body.

The kissed warmly as if sharing something no two other human beings had in

165

common. Sheila moved her thigh up between Martha's legs and they began to groove together, kissing each other wildly and working up to the great moment - each imagining that it was Boris they were making love to.

As the night moved on, Martha talked at length about her six months with Boris and about his unexpected disappearance.

"He told me" she said "that he wanted me to go to Paris and meet with a man he thought was the successor to the Gueverra. I was supposed to bring
him back to Toledo to meet with Boris about a movie they were going to make in Algeria. Boris saw me off at the train station in Madrid. A week later, ! returned with the man and Boris was gone. I never heard from him again."

The father of time was also the father of sorrow and sadness, of shuttering emotional loss and empty boats gloating without direction. The salt twisted the wood until its domain became those trapped inside. But it would be over some day - it always was although Sheila and Martha knew that now, sadness would be more a part of their life.

Sheila left the following morning to return to Canada. It wasn't that she didn't wish to continue, she did - but to where and to do what. She had •s gone as far as her mind and her Imagination could take her. Now, she felt that
she must regroup and rebuild - maybe for some future journey or possibly to rebult her life


Marcel sat in his cell I flashing back over his I ife. It was as if he was watching a movie, and the camera was focusing in on different scenes in a wild speedy ha Iucinogenic trip. First he imagined the camera shooting in on a large church where a funeral was taking place. Marcel saw himself standing beside the alter, the epitome of the innocent alter boy. His hands were folded gently on his chest and a spirituality glowed around him. Then suddenly, his mind switched to another scene. The scene showed the face of an attractive and sensual woman against the background of a pillow. Her face was laying sideways against the pillow and expressed a conbination of anguish and pleasure. Suddenly the scene widened to include a man and the woman having intercourse from a sideways - behind position. Marcel sat up on the edge of his bed staring at the wall on which he imagined the movie to be taking place. He heard sounds of sexual pleasure emenate from the woman and the man began breathing heavily. Marcel screamed out,

"Stop! stop the picture." He put his hands up over his eyes but the movie would not stop. The scene went on until a child voice was heard' saying "Mama, can't we go now". The scene then widened to show the alter boy standing by the door of the small dingly hotel room. Marcel yelled out agina but the scene continued as the man said, "Look kid, pick that ten dollars up off the floor and get out of here."

Marcel threw himself on the floor of the cell and began pounding his head. He lay there until he was exhausted.

Taras sat down and drank a glass of grapefruit juice that Sheila had squeezed for him. it was a clear, pleasant day, Taras noted, as he looked out of their apartment window high above English Bay in Vancouver. He looked at the headlines of the morning paper and called out to Sheila in the kitchen.

'"There's been another hijacking from the Toronto airport this time.

"Oh" she said "is everything all right?"

"They had very little information about it at time of press - I suppose it will all be in the evening paper."

Sheila walked In from the kitchen carrying a plate of eggs and toast.

She set them down in front of Taras and sat down to sip her coffee. The telephone rang, and she reached behind her and pressed a button below a speaker that was set in the wall.

"Yes?" she said.

"This is Carlos - can I come up?"

"Oh - good morning Carlos. I'll let you in." Sheila said as she pressed another button.

He came in appearing somewhat startled. Sheila offered him coffee and he sat down as if in some way relieved from what he was struggling about. After a long pause in which both Taras and Sheila looked intently at him, he said,

"1 don't want to arrive at any irrational conclusions, but 1 feel that I must inform you that the man who hijacked the plane this morning has been positively identified as Marcel Lamont. He escaped while being transported to a mental hospital."

For a moment, they were all quiet as they pondered the implications the event might have for Boris.

"Well" said Taras "nobody knows where Boris is so there shouldn't be anything to worry about."

Sheila stared straight ahead of her as if dazed by the return into her life of anxiety over Boris.

"V/herever that plane goes, Mm going too." she said without emotion

Carlos and Taras looked at her and Taras began to speak but stopped realizing that she would continue to express her guilt and love in what might be a search that would last for the rest of her life.

Marcel stood In the cockpit of the aircraft hallucinating and flashing back to a scene fourteen years previously between he and Boris.

They v/ere sitting in the pub of an old hotel in Fort Qu'Appelle, Saskatchewan. It was late in the evening and Boris was very drunk. Marcel's mind was floating around the scene and he kept coming back to one thing Boris had said.

"You know Marcel" Boris had said chuckling at bit. "if I can't find the means through my work to uplist all of man, I'm going to join my brothers in the rice fields rather than live better than them. i was travelling through Burma a couple of years ago and I picked out a little field to the East of Rangoon. Don't be too surprised if I'm not there some day."

Marcel didn't know why he hadn't remembered it before, and he realized that he knew something that nobody else did.


The people of Rangood had rarely been the center of international attention and it altered the mood of the city to have almost an historical event on their hands. The police chief sat in his office reviewing the story in the afternoon paper. The headline read:

'NOBEL PRIZE WINNING AUTHOR HUNTED BY SKYJACKER'

The chief gazed down the page and he noticed something that caught his attention near the end of the story. It read:

'TARAS MOLIERE AND HIS LONG TIME CCMPANI AN, SHEILA MONET ARE IN RANGOON AWAITING THE OUTCOME OF THE ORDEAL. THEY ARE WITH CARLOS SERRANO WHO IS IN CHARGE OF THE CANADIAN DIPLOMATIC DELEGATION OVERSEEING THE INCIDENT.

AN UNIDENTIFIED BUT RELIABLE SOURCE HAS SAID THAT MR. MOLIERE WAS A FORMER FRIEND OF MR. ANDRE'S AND THAT MISS MONET WAS THE WOMAN MR. ANDRE DEDICATED HIS LAST AND MOST FAMOUS WORK TO. CANADIAN VICE-PRESIDENT BARRY MARTIN, A FORMER ASSOCIATE OF

MR. ANDRE'S AS WELL, IS DUE TO ARRIVE THIS EVEN ING.*

The Rangoon police chief was a man whose thought patterns worked in an opposite manner than most. He would look at things upside down and then from the side and so on, and it was probably this factor that had

caused him to solve so many crimes and rise to be chief at the age of

twenty-eight. Although he was sixty-two, he still held the post. Some of his younger officers secretly whispered that he was senile and had lost his mental agility.

He turned around in his swivel chair and reviewed the first portion of the hijacking story. It read:

'MARCEL LAMONT, WHO ESCAPED FROM A CANADIAN PRISON, HAS HIJACKED AN AIR CANADA DC 10 TO RANGOON. HE ALLOWED THE PASSENGERS TO LEAVE THE PLANE ON A RE-FUELING STOP IN MONTREAL, AND IS HOLDING THE THREE STEV/ARDESSES AND PILOT AS HOSTAGES. AUTHORITIES REVEALED THAT HE IS DEMANDING THAT THEY HAND OVER TO HIM THE AUTHOR, BORIS ANDRE, WHO DISAPPEARED ELEVEN YEARS AGO. LAMONT CLAIMS THAT ANDRE IS IN A RICE FIELD TO THE EAST OF RANGOON. ALTHOUGH AUTHORITIES SAY IT IS POSSIBLE THEY DOUBT THAT THIS CLAIM IS ANYTHING MORE THAN THE RAVINGS OF A MAD MAN. THE PLANE IS PARKED IN FRONT OF THE TERMINAL AT RANGOON INTERNATIONAL AIRPORT.

ALTHOUGH THE LiKELYHOOD OF ANDRE BEING IN BURMA IS REMOTE, CARLOS SERRANO HAS INSISTED THAT A WIDE SCALE SEARCH BE UNDERTAKEN AND THAT THE STORY BE WIDELY PUBLICIZED.'

The police chief put the paper down and rested his chin on his hand. He thought for a minute and then said to an aid who had been waiting for insturet ions:

''Tell me again what Mr. Serrano said to you."

"He said his police contingent was sufficient to handle security precautions and they were not needed. He also said that if Mr. Andre came forth, that we were to let him go through to the plane." the aid replied.

"Very strange" said the chief.

''What is?" the aid asked.

"You would think he would want the maximum possible security and you wou l d think that he would be concerned enough about Mr. Andre's life to stop him from going to the plane if he comes forth. l think we must pay this

Carlos a visit." said the chief as he stood up.

They arrived at the hotel v/here Carlos was staying and moved up the old staircase to the second floor. The hotel clerk was with them.

"Is there an open room next to his?[11] the chief asked.

"Yes there is" the clerk replied.

"Let's go there first." said the chief.

The clerk led them to the room and opened it with his master key. They entered and closed the door.

"His room is through that door."

"Okay - keep your voices down." said the chief as he and his aid moved over to the door. They stood there listening. A conversation was taking place in Carlos' room between Carlos and Taras. There voices were somewhat faint, but they were able to overhear. However, a knock at the door interrupted them. It was a reporter from the New York Times who had seen the chief enter the room.

"I don't want to disturb you" he said, "but has anything new broken on the story."

The chief motioned for him to come in and he joined them listening at the door."

Taras was talking to Carlos.

"Carlos, I have already betrayed everything I am for the sake of this revolution - and what have they done - given us a dictatorship and now they're trying to turn us into murderers. You have no idea how hard these years have

been on me - on my conscience." And then raising his voice, "and on my soul. Yes, that's right i have a soul." There was silence for a few minutes and then in a quieter and almost emotional voice Taras said,

"! am an artist and I have broken my own spirit by becoming what I am not." and then in a louder voice, "but I will not also become a murderer least of all for those selfish vain puppets in Ottawa. Don't look surprised Carlos - sure I believed in the revolutions as strongly as you did, I falsely fained love for Sheila so that she would not join Boris, and Boris was one of my kind - his spirit was my spirit. We hoped that being without Sheila would drive Boris insane and possibly to suicide because a couple of idiots considered him an enemy of the people's government." s He paused for a minute, "and now Barry has conjured this plan to finally kill Boris."

Then Taras raised his voice.

"And worst of all, we were all his friends. Well I'm going to stop him and I'm going to tell the world what is really going on In Canada as Boris would have."
"No you're not Taras" said Carlos.
At that second the chief banged the door open and pu! led out his revolver. Carlos was standing over Taras with a gun. The chief fired two shots In Carlos' stomach, dropping him to the floor.
"Get an ambulance" he said to his aid "we want him to live."
Later In the day, at an international news conference, Taras told the story.
"The government had learned that Borⱼs' ideas had changed even more radically against them than when they first took power. Boris had achieved an Infernational reputation and they feared, if he ever started writing again, that he would ruin their delicate international relations which were
so important economically. Canada has become a very poor country.
Vice-President Martin handled matters pertaining to Boris, personally."
Taras paused as he noticed Shei la enter the back of the room. He looked at her for a minute and then continued.
''Boris wrote a letter to a former close friend named George Masdane. Masdane's mail had been carefully screened for many years because Martin realized that Masdane v/ou I d have no part of our plot against Boris, and it was likely that Boris would choose him to get in touch with.
In the letter, Boris asked Masdane to meet him in Los Angeles at the home of a fi lm producer. He implied that he was going to make a movie portraying the reality of life in Canada. The government did not let the letter go through and sent its own agents to meet Boris. But Boris never showed up.
Somehow a second letter from Boris got through to George without being detected. This letter was later found in a search of George's apartment.
In the letter, Boris mentioned his first letter and that he would be delayed getting to Los Angeles. George figured out that something was up and set out to attempt to warn Boris. So Martin arranged to have him killed.
It became clear by this time that Boris was remaining wherever he had gone in order to complete his work. Therefore, we had to get to him before he could market it." He stopped again as he noticed Sheila break down in tears. He began to cry a bit as well, but pulled himself together to continue.
"Lamont was under heavy psychiatric care and we had found out that Boris had become the symbol of all his hatreds and frustrations. We knew that he would kill Boris if given the opportunity.

One day, a couple of months ago he said that Boris had told him where
he would be. We didn't know whether to believe him or not, but finally decided
to give it a chance. The psychiatrist placed the hijacking idea in Marcel's head
and we arranged a situation that would allow him "to escape easily.
We also knew that Boris' humanitarian ideals would bring him out in the open
to save the lives of the hostages, wherever he was in the world."

Taras paused again and then added, "The rest you already know." He got up
and left the room, as if something had suddenly overtaken him. A few minutes
later he was in a taxi on his way to the airport.

The clouds had darkened a bit as dusk was setting in and a cool breeze
was chopping at the humid heat of the day.

Taras pushed his way through the crowded terminal and walked pas the
security forces surrounding the plane. He stood at the bottom of the ramp and
called to Marcel. Marcel came to the door with one of the stewardesses
in front of him and a shotgun resting on one of her shoulders pointed at
Taras.

"Listen to me Lamont," said Taras, "we planned the entire thing - you and Boris
have common enemies. It was all a plan to ki I I Boris by the government."

Lamont became very confused and began grunting. Suddenly the shotgun
blasted out at Taras. He smashed back against the runway - blood spraying
everywhere.

Marcel screamed out.

"Get Andre here in an hour or I'm going to vlow us all up."

When the news filtered back to Canada there were uprisings in three of the
major cities. The wire services reported that a strong new revolutionary
movement was afoot.

Marcel had been talked into waiting another day by the Rangoon police chief,
but he had said that by 6 o'clock the plane would blow up. He had set a time
charge.

Sheila had gone into a complete state of shock and withdrawn into herself. She
was hospitalized by the police chief and was given very little chance by
Rangoon doctors of ever coming out of herself again. They had never seen the
spirit and mind of a human being so dead. It was sort of a state of sick
nervousness - with its full double meaning, enlightenment or obIi v i on.

The chief was standing over her bed, a bit spaced out himself over the tragedy.
As he walked out of the room, he noticed an odd figure making its way down

the hospital corridor. It was sun-darkened Caucasian dressed in Burmese rags. The chief stopped, realizing who it was.

So this was the man, he thought, that had endured the winds of tragic life to become an almost Christ-1 Ike figure to the people of the world. This was the man they had planned to crucify because he wouldn't endorse the petty ideals of a few men in an insignificant country somewhere on the other side of the world.

Boris walked into the room and over to her bed. He stood there staring at her, tears running down his face. One of the doctors came in and whispered to him,

"I'm sorry, but I think she's beyond ever coming back."

Boris called to her - and then screamed for her to come to. But she just layed there her eyes open, but glazed and unseeing.

He v/a I ked to the end of the bed v/eeping. His mind began fo drift through the years - back to when they had first met and were living together. He had just completed his first book.

The sun was shining into the apartment as Boris lifted his head up and looked around the apartment. Sheila was still sleeping. He walked into the kitchen and put a kettle of water on and then returned to bed.

"Did you have a good sleep?" he asked her smiling and chuckling.

"Oh God .ʳ - can't you find something else to ask me in the morning?" she replied without opening her eyes.

Boris began to laugh and said again.

"Did you have a good sleep Sheila?"

"Sh, Sh" she replied as she pulled the covers up over her head.

"You're so silly in the morning."

"Be quiet, I'm thinking about something."

"Okay, but we're getting up together. It isn't any fun moving into the day by yourself. You're the one that's always complaining about not doing things together and not sharing our experiences.

"Oh, shut-up" she said as she threw the covers off and got out of bed.

Boris watched her warmly as she went into the kitchen. He then got up and put some clothes on as she returned and began making the bed. She was just wearing panties and he walked over to her and put his arms around her.

"I love you" he said as he lifted her head up to look into her eyes.

She smiled and he walked over to a table in the corner of the apartment.

Books and papers were haphazardly strewn on it. He sat down and began to page through a large stack of typed papers. She stood fhere, watching him, with a gentle loving expression on her face.

"Do you think they'll publish it?"

"Yes⸴ she said, "its so good, and I'm not just saying that because I'm in love with you. It's the most contemporary work of literature that I've ever read. Mi I ler and all these people seem to be talking to us from another planet - a dead planet - and what you've done is today."

"Yah, I don't know. It's hard for me to evaluate my own work. Sometimes I think it's great and other times l just shake, wondering whether anybody wi1 I ever read it or care about it. It's so important to me because it is me. It's my functional talent - it's v/hat I want to give to the world - it's my essence, my sense of life - everything," he said, "and if they reject it -" then what?"

"You'll write another one, and another one after that. You're a genius. It's just a matter of time and plugging into the right circuits."

"It isn't that simple. It's one thing to create an original and great work of art, but it's quite another thing to get that work of art out into the world so that it can have its play with man's mind." he replied.

"Well, don't take it that seriously. We'll live and love and survive because we know how irrelevent any one second in history is." she said.

"You're right, but in the short term, you have to block out your total view of things in order to get something done. One has to become serious in the narrowest of ways while retaining a slip of paper to remind oneself of infinity." He paused for a minute and then became a bit angry.

"It's easy for you - what do you have to worry about? But this is where I've decided to fight my battle." He looked at her and then added., "Maybe that sounds ridiculous to you, but you'll understand when you get to this point in your evolution."

"Oh bull shit" she said.

Borls walked over and grabbed her arm.

"Look, this is the one time in my life when I'm not turning away. This is the field I'm going to fight on and this is the battle I want to win. There aren't any other battles, this is it for me - I win or I lose. I am or I am not. I've assembled my forces and collected together my strengths and I'm fighting the only and last battle of my life."

Sheila lurned her head away and said,

"There'll be other battles."

"You bitch, you can't understand. Either I win this one and break through and become a human being or lose, like most others and just fail into a life pattern In some drone society. I'm at the point that everyone reaches sooner or later when they're either going to assert themselves and be or slike away with the mob In cultural assimilation and sublimation of self. This is it," he said as he became very emotional. "I'm fighting here today, this battle, this book, this field, these troops, this issue - not tomorrownot yesterday. Today' Now! Me! Life! - and I'm going to win, with or without you." He stopped as if something was wrong.

"No," he continued "I take that back. It's with you, even if you're a cannon that doesn't function and slows me down and brings victory into question. I'm going to drag you with me, because I love you."

His emotions calmed down and then he added somewhat pensively.

"One can't turn away forever - when one confronts something that is finally important enought to fight over - one's got to fight because not that many things come along that are worth winning - and if one is lucky enough to find something when you're as young as I am, then you fight until you win or until you die. There isn't any such thing as losing, now that 1 think about it."

Boris was sitting in a coffee shop. Suddenly he got up as he noticed Shei la walk by. She turned her head and noticed him as he waved to her to come in. She walked through the open door and joined him at his table. They smiled warmly at each other and he asked,

"Well? Did you get to the hospital?"

Sheila was in a giggling mood and said in an evasive manner.

"No, well, yes. But I've got my own doctor. He$^T$s really too much."

"For Christ's sake Sheila, areyou pregnant?"

"Weil, this young doctor referred me to a doctor who had recently arrived from England and was taking on new patients. But he couldn't see me until 12:30 because he doesn't work in the morning. He sort of stumbled info the offIce."

"Dam it - are you or aren't you?"

Sheil a laughed.

"Wei I, he asked me if Í was getting Irritable? and I said .yes - if my breasts were getting larger? and I said yes - If I didn't feel like doing anything and if 1 was goint to the bathroom a lot and..."

175

"And you said yes - so?" said Boris.

"I'm pregnant."

"Wow" he said as he leaned over and kissed her. They both sat there grinning like children at each other.

Boris' mind drifted back to the hospital room. The chief watched him as he reached over and touched.Sheil a's hand, wishing that he could change it ail.

Boris turned and began walking out of the room. The chief's aid, who was standing outside the door, put his arm out and said

"Wait. If you are going to the plane there is something that you should know."

Boris looked at him for a second and then moved on down the corridor.

The aid yelled out for him to stop, but he didn't.

As he watched Boris disappear at the end of the ha 1 1 the chief looked over at his aid and said,

"You have yelled stop to one of the few men who can never be stopped. He is a man who has gone his own way - he isn't going to change now."

The chief arrived just as Boris was walking up to the plane. He could see that Marcel was in a rage - screaming and yelling at Boris. But Boris just stood there with an intent but understanding look on his face. He was standing slightly sideways, not even looking at Marcel. His eyes looked off towards the horizon somewhere afar where the sky and ocean seemed to meet.

There was an expression on his face that reflected the sorrow and misery of half the population of the world. He stood there motionless as Marcel unloaded the shotgun. The crowd began to sob and cry, but above their cries could be heard the wailing and screaming of a woman, who had just pushed her way through to the front. It was Martha.

Marcel gave himself up as the ambulance put Boris' body on a stretcher as if that would bring him back to life.

The police chief asked them to stop for a second as he took a piece of paper out of Boris' tightly clenched hand. He opened it and read It. It read: , .

1 HAVE A DAUGHTER. SHE WAS TAKEN BY THE GOVERNMENT WITH ALL OTHER CHILDREN WHEN THEY ASSUMED POWER. PLEASE GIVE HER MY LOVE AND TELL HER THAT HER MOTHER LOVES HER TOO.

Tears rolled down the old chief's face as he nodded his head over and over

176

again saying, "I'll tell her."The Rangoon police force had suddenly begun to look upon their chief as an internâtional hero, and as he and his aid walked through the building to their office, people smiled and looked after him with a new-found respect.

As the evening wore on, and the episode began to crunch in, thé aid became increasingly puzzled.

"Why would a man do that?'[1] he asked the chief.

The chief was sitting back in his chair with his hands folded on his stomach. He tilted his head up in disbelief of the question.

"Do you know what that man said eight years ago in his only public appearance in the world in the last twelve years?"

"No," the aid answered.

"He had won the nobel prize for literature and at the last minute he unexpectant 1 y appeared at the podium. I remember cutting his address out. I've got it here in front o f me. Do you want to hear it?"

"Yes" said the aid.

The article says that he walked up to the podium and said,

'When I was gentle and kind - when I gave of myself and all that 1 was,

I was scorned and ridiculed. When I loved and lived trusting all, even though I knew I was being abused, | was called a fool.

And now that I have carved out my ov/n selfish v/orld and learned to hate - you call me a great man. Now that 1 have learned to not be concerned with means, but only with ends - now that 1 have used, rather being used, you sit there and wish to present to me the world's highest artistic award in Ii terature.

Never at any other moment in my life have been more aware of the psuedo - pomp and elitism that promote and congratulate a world of competative hatred. 1 want no part of your award.

It would only be iogicai for me to continue this process of thought to conclude that' if you applaud hate in this manner, you would probably react to my learning to love again, by ki !ling me.[1]

"I would like to read to you a story that my father wrote a long time ago. I think it would be a fitting tribute to this, anniversary of his death," said Carmen Andre.

"This is a story that he decided not to publish because he considered it his highest accomplishment in literature.

He left a note with it saying that he refused to have it dealt with by the market place consciousness, but that he wished others to hear it in some future age. I am glad that I am able to present this to you."

There was r, mild applause in the room. Over fifteen hundred people were gathered in the large hall and the world watched-.through live satellite television. As she began to read the story, their minds drifted with it as if they were watching a movie.

"The title of the story," she said, "is, 'Beyond the last House*, and it begins," she paused for a minute and then read the story.

"floating up, and then emerging above the crest of overcast, the plane slid away from its arc as it directed its course east. It pursued the sun, which was now less noticeably sinking away.

Sitting in seat D, Row 23, on this wew York to Lublin flight was Peter Haller - adventurer, taxi driver, writer and sometimes business executive. Ke was a young man, ever pursueing self-transcendence. **He** liked to think of himself as being a part of something beyond his own life - on some days a revolution, on others as a member of a productive and great Society and on others as merely a transhistorical entity in the on-going process of evolution.

A week's holiday from the terror and lunacy of New York.

A week to re-discover life, to begin again. Maybe it would happen in Dublin.

''Do you live in JN'ew York?" blonde pubic chaos began asking him as he was licking a large pint of heavy Irish beer.

"I didn't travel four thousand niles to get layed - I can do that in Hew York," he blurted.

The good clean wood - old, but real. An Irish pub - nothing like it. The upturned wrinkles of men with spirit - who love life and seem to twinkle and laugh through it all.

"I came here to find my soul," he responded quietly.

"Did I help," she later said as her lithe naked white skin slowly concealed itself in the darkness of his hotel room.

1 ·'I can't say I felt any pain," he replied as they both found their sense of humor for the first time, again.

She poured a couple of drinks wondering whether to tell him or not. If he knew he might just disappear as quickly as he had arrived in her life.

"You pour the good drink.

"Thank you."

"How, how are we going to begin?"

" v/hat do you mean?"

"I mean, I know that cat who interrupted us is into
something heavy, and in a small way so are you - what is it?"

"Uh...okay...we ¹ re both Catholics - we believe that man is a prisoner of the
institutions he has created, ana we ᵀ re dedicated to changing all that."

"But you*re both catholics - I see," he replied and laughed.

" Well, I guess I could have left that out."

"You sure could have - I'm tired of running Into revolutionaries
who are trying to liberate this and that segment of society -
when you talk of revolution you should be speaking of liberating everybody."

"Well, we are."


"Oh, shit, you'r right out of a magazine - a product of your times and its
fashions - nothing more. You have no more individual reality than the girl in
the toothpaste commercial."

He moved lightly off the bed and began putting his clothes
on.

"Do you want me to leave, too?" she questioned as she lifted the smooth skin
of her thighs up, concealing the warm redness between her legs.

"I don't care, do whatever you want to do. I'm going on an evening sojourn."

When he had left she stretched out - enjoying her fulfilled sensuality. However,
she walked out soon after.

The V-buildings, the small lanterns, the fresh air - and the warmth underneath
Dublin moved his being past his own subjective world into thinking for a
moment that the Holy Grail just might be here. The rusty barbarism of Worth
American youth contrasted politely with the detached but romantic surge
following a new generation of St. iatricks,,

".There's it at, man?" The brown checkered shirt, peaked gray hat and clumsy
work boots clothed a human being.

Haller had already noticed. The guy kept banging his glass on the bar and
spilling spray where it wasn't supposed to go.

"Shut up," Haller replied.

"Look, man - I want to know."

"Go up to Belfast and throw a bomb."

Danny always arrived at the best point in a conversation.

Haller and his antagonist smiled.

"This guy thinks that it's at somewhere - where as I was under the impression that it always stayed in one place,"

Haller said as he kicked the antagonist in the balls.

An hour later in a small 17th century pub on the fringe of Dublin, Haller sat wiuh Danny and his blond bitch. She kept looking over at him with a 'he doesn't know I fucked you'

look, followed by a 'don't blow it[1] loci;.

"Germs are actually space ships sent into outer space

to explore atoms larger than themselves," Haller responded to Danny's whimpering about his cold.

"And you're a blind man who has fashioned a beautiful

world - everything and everybody are beautiful to you - but

I've got the new medical discovery. I can make you see - do you want It or not?" replied Danny with a sarcastic smile.

"Come on, Danny," the bitch twitched.

"iTo - we[1] re going to talk - and maybe one of us is going

to die. .but that's only if one of us is living on his knees.

If you're standing up straight, man, there's going to be no trouble . "

He paused, smiling a little.

"You call yourself a writer, an artist. Is that right?"

" Ye s ."

"Okay - I say art is neurosis - what do you say?"

"If that were true everybody would be an artist because everybody is neurotic. The artist creates what might be, as well as to explain to the captive fimctionaries of culture - such as yourself - what is," replied Haller.

"So you think I'm a functionary of this culture?'"

"Ox the negative culture - yes - it's the same thing as being a part of it - you're equally as irrelevent."

Danny was hurting and Mailer knew it - but if he- was living on his knees he had to get hurt in order to stand up.

"I fucked your bitch," halier said.

Red crunching chaos - vibrations zinged all over - the wood creaked.

Danny jerked, then hung on to the table. His head leaned down Into his hands and he whispered,

"Okay, you're for real - there isn't going to be any trouble."

The dancers, as always, seemed mad to those who couldn't
hear the music. Haller remembered the last words written by so many writers,
"I have spent the years looking for peace.
I found ecstacy; I found misery; but through the long years,
I did not find peace."

The effervescent clouds that only sizzle and come s.live in the waters of one's
own mind. Tne satire ebbed from comedy to tragedy - frora neurosis to life -
to art and back a vain.

7/hen one grew, as Haller had, beyond the vision of those that spurned the seed,
one became one's own seed and one's own creation. To then interact with those
that were still the product of the clumsy chaos of sociological beginnings was
indeed easy - but it was empty and it left nothingness.

The morning wisped in mist around and by the bicycle rider venturing into the
trees and flowers of the Irish countryside. It was Halier at .-seven-thirty in .
themorning going to the unknown.

The limp and the lisp were no longer excuses. He would crush himself in
lisping terror, or walk away limping'forever. The small splash of water just
above the light sand asked him to hope for another way - another pub - another
mother - another world. "I want a new life!" he screamed to the meadow as it
rolled away a.nd away.

"I'm tired of my heritage," Haller finally admitted to the white beard and
shining soul across from him - a country pub, and an old man out of the bible.
A small coach inn and a farmer from the fields.

"And," Haller continued, "I'm bored with the western experience; I'm
exhausted by the occidental approach to life  and knowledge

"'here you are thinking you could go to change that?" his countryside
acquaintance asked.

"I would like to immerse myself in something beyond an anti-thesis or a
synthesis to the present perception of the evolution of man. I would like to be
tingled by a. new world and a new human experience . "

The old man chuckled and sipped from the mug he had been drinking from
since 1890 in this little untouchable paradise.

They laughed and talked for a long while. Haller caught a flash of something.
.ʳ. . . . in other words nobody has lived my life before - so that's it . I'm going
to live my life.

The wrinkled brown face strolled up above the still clear bronze eyes.

ᶠIt didn't take men in my youth long to come to that conclusion. v7e didn't need Kegel or anybody else to teach us dialectics. 7/e breathed and laughed and worked. .... .and lived."

Haller later floated out of the inn. ne passed by some children playing on the cobblestone. The house next to the inn was welcoming a thirty-fiveish family man back tc his home at the end of the day. ne stopped tc light a cigarette in front of the next house as he smiled at the two middle a₀ea occupants who were sitting in chairs on the veranda.

As he walked by the following house, he noticed the old man from the pub rocking away in the front. They smiled at each other, he had now reached the corner. There weren't any more houses."

WAR

AND

AFTER

FIRST EDITION

Copyright © 1972 by Terrence F. Hill

Published by Vantage Press, Inc.
516 West 34th Street, New York, New York 10001

Manufactured in the United States of America

Standard Book No. 533-00271-0

### THE AMERICAN DREAM

It is found in those majestic words of the Declaration of Independence, words lifted to cosmic proportions: "We hold these truths to be self-evident, that all men are created equal, that they are endowed by God, Creator, with certain inalienable Rights, that among these are Life, Liberty, and the pursuit of Happiness." This is a dream. It's a great dream.

If we are going to make the American dream a reality, we are challenged to work in an action program to get rid of the last vestiges of segregation and discrimination. This problem isn't going to solve itself, however much people tell us this.

We have a great dream. It started way back in 1776, and God grant that America will be true to her dream.

I still have a dream this morning: one day all of God's black children will be respected like his white children.

I still have a dream this morning that one day the lion and the lamb will lie down together, and every man will sit under his own vine and fig tree and none shall be afraid.

I still have a dream this morning that one day all men everywhere will recognize that out of one blood God made all men to dwell upon the face of the earth.

I still have a dream this morning that one day every valley shall be exalted, and every mountain and hill will be made low, the rough places will be made plain, and the crooked places straight; and the glory of the Lord shall be revealed, and all flesh shall see it together.

I still have a dream this morning that truth will reign supreme and all of God's children will respect the dignity and worth of human personality. And when this day comes the morning stars will sing together and the sons of God will shout for joy.

"We hold these truths to be self-evident, that all men are created equal, that they are endowed by their Creator with certain inalienable Rights, that among these are Life, Liberty, and the pursuit of Happiness."

*Dr. Martin Luther King, Jr.*
*Delivered at Ebenezer Baptist Church, Atlanta, Georgia, on 4 July 1965.*

*TERRENCE F. HILL*

WASHINGTON, DC MARTIN LUTHER KING, JR.
NATIONAL MEMORIAL PROJECT FOUNDATION

# FOUNDING SPONSOR

$8.95

# WAR AND AFTER

By

## Terrence F. Hill

*War and After* is another book about Vietnam, but there ends any comparison between war experiences in Indo-China and Terrence F. Hill's service as a fighting member of the U.S. Marine Corps in that theatre. This is about involvement and evolvement, about survival and, about living for a day, a few days, or living forever. It exists in the jungle and back home, in memories and stubborn determinations, but it spends not one second on hope. Reality is the starkest value present—but it is somehow made acceptable in the minds of those who will to survive.

In its paucity of conversation and absolute lack of any of the verbal exchanges for which the fighting-forces of World War II are remembered on the book, late shows that absolutely indominable humor that enabled Allied troops to live with this war is this homely lie—the creeping conviction that reaches the reader: nothing like Vietnam has ever been experienced in time, or place, or state of mind. Everybody in this book is thinking hard; if he doesn't, he's brushed aside, and we hope luck goes with him.

*(Continued on back flap)*

1973, "AFTER FOUR MILLION YEARS of EVOLUTION - IT WAS THE dawning of INTELLIGENCE"

Terrence F Hill

*(Continued from front flap)*

The resulting picture goes deeper than the mere facts, either group, and averages candidate. It's easy going to dazzle prose; and enough, the author's holistic prose makes it all run together in a way smooth stream: you accept and want and realize almost subconsciously. Yet anyone who wonders undecided, who finds it difficult to accept the veteran's view who just to react to know, war and freedom, and then, will be sharp. Published by Torollay Press, Inc., 516 West 34th Street, New York, N Y 10001.

COMMITTEE:
ENERGY AND COMMERCE

SUBCOMMITTEES:
CHAIRMAN, COMMERCE,
MANUFACTURING AND TRADE

COMMUNICATIONS AND
TECHNOLOGY

ENVIRONMENT AND
ECONOMY

**Mary Bono Mack**
**Congress of the United States**
45th District, California

WASHINGTON OFFICE
1721 LONGWORTH HOUSE OFFICE BUILDING
WASHINGTON, DC 20515
(202) 225-5330
FAX (202) 225-2961

DISTRICT OFFICES
36-955 COOK STREET
SUITE 100
PALM DESERT, CA 92211
(760) 320-1076
FAX (760) 320-0596

1600 EAST FLORIDA AVENUE
SUITE 301
HEMET, CA 92544
(951) 656-6310
FAX (951) 652-2562

October 25, 2012

Ms. Judith Appelbaum
Office of Legislative Affairs
Department of Justice
Washington, DC 20530

Dear Ms. Appelbaum:

My constituent, Terrence Hill, has requested my
assistance regarding justice issues. I have enclosed the
original request, which I received from Mr. Hill for your
convenience.

Thank you for taking the time to investigate this matter. Please
forward any correspondence in care of Kyle Christian, in
my Washington, DC office.

Thank you for your assistance in this matter.

Sincerely,

MARY BONO MACK
Member of Congress

MBM/kc

27 March 2014

Terrence F. Hill
hillterrencef@gmail.com
Tel.: +39 3394341623

"Jesus, why did the
birds stop singing?
TFH 2014

It's not me, and no one
is asking me who I am

Poem-Story

Who wished to be poets
so hard that they were
willing to live in hell hitself
and violate every value
and law, even imagined by
the people and civilizations
of the world

Violated even the centuries
of soldiers leaving their mothers
to fight for some idea called
Freedom
which hell called licentiousness
and other hells called
an unlucky roulette wheel
for mankind

Some blamed the murder of children
and the hunger of mankind
on this one word, Freedom.
And it's conseguences
distrusting the invisible hand
that had given these
people everything, even their soul.

Written by
Terrence Hill
September/2013

187

*Copy for Jan Koos -Press*
*officer Human Rights Watch.*
*Brussels*

Terrence Hill < hillterrencef@gmail.com>

**wishes from fr yesu**
1 message

*7 april 2014*

yesu karunanidhi < yesu@live.in>
To: "hillterrencef@gmail.com" <hillterrencef@gmail.com>

Mon, Mar 31, 2014 at 10:17 PM

Dear Mr. Hill,

Good evening.

How are you?

Wishes and love from Fr. Yesu, Parr. San Giuda Taddeo, Rome.

It has been a moment of God-in-work talking to you during the weekends.

I went through your writings. You are expressive, innovating and enlightening.

May God bless you today, tomorrow and always.

Wish you a happy month ahead.

Good evening.

Truly yours,

Yesu Karunanidhi
Parrocchia San Giuda Taddeo
Via Amedeo Crivellucci, 3
00179 Roma, ITALIA

+39 389 8438218

*Alexander Solzenitzen walked*
*out of the prison and thanked*
*the prison because He found*
*God there. Then He looked*
*at the graves around the prison*
*- and they shouted back at him*
*"you made it out - we died in that*
*prison."*

*We leave the results to God*

*"God did not give David*
*a sword"*
*TH sept-2013-Roma*

188

THE WHITE HOUSE

August 14, 2012

Mr. Terrence F. Hill
112 Castellana West
Palm Desert, California 92260

Dear Terrence:

Thank you for sending me materials to review. I appreciate hearing from you.

I am encouraged by the outpouring of messages and suggestions from Americans across the country. Some comments are supportive, others are critical, but all reflect the desire of Americans to participate in a dialogue about our common concerns and challenges. To learn more about my Administration's agenda, please visit: www.WhiteHouse.gov.

Thank you again for contacting me and for your continued participation.

Sincerely,

189

June 26, 2014
כ״ח סיון, תשע״ד

Mr. Terrence F. Hill
Via Tommaso Inghirami 85
apt B-10
Roma 00179
Italy

Dear Mr. Hill,

On behalf of Prime Minister Benjamin Netanyahu, we acknowledge receipt of your letter dated June 8, 2014, and the copy of your book, "The Heart of a Poet".

With warm greetings from Jerusalem,

Sincerely,

Jonathan Schachter
Senior Advisor

*THE GREAT HEBREW CIVILIZATION of THE POETS - NATHAN AND ISAIAH*

רח' קפלן 3, הקריה, ירושלים מיקוד 91919 טל: 02-6705555, פקס: 02-5664848

3 Kaplan St. Hakirya, Jerusalem 91919, Israel Tel. 972-2-6705555, Fax. 972-2-5664848

So I was well regarded as young writer in New York, London, Heidelberg, Paris and
Madrid AND WAS CALLED ONE OF THE GREATEST
WRITERS OF MY GENERATION, AND EVEN
A NON-POLITICAL THINKING PERSON.

SINCERELY, IN CHRIST

Jerrold Hill

10 APRIL 2014
ROMA ITALIA

FROM 1976

WHAT NATION OR PEOPLE
WOULD INTERFERE WITH
LIFE - WHEN NOT EVEN
GOD WOULD INTERFERE
WITH LIFE

SINCERELY,

WHEN NO MAN OR GOVERNMENT
CAN ACT
WHEN NO MAN OR GOVERNMENT
WILL ACT
SOMETIMES, IN LIFE ON EARTH
GOD HIMSELF ACTS SINCERELY,

MAMA AND PAPA ARE
MORE IMPORTANT THAN
ANY ARMY ON EARTH

SINCERELY,

191

Terrence F. Hill
304 - 1425 West 6th Avenue
Vancouver, BC  V6H 4G5

Telephone
Area Code 604
732-9350

Friday, July 16, 2004

McClelland and Stewart
481 University Avenue
Toronto, Ontario  M5G 2E9

Dear Sir:

I have been writing for 40 years and have completed a number of novellas and plays.  I am also a poet.  I am enclosing some of my poetry for your consideration to be published.  Maybe a volume of poetry of mine could be published.

Also, I have enclosed a few chapters of my new novel "Window to Heaven".  Hopefully you will be interested in publishing my new novel.

Thank you.

Sincerely,

Terrence F. Hill

TFH/cli
Enclosures

www.hrw.org

Mr
Terrence F. Hill
Via dei Gracchi 278
Scala A. Interno 12
Roma 00195
Italia

Zürich, 30. May 2013

**HUMAN RIGHTS WATCH
Komitee Zürich**

Baurstrasse 24
8008 Zürich
Tel. +41 (0)44 380 8018
Fax +41 (0)44 380 8019
zurich@hrw.org

**Spendenkonto**
CH 88 0024 0240 3505 3302 P
UBS AG
1227 Carouge
Swiss Foundation in Support of
Human Rights Watch, Genf

**Returning your documents**

Dear Mr Hill

We received your documents from the 21. May 2013.
Thank you for contacting Human Rights Watch on the matter in question and having shared your story with our organization.

Owing to our mandate Human Rights Watch researches transparently and neutrally on social plights. Our organisation works against widespread and systematic violation of human rights and does not investigate on individual basis. Therefore we cannot assist you in such an isolated case.

We enclose your submitted documents to this letter.
We truly hope the sorrowful situation will be improved and that you will find answers to all of your questions.

Yours faithfully
**HUMAN RIGHTS WATCH
Zürich**

Christina Affolter
Development & Outreach, Zürich

THE DERILECT

A POEM
by TERRENCE F Hi.

I AM A DERILECT THAT
PEOPLE PASS by ON THE STREET
YET, I AM AT THE CENTER of THE
BANKING SYSTEMS of THE WORLD
AND AT THE CENTER of EVERY
GOVERNMENT, of EVERY PEOPLE
AND CIVILIZATION ON EARTH, YET

I AM A DERILECT THAT
PEOPLE PASS by ON THE STREET

P.S.
My PLAYS, NOVELLAS, POETRY, FILM TREATMENTS,
ARE ABOUT THAT WHICH TRANSCENDS ANY
PARTICULAR CIVILIZATION — THEY ARE
ABOUT THE LOVE AND TRAGEDY THAT IS LIFE.

by TERRENCE F Holl

194

E MAIL AND Hill Terrence F@gmail.com    TERRENCE T HLL

THE CRY OF ST PAUL WAS HEARD DOWN THROUGH THE CENTURIES, FOR SOME KIND OF FAIRNESS AND MERCY IN OUR LIVES THE CRY WAS HEARD IN THE HISTORY OF EVERY PEOPLE AND CIVILIZATION ON EARTH AND

IN OUR LAWS IN OUR CONSTITUTION IN OUR ENTIRE STRUGGLE FOR DIGNITY AND FREEDOM.

DEAR JESUS IN OUR NEW 21TH CENTURY, WE ARE STILL LOOKING TOWARD THE IDEALS OF OUR LAWS ( WE MUST, AS HUMAN RIGHTS WATCHER DOES THROUGHOUT EUROPE AND AFRICA), REMIND OUR SOCIETIES OF OUR LAWS ASSURING THE ENJOYMENT OF FUNDAMENTAL RIGHTS FOR ALL PEOPLE.

MONSIEUR HOLLANDE SAID IN SEPTEMBER 2013, IN FRANCE:

"THE POISON THAT CAUSED SLAVERY , IS STILL IN THE HEARTS OF MEN"

PRESIDENT OBAMA SAID TWO YEARS AGO IN AMERICA:

"NO AMERICAN WILL BE LEFT BEHIND, NO AMERICAN IS OUT THERE IN HIS OWN.

THAT LIFE ISN'T A CRAP-SHOOT FOR AMERICANS, AND THAT, THE GENETICAL LOTTERY

DOES NOT DETERMINE AMERICAN RIGHTS OR OPPORTUNITIES,

THAT THE UNALIENABLE RIGHTS AMERICANS ENJOY COME FROM THE HAND OF GOD

FROM THE LIGHT OF THE TWO CANDLES ON EARTS, FRANCE AND AMERICA.

14 MAY 2014

DEAR MICHELLE OBAMA,
PLEASE MICHELLE SEE IF,
AS A WRITER-ARTIST, I HAVE
ANY MISUNDERSTANDINGS WITH
THE U. S. GOVERNMENT - AND IF
I DO, TELL THEM THAT I AM
A RESPECTED, RETIRED U. S NAVY
VETERAN - A NON-POLITICAL AMERICAN-
CANADIAN WRITER-ARTIST, - AND
NOW RETIRED IN ROME. I EARNED
MY LIVING AND FED MY CHILDREN
WORKING AS A LABORER AND CLERK
MOST OF MY LIFE I RECIEVE THE CANADA
PENSION - A NATIONAL PROGRAM THAT HAS
— n-I... in Ho WE ARE AS CANADIANS:

195

JEFA DE LA SECRETARÍA
DEL PRESIDENTE DEL GOBIERNO

Madrid, 25 de julio de 2014

Sr. Terrence F Hill
Via Tommaso Inghirami 85. Apt B.-10
ROMA 00179 (ITALIA)

Estimado Sr. Hill:

Siguiendo las indicaciones del Presidente del Gobierno, tengo el gusto de agradecerle el ejemplar de su libro "The heart of a poet" que ha tenido la amabilidad de obsequiarle y dedicarle.

Atentamente,

*SUCH AS MEMBERS
of OPUS DEI—
ONE CAN CHOOSE
A CERTAIN STOICISM
— EVEN WITH CELEBACY
AND FIND AN INNER
PEACE AND JOY.
SINCERELY*

*THE GREAT SPANISH
CIVILIZATION of Lopa de Vega*

## AMENDMENT III
*Housing of soldiers*

No Soldier shall, in time of peace be quartered in any house, without the consent of the Owner, nor in time of war, but in a manner to be prescribed by law.

## AMENDMENT IV
*Search and arrest warrants*

The right of the people to be secure in their persons, houses, papers, and effects, against unreasonable searches and seizures, shall not be violated, and no Warrants shall issue, but upon probable cause, supported by Oath or affirmation, and particularly describing the place to be searched, and the persons or things to be seized.

## AMENDMENT V
*Rights in criminal cases*

No person shall be held to answer for a capital, or otherwise infamous crime, unless on a presentment or indictment of a Grand Jury, except in cases arising in the land or naval forces, or in the Militia, when in actual service in time of War or public danger; nor shall any person be subject for the same offence to be twice put in jeopardy of life or limb; nor shall be compelled in any criminal case to be a witness against himself, nor be deprived of life, liberty, or property, without due process of law; nor shall private property be taken for public use, without just compensation.

## AMENDMENT VI
*Rights to fair trial*

In all criminal prosecutions, the accused shall enjoy the right to a speedy and public trial, by an impartial jury of the State and district wherein the crime shall have been committed, which district shall have been previously ascertained by law, and to be informed of the nature and cause of the accusation; to be confronted with the witnesses against him; to have compulsory process for obtaining witnesses in his favor, and to have the Assistance of Counsel for his defence.

## AMENDMENT VII
*Rights in civil cases*

In Suits at common law, where the value in controversy shall exceed twenty dollars, the right of trial by jury shall be preserved, and no fact tried by a jury, shall be otherwise re-examined in any Court of the United States, than according to the rules of the common law.

## AMENDMENT VIII
*Bails, fines, and punishments*

Excessive bail shall not be required, nor excessive fines imposed, nor cruel and unusual punishments inflicted.

## AMENDMENT IX
*Rights retained by the people*

The enumeration in the Constitution, of certain

25

THE above, FROM THE CONSTITUTION of THE
UNITED STATES of AMERICA (1776)
ALONG WITH THE declaration of INDEPENDENCE

WE Hold THIS TRUTH TO be
SELF-EVIDENT - THAT ALL MEN
ARE CREATED EQUAL
AND THAT MAN IS endowed WITH
CERTAIN UNALIENABLE RIGHTS
AMONGST WHICH ARE LIFE, Liberty
AND THE Pursuit of HAPPINESS -
WHICH COME FROM THE HAND
of God (NOT ANY STATE ON EARTH)

THIS IS WHAT I defended IN WAR,
FOR AMERICA AND ANOTHER PEOPLE
1968-1970
THE U S MARINE
COR;

197

### THE SHAW PLAY AT THE MANITOBA THEATRE CENTRE

" YOU NEVER CAN TELL ", now on stage at the Manitoba the Centre is a light, un eventful comedy in which George Bernard Shaw reminds us that many of the conflicts of our age are by no means novel or peculiar to our times. The play is about the reconciliation of a woman and three children with the husband and father they have been separated for eighteen years. There re-encounter is quite by chance and involves a young dentist and the eldest daughter in a love affair that brings to focus the central conflict of the play – man versus woman.

Fighting for the traditional role of man and attempting to alter the traditional role of woman, the characters interact with an unyielding individuality that makes this one of Shaw's funniest play. It is simply light and in that very entertaining.

oF wHAT

Shaw wrote it in 1897 as the last he called "Four Pleasant Plays", but is not a masterpiece. The dramatist, on this occasion didn't surprise anybody. All of the action it's easily anticipated, but the audience is held, non of the less, by the master full craftsmanship of the artist and a truly brilliant performance by Paxton Whitehead.

We are told quite forcefully of the second major conflict in the play, that "there are two sorts of family life......one that is based on mutual rispect , on recognition of the right of every member of the household to independence and privacy......but there is an other sort of family life- a life in which husbands open their wives letters and call on them to account for every farthing of their exspenditures, and every moment of their time; in which women do the same to their children; on which no room is private and no hour sacred; in which duty, obedience, affection home, morality and religion are detestable tyrannies, and life is a vulgar round of punishement and lies, coercion and rebellion, jelousy, suspicion and recrimination.

IT IS OF COURSE, by THE growTH
of THE CHARACTEES THAT THE
MISUNDERSTANDINGS ARe Resolved.

198

Printed in the month of May 2015
on behalf of Youcanprint *Self - Publishing*

www.ingramcontent.com/pod-product-compliance
Lightning Source LLC
Chambersburg PA
CBHW050842180626
46814CB00007B/2578